Lifetime Achievement
award winner and author of
over 40 novels

RUTH LANGAN

"Fans of Jude Deveraux's Velvet Series will be
captivated by Ruth Langan's charming and
colorful love story...."

—*Romantic Times*

Talented rising star

MARY McBRIDE

"Mary McBride wraps her story around
every emotion.... I can hardly wait for her
next one. She's great! 5★s."

—*Affaire de Coeur*

OUTLAW Brides

ELAINE COFFMAN
RUTH LANGAN
MARY McBRIDE

Harlequin Books

TORONTO • NEW YORK • LONDON
AMSTERDAM • PARIS • SYDNEY • HAMBURG
STOCKHOLM • ATHENS • TOKYO • MILAN
MADRID • WARSAW • BUDAPEST • AUCKLAND

HARLEQUIN BOOKS

ISBN 0-373-83315-6

THE BRIDE OF BLACKNESS CASTLE
Copyright © 1996 by Elaine Coffman

MAVERICK HEARTS
Copyright © 1996 by Ruth Ryan Langan

THE BALLAD OF JOSIE DOVE
Copyright © 1996 by Mary Myers

Printed in U.S.A.

CONTENTS

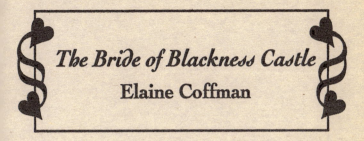

The Bride of Blackness Castle

Elaine Coffman

Prologue

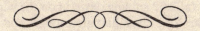

Scotland, in the years
following the battle of Culloden Moor

He was not taller than any mortal man, but the curses and dark prophecies that haunted him made him seem that way. He was the last laird and sole survivor of what had once been known as "the mighty clan Macqueen."

Alone and bitter, he walked the walls of Blackness Castle—long ago a stalwart fortress, now neglected and partially roofless. Yet, like the broken man who possessed it, it was noble in its desolation—a heap of crumbling griffins and grotesque carvings that rose majestically from a base of tumbled-down stone.

Night after night he was there, crouching against the salt-laden winds to gaze far out over the ocean toward the Arctic, looking as wild as the island he lived upon, as fierce as his Celt and Viking ancestors, and as cold and unforgiving as Scotland itself.

There had been a time when he had laughed and loved, a time when he was known by his Christian name, Robert Macqueen. But those who had called him that were gone, lying as cold and silent as the Stones of Callanish. Only he was left behind—a man, once so capable of emotion, now dying inside. A man who hated as deeply as he had once loved.

To those who lived in the Shetlands, he had become the Wolf of Blackness Castle. Many thought the name appropriate, for it was rumored that when the moon was full and shining down upon the windswept parapets, his long black hair grew longer and his eyes changed from blue to tawny yellow.

They swore by all that was holy that what they said was true, for there was not a soul on the island who had not heard the eerie notes of his mournful howl as it came rolling across the bogs and peat moors, a sound as chilling, and as lifeless, as the fog.

"He searches for his lost mate," they would say, for everyone in the islands knew the tragic story that haunted the last laird of the clan Macqueen.

He was a man of myth and legend, a man they whispered about behind locked doors, a man they pitied, a man they feared. For he lived in a magical place, where the Atlantic met the North Sea, where roaring and swirling currents turned the giant millstones beneath the water, grinding the salt that flavors the sea.

Perhaps the castle was haunted, just as the village folk believed. Perhaps, too, it was the place where the water horse lived—a malicious Shetland spirit that drowned anyone who tried to ride it....

Anyone, that is, save the Wolf of Blackness Castle.

Chapter One

Be not forgetful...
some have entertained angels unawares.

Lady Anne Crofton sat demurely in the boat. Her manner was deceptive, for there was absolutely nothing demure about Lady Anne.

She kept a sharp eye upon the ruffian who rowed the small craft toward shore. It was obvious his brain was as rum-soaked as the ship's captain. She should have known better than to book passage on a ship named *Misadventure*.

A wave slapped the boat and threw a shower of water over her, drenching her best clothes and her parasol, and soaking her only hat. The toothless brute on the working end of the oars had the audacity to laugh. Her patience was wearing tissue-thin, and she swore inwardly that if he did one more thing to irritate her, she would find another use for her parasol.

They were drawing closer to the shore, and Anne searched the land with mounting excitement for the home her father had written her about, a place called Ravenscrag Castle. But the island looked completely deserted, save for a roofless ruin of a structure that must have dated back to the days after King William.

"Are you certain we're in the right place? I don't see anything that looks like the castle my father described."

"Eh . . . it's wot the cap'n said, miss. This be the place."

Anne could barely understand a word he said, perhaps because she had never heard anyone completely toothless speak before. It sounded as if he were speaking a foreign language.

The boat struck bottom and scraped across rocks to come to a stop. The seaman leaped out, then took her bags, one by one, and stacked them just beyond the edge of the water, on the shore. Then he climbed back into the boat and looked at her, as if she were holding up his departure.

She closed her parasol and rose majestically to her feet. "I did not relish being carried to shore by a smelly brute, anyway." With that, she yanked her skirts up to a modest length and climbed out of the boat into water that came to her thighs. When she caught him leering at her, she smacked him, hard, beside the head with her parasol. "If you don't want your bloody eyes to be as gone as your teeth, stop your leering and weigh anchor!"

She knew the rowboat did not have an anchor, but he seemed to get the message, for he did as she ordered.

Once he started rowing, she turned her back on him and the ship anchored offshore and concentrated on making the last few feet to dry land. Walking through deep water wasn't easy, especially dressed as she was.

Once ashore, she surveyed the area around her. She fervently hoped the ruined castle was not her new home, but as it was the only choice she had for making inquiry, she decided to leave her baggage where it was and head in that direction.

As she walked along, her shoes squishing with each step, she saw someone riding toward her. The dark chestnut horse drew closer and she could see the rider was a man. His hair was long, and as black as the cape that hung around his shoulders. When he drew even with her, he stopped.

He did not dismount, but sat towering over her, with the most piercing look in his eyes—eyes that were as hard and blue as sapphires. He was a handsome man, but his brooding male vitality held her at bay. There was a dangerous quality to him that set her heart to beating faster. It also made her wary.

This was not a man she would be able to crown with her parasol. Just the thought gave her a sudden vision of him yanking her parasol out of her hands and breaking it over his knee. She decided that she would be wise to be guarded around him, for she knew he would not hesitate to use anything he learned against her.

"What in the hell are you doing here?" he asked suddenly, his voice so hard and brittle that she flinched and took a step back. "You are on private land."

Anne's first instinct was to turn tail and run, but she was too terrified to do more than squeak out an apology. "I do beg your pardon, sir." She cupped her hand to shield her eyes as she stared up at him.

He looked her over with thorough devotion, and she had a feeling he knew one of the buttons on her drawers was missing. There was something in that look that made her aware of him as a man. If he had the same awareness of her, she was doomed. She knew what could happen to a woman alone in a deserted place.

He obviously thought her an intruding inferior. Why not let him add *simpleton* to the list? "It was not my choice to be left here, sir. You see, the ship's captain was too drunk to find his head in broad daylight, much less my destination. I fear they have set me upon this place by mistake." She paused for a shaky breath. "Where am I?"

"Where are you going?"

"I am on my way to see my mother. She is a widow... That means she doesn't have a husband, that is, not at the present time. Widows were married once, you see, but their husbands died, and that is what made them a widow."

Anne was feeling pretty good about the way things were going, until he pinned her with a cold, angry look. She melted into a quivering lump of fear. "I am all she has in the world."

"How unfortunate for her."

She smiled at him and dipped in a hastily modified version of a curtsy. "Thank you."

She saw him squeeze the reins in his hands so tightly that his knuckles turned white. "You...are...*English*."

He obviously hated everything English, including the word, for he literally spat it out. She decided to nail down a few Scots ancestors and family members before he put those white knuckles around her throat. "My speech has lost its Scots flavor, I fear. After my father died, my mother sent me to her aunt in England."

He seemed restless, anxious to have this conversation over and her on her way. "So, where does this unfortunate woman live?"

"In a house, of course. It is a modest cottage with a thatched roof. It is quite small...barely big enough for two. The garden is tiny, and she has only one cow, three chickens—"

"Enough!" His eyes seemed to glow with anger, and she wondered if she had come face to face with the devil himself.

She took a step backward.

He leaned forward, catching the bottom of her chin with the handle of his whip. While she stood there in terrified silence, he lowered the handle, dragging it along the neckline of her dress. "I would caution you to stop playing games with me, mistress. I am not some callow youth with an Adam's apple bigger than his brain. I tend to get nasty when I am angered, and it isn't a pretty sight. I asked you where your mother lived. I expect to be given a location, not a description of her house and everything in it. Now, I will ask you one more time. Where are you going?"

"I...I..." The words came out in a gravelly croak. Terror had sucked the moisture from her throat. She couldn't have spat if he set her on fire. She knew she had better get to talking fast, or he might be tempted to do just that, so she took a deep breath, giving her mouth just enough time to recover, before she tried again. "I do not have anything exact, sir. I only know my mother wrote that her cottage is not far from a castle."

"And the name of the castle?"

She looked around her, as if frantically searching for something. "Oh, no, I think the captain has kept my paper . . . the one with the name written on it. Oh, dear! What shall I do?''

''You might try thinking.''

''Oh, I didn't think of that.''

''Obviously.''

She rolled her eyes in her best imitation of deep thought. ''It's no use. I can't remember anything. . . .''

He leaned forward and looped the whip around her head and pulled her toward him. ''You'd better pray something shows up fast, otherwise I might he forced to take other measures.''

''Oth— Other measures?''

He smiled nastily. ''Of a passionate nature.''

''I remember now.''

He withdrew the whip. ''Somehow, I knew you would.''

''I remember only that part of it contained the name of a bird. . . . Something like Sparrowcroft . . . No, that's not it. . . . Wrenfields . . . No, that's not right, either.'' She shrugged her shoulders and smiled at him. ''Wrong again.''

''Ravenscrag,'' he said through gritted teeth. ''Ravenscrag Castle.''

''That's it! I am certain that's it. Are you familiar with it?''

''I am familiar with it. The question is, are you? The castle there is haunted. It is a place of great tragedy. There is a man who is reported to be a monster. He turns into a wolf at night. Are you certain you want to go there?''

''Is this monster dangerous?''

''No one who has seen him has ever come back, so who's to say?''

"I think I will bypass the castle and go straight to my mother's cottage. Am I very far away?"

"No. Ravenscrag Castle is on the other side of this island. Across the bay. The place you seek should be beyond that."

She wrinkled her nose as she looked at him. "This is an island? But I was going to an island. One called Shetland."

"The Shetlands are a group of islands. The one you seek is across the bay." His voice held a warning. "There are no villages here."

"You mean to tell me I have been dumped, parasol and baggage, upon the wrong island?"

"Catastrophic, isn't it?"

"How will I ever get off of this island, if no one lives here? I can't very well swim…. What would I do with my baggage?"

"It will be a pleasure to help you on your way. I will have someone take you across."

"I don't want to be a bother."

"You are a bother now, mistress, and I am anxious to rid myself of you…one way, or another. I do not take to having strangers snooping around my island."

"I have yet to snoop," she announced.

"You are a woman. You will snoop."

"I am a different sort of woman than most."

"For once you have spoken with something that resembles wisdom."

"If I am such a bother, sir, I will see myself off this island, even if I have to swim across. I shall leave my baggage here, and send someone for it later. Good day."

She opened her parasol with a fluttering snap, and held it over her head as she turned and marched with as much dignity as she could muster, through the rocky sand. She had walked a fair distance when she heard the thundering sound of a horse approaching. A second later, a strong arm whipped out and grabbed her. Suddenly she was airborne, uncertain whether she was more terrified that he might take her with him, or drop her on the spot.

"You aren't going to kill me, are you?"

"The thought crossed my mind. Now, be quiet, or I may start thinking about it again."

She snapped her mouth closed, unable to see anything but the ground beneath them for quite some time. When he finally stopped, he yanked her from his horse and stood her on her feet. When she gained her balance, she saw two men standing in front of the ruined castle, staring at her.

"This baggage has more baggage waiting where she came ashore. Get it, and take her across the bay. She lives not far from Ravenscrag."

The men left to do his bidding and he turned to her. He was unbelievably tall. "I will ask you this once. Do not lie to me, for if you should, I can promise you will not like what I do to you. Do you understand?"

Anne was terrified he knew she had passed herself off as something she was not. "I understand."

"Why are you here?"

She looked at him blankly. "But...I told you. I have come from England..."

"To spy on me?"

She blinked. "I am not a spy, sir. Do I look like a spy?"

"No, but you have the brains for one."

"I am no spy, and that is the truth."

"It had better be. I detest lies, and I do not deal mercifully with those who tell them. For your sake, I hope you have been truthful with me, for if you have not, there is no place safe where you can hide. I am not making light with you, mistress. Believe me when I tell you, I am not a nice man."

She gulped. "I believe you . . . with all my heart."

"Good."

Chapter Two

Darkness was where he belonged. It was his comfort, his strength, the place of refuge where he could go and remember. In the deepest part of his heart existed a tomb and a dungeon, and when the darkness came, their doors were thrown open and he was consumed with grief—and filled with an insatiable thirst for revenge.

It was night, and the darkness was all about. The new maid, Marta, had come by to light the candles, but that had been some time ago. They were all burned down now, and they sputtered and flickered, leaving a legacy of tawny shadows to dance upon the wall.

Marta looked at the lord of the castle and moved closer to the housekeeper, Grizel. "Do you think the devils will come for him again tonight?"

"They cannot come for him, lass. They are already here. His devils come from within. It is only at night that he lets them out."

Marta shivered and looked around her. She rubbed her arms. "It grows colder, I think."

"Aye. The wind of remembrance blows coldest when it comes from the graves of those who cannot rest."

"What graves?"

"The ones we spoke of earlier."

"Oh . . . you mean the graves of his wife and son?"

"Aye, and those of the entire clan . . . save the laird, of course."

Marta glanced back at the Macqueen. "He must be very sad and very lonely."

"Aye, he lives in the dark part of his soul, where pain and torment wait."

A look of compassion swept over Marta's face. "Have you ever heard him laugh?"

"Not since the tragedy, but before that, yes." She closed her eyes as if remembering. "I can still recall the sound of his laughter shaking the very walls of Ravenscrag Castle."

"Ravenscrag? He did not live here, at Blackness?"

"No. He came here only after Ravenscrag was taken from him by the English."

"The English . . ." She spat on the floor. "The curse of Cromwell be upon them all!" Marta narrowed her eyes and looked back at the somber figure hunched over his tankard. "I can't imagine him ever laughing."

"No, I don't suppose you can, any more than you can imagine the way he has suffered. Everything and everyone he loved—all those he was closest to—they are all gone."

Tears slipped down Marta's rosy cheeks.

Grizel gave her arm a pat. "Don't cry for the dead, lass. They are at peace."

Marta sniffed. "I'm not." She took the corner of her apron and wiped her eyes. "I was crying for the Macqueen."

"You could not cry enough tears to equal his grief. His pain is too deep." Grizel picked up a candle and held it toward Marta. "Go to your room, lass. Try to get some rest. In time, you will learn, like the rest of us, to live with the constancy of his torment. Go on, now. I will snuff out the candles."

Marta reached for the candle, then paused, her gaze going back to the Macqueen. "If you don't mind . . . I think I would rather wait for you."

Grizel's expression softened, and she nodded. "Come along, then," she said, and the two of them put out the candles and slipped quietly from the room, leaving the master of Blackness Castle to grieve alone in the darkness.

The Macqueen sat at the head of the table in his great carved chair, his head bowed with grief, his mind focused not upon what was happening around him, but upon what had already passed.

His eyes were cold and lifeless, and his face was unshaven. His gaze was fixed upon the rich burgundy of the liquid inside the tankard before him. Upon its dark, glossy surface danced the image of Ailis, his wife. Ailis, with her long flaxen braids, their small son, Colin, held fast to her side. Ailis and Colin, radiant and happy, floating on the surface of the wine. Ailis, forever silent, cold as clay, and Colin, sleeping eternally in a grave no bigger than his tiny bed.

With a ragged curse, he reached for the crystal decanter of wine and knocked it from the table. Crying out in agony, he buried his face in his hands.

The sound, more mournful than the howl of a wolf, echoed down the long corridors and empty hallways, then faded away. Nothing moved. Not a sound could be heard. For some time, he sat motionless, and then, after a while, he lifted his head.

The darkness of the night called out to him, and he rose from the table, the heavy legs of his chair scraping across the uneven stone floor. He lifted the tankard to his mouth and swallowed the last drops of forgetfulness and tossed the goblet to the table. It rolled to the edge, teetered, then fell to the floor with a hollow clang.

Standing silently near the door, Manus Finlay stood in the shadows and watched, as he always did. He had been the Macqueen's friend and faithful ally since he had found him lying wounded upon the bloody fields of Culloden Moor, some five years before.

As the Macqueen approached, Manus removed his friend's cape from a peg, and he handed it to him as he passed by. As if in a trance, the younger man took the cape and threw it around his shoulders. A moment later, he had disappeared through the door.

Once he was gone, Manus turned to follow in silence.

Chapter Three

Lady Anne Crofton went to bed with a glass of warm milk. She could not sleep even after drinking the milk, so she lay in the darkness, watching eerie shadows move silently about her room. Something about them reminded her of the stories she had heard of the haunted island across the bay.

She wouldn't have given those stories a second thought, had it not been for two facts. The first was that her father was somehow involved, and the second, that she could not stop thinking about her frightening visit to the island.

It was that tall, dark man with the piercing eyes and the angry set to his jaw who had first told her about the beast. But when she had inquired about the story, she had learned that the beast the man on the island had talked about did not live here, at Ravenscrag, as he had led her to believe, but on the island where the crumbling old castle lay in ruins. She shuddered at the thought. No wonder he had wanted her off the island as soon as possible, or that he had been suspicious of her, accusing her of being a spy. And then there was the matter of the way he had threatened her with what he would do if he ever learned she had told him a lie.

She trembled at the thought. The truth was, she had told him nothing but lies. And she had a suspicion her father had told her a few of them as well.

Try as she might, she could not remember more than a few snatches of the conversation she had had with her father. They had talked of the enmity between him and the half-mad creature who lived on that devil-possessed island, but her father had not revealed much, keeping the discussion vague and, obviously, from his own point of view. Lady Anne was a woman who formed her own opinions. Just because he was her father, that did not mean she trusted him. In truth, she hardly knew him, having seen him for the first time since she was a baby when she came to the Shetlands only a few weeks ago, after the death of her mother in Cornwall.

Because of this, she thought it prudent to be cautious. After all, her mother had disliked him enough to leave him, and she had continued to hate him until the day she breathed her last. And now that he had sailed for England, it would be longer still until she and her father got to know one another.

By the time Anne finished that thought, she was hoping she'd find someone to tell her the truth about what had happened between her father and the creature who lived in the ruins of Blackness Castle before he returned.

Blackness Castle... Why did the very name intrigue her? The sound of it haunted her dreams at night. Even now, she could feel its pull... something magnetic that drew her like the power of suggestion.

Throwing the covers from her body, she combed her fingers through her mane of thick black hair, pushing the long length of it behind her as she climbed from the bed. She went to the window and drew back the drape. Darkness surrounded the island, making its outline vague. Not that it mattered. She could feel its presence.

Above the island, the moon danced among the dark, brooding clouds that rolled restlessly overhead. A cold rush of wind swept over her, as though a door had been left open somewhere in the house. A breath later, she thought she heard someone calling her name.

Anne... Come.... Come into the darkness.... Come and share your warmth with me....

What she heard was only the wind making eerie noises as it blew through the old, drafty turrets and crenels of Ravenscrag Castle. Yet she could not shake the feeling of a presence.

She gave in to a bit of self-admonishment. "You have been listening to too many ghost stories. Keep this up and they will lock you away in an oubliette and leave you there to forget." The reminder sent a shiver up her back, which was followed immediately by an unquenchable thirst to know even more. One step was all she took. Now she was closer to the window. Pressing her nose to the pane, she searched the darkness that lay beyond.

Was he out there? Now? Was that what she felt? His awful presence? Did he lure young women to their deaths among the treacherous rocks?

Logic told her that was ridiculous. Curiosity said the best way to answer her questions was to go to the island again, where she could see for herself.

Yet the thought of going to the island caused an uneasiness to sweep over her. She had been frightened the day she was there, and she was famous for being too curious and too headstrong for her own good. Even now, her mother's word of caution reached out to her: "God fashioned hell for the inquisitive."

Anne stood at the window, staring at the grotesque outline of Blackness Castle. Its broken towers and jagged walls were as black as the name they bore. He was there, she knew, walking the walls as the village folk said, with his hair wild and flying about him. A madman. A howling beast . . .

The Beast of Blackness Castle.

She heard the door open, and although she knew it would be her maid, Fanny, she quickly dropped the drapery and turned away.

Fanny stopped and looked at her bed. "Were you in the bed, milady, or did you leave the window open when a storm blew through? What a frightful mess! The covers are going every which a way."

"I couldn't sleep."

"I would never have guessed."

The two of them laughed, and Anne was reminded that laughter was, indeed, good for the soul.

"I'll straighten it up and then you'll sleep better," Fanny said. She turned to the bed and busied herself with setting it to rights, clucking and tsk-tsking as she did.

Anne stayed where she was, waiting for her heart to stop its rapid pounding. She took a deep breath.

"Have you been staring at that devil again, milady?"

Anne glanced back at the window, thankful she had allowed the drape to fall back into place. She did not want to look at the darkness or see that awful place the beast called home. "Fanny, do you believe the stories they tell about him in the village?"

"Of course I do, milady."

"What kind of stories do you hear?"

Fanny punched the pillow into a nice puff. "Horrible stories. It is said that he offers sacrifices of young virgins and he drinks their blood. That is what makes him go mad—virgins' blood."

Anne laughed. "Oh, Fanny, surely *you* don't believe such stories . . . do you?"

Fanny looked a bit shamefaced. "I . . . I don't know, milady."

"Have you ever seen him?"

Fanny looked properly horrified. "Oh, no, milady. And I wouldn't want to. They say he has a curse upon him, you know. He has the evil eye."

Anne did not bother to hide her amusement. "I think he is probably a poor, miserable man who has gone slightly mad—more to be pitied than feared."

"I don't believe that for a minute. There isn't a soul in the village what isn't afraid of him and his devil's lair. People who go there never return."

Anne scoffed at that. "I was rowed to the island when I first came here, and I survived, as you can see."

"You went to Blackness Castle? Alone?"

"I was left on the island by mistake. I was supposed to be taken here, but the captain of the ship was a fool."

"It was the perfect time for the beast to put his curse upon you." Fanny eyed her with an open air of speculation. "Lord protect us! You do seem intrigued with him and his wicked castle, more and more. Oh, milady..."

"Fanny, I am not bewitched. I am simply a curious sort, and certainly not on the receiving end of any curse." She tapped her finger against the side of her face. "I would give anything to know what the bitterness is between the beast and my father. Have you ever heard anyone speak of it?"

"Not to any great length. All I know is that his family was murdered. They are all buried here, you know... at Ravenscrag."

"His family? You mean his wife and children? Or his parents?"

"I don't know, milady, but I think I remember hearing someone say it was his wife and child. Murdered, they were, and by the English, it is said."

Anne turned her head away. "Oh, how awful! Did it happen here, do you think?"

"Yes, it was here... perhaps in this very room."

"I asked for information, not white hair. What are you trying to do, frighten me?"

"The more you know about the enemy, the more you can withstand him, I always say. Will there be anything else, milady?"

"No, that will be... Wait a minute. Take that empty milk glass when you go."

Fanny bobbed downward in something that faintly resembled a curtsy, while brilliant red strands of her hair fell down across her eyes. With a quick puff of air, she blew them out of her face. "Yes, milady." She picked up the glass and headed for the door. As she passed through it, she said, "Good night, milady. Don't worry about the beast coming to get you. I hear he never leaves the island. They say he cannot, for his heart is buried there and he cannot leave until he finds it."

"Good night, Fanny. I am *certain* I will sleep now."

When Fanny closed the door, Anne turned toward her bed. "Well, with that bit of cheerfulness, I suppose I will try to get some sleep." She climbed into bed and doused the light. She closed her eyes and waited for sleep.

. . . he never leaves the island. . . . he cannot, for his heart is buried there and he cannot leave until he finds it. . . .

Anne pulled the covers higher over her shoulders and lay in the darkness, staring at the drape that covered her window. She wondered what was going on across the bay—on that tiny island where a man existed who was as steeped in mystery as the great ruins of his castle. And what the connection was between the man she had met that day and the beast.

As always when she thought of the beast, a cold draft of air seemed to move over her. Her body trembled in response. She found herself wondering what he was like, and yet, deep inside her, she knew that she really did not want to know.

She closed her eyes, refusing to think about the crumbling castle and the man who haunted it. Instead, she focused her thoughts on her father and wondered when he would be home.

Chapter Four

The old longing was back, and the thirst for revenge was strong. The Macqueen stood on the castle wall and stared out across the expanse of thrashing black water toward the battered coast of the Shetlands, his gaze locked upon the dim glow of lights from the windows of Ravenscrag Castle, the ancient home of the lairds of the clan Macqueen. His home ... until it, and everything else he loved, had been taken from him by the English.

The pain of remembrance caused him to throw back his head and shout. It was a long, mournful cry. The wind ripped the ribbon from his hair, sending the long black mass swirling about his head. Hard drops of freezing rain pelted him and splattered upon his face.

The rain came down harder and faster. The wind rose and whipped his great black cape about him. Overhead, black, boiling clouds blocked the moonlight and cast the world below into complete darkness. Not even the torches that burned along the castle wall could penetrate the inky cover of black. Below him, the angry sea pounded against the rocky summit and sent a fine mist shooting upward, where it leaped the parapets to settle upon his cape, but he did not seem to notice, any more than he noticed the deafening sound of the towering waves that slammed against the rocks.

A storm was settling in. He had known since early this morning that this storm would be worse than all the others, for the throbbing ache in his old wounds had awakened him even before daylight penetrated the gloom of his chamber. Even now, he could feel the pain more intensely than he had this morning, and he prayed it would grow stronger still. For then, and only then, would he be certain that he would never forget.

One by one, the lights of Ravenscrag began to disappear as the storm worsened. A blinding bolt of lightning ripped across the sky. A second later, an exploding crack of thunder sent a stab of pain deep inside his ears. To his right, a dull beam of light penetrated the darkness as a lamp appeared.

Manus stepped through the doorway and shouted, his voice barely audible over the roar of the wind and the waves. "I ken we've a bonny storm brewing! Would you be coming inside now?"

The Macqueen stood with his legs widespread as he faced the wind and stared into the heart of the storm. He did not turn his head to look at Manus. "Go back inside, I'll—"

The words froze in the Macqueen's throat, for just as he was about to speak, he saw the faintest glimmer of light reaching out from the wildly thrashing sea. As quickly as it had come, the light disappeared. For a moment, he thought his eyes had deceived him, for he could see nothing. Then, suddenly it appeared again, the faintest gleam of light.

A ship. Before he could think further upon it, Manus quickly covered the distance between them and reached his side. He held the light aloft and stared into the Macqueen's face. "You look like you have seen a ghost."

"No ghost, but a ship...floundering not too far offshore."

Manus glanced in that direction. "Will she be coming aground, do you think?"

"Aye. She will be upon the rocks before we can get down there. Alert the men."

Manus grumbled something inaudible, then said, "You know what they will be saying...that it was you and your curses that caused the wreck. You will receive no thanks for risking your life." Manus paused to watch the great black cape of the Macqueen disappear through the doorway.

Grumbling, he turned away and did what he had been doing for five years: He followed the Macqueen.

Chapter Five

It appeared that all aboard were dead by the time they reached what was left of the ship. Robert and his men searched among the rocks and wreckage for survivors, fighting the waves to reach each body, only to discover that the life they hoped to save was already gone.

"We're too late!" Manus shouted through his cupped hands.

"Aye!" Gavin McDougal shouted back, holding a lamp aloft.

The Macqueen was about to tell his men to return to the castle when Gavin held his lamp aloft and waded out into the water. "Look! Over there...is that someone clinging to a piece of drift?"

Already the Macqueen was making his way between the rocks to wade deeper into the water, fighting his way, inch by inch, falling and being driven back by the sheer force of powerful waves. When he reached the driftwood, he threw his arm around the man. This time, he fought against the weight of a limp body and the water's power. At last, he pulled the man to shore.

Weak and trembling from exertion, the Macqueen stared down at the body stretched out on the sand before him. "Gavin! Bring the lamp!"

Gavin hurried to his side. "Is he dead?"

"I don't know. Hold the lamp higher."

Gavin raised his arm. The lamp cast a small circle of light upon the face of the man Robert Macqueen hated more than anything in the world: Sir John Crofton.

Manus approached. "Is he dead?"

Robert could not take his gaze from the devil's own face. "Aye, much to my sorrow, I think he is."

Manus looked down at the man and gasped. "Sir John! 'Tis the murdering bastard himself."

"Even in death he has cheated me."

"At least this way you won't have his blood on your hands."

"I can think of nothing I would like better." He nudged the body with his boot. There was no movement, no response.

Manus stared down at the despised face, then looked around at the bodies scattered upon the sand. "'Tis a pity we couldn't save even one of them."

"It is a greater pity that we couldn't save *this* one."

"What do you want to do with him?" Gavin asked. "Shall we leave him here for the scavengers?"

"No. Bring him back to the castle. I'll hang his black heart from the tower."

Gavin wedged his lamp in the sand, then picked up the body of Sir John, his brawny arms flexing as he heaved the Englishman's scrawny body over his back. Suddenly a gush of water rushed from Sir John's mouth. It was followed by a choking cough.

Gavin started and glanced at Manus, who turned to look at the Macqueen. "He lives," Manus said, in a disbelieving voice. "What shall we do with him, now?"

"Take him to the castle. Nothing has changed," Robert said. He said nothing more as he stood with his arms crossed in front of him, but he never took his gaze from Sir John's body as Gavin hauled it toward Blackness.

Manus gave him a questioning look. "What will you do with him? Toss him into the dungeon?"

"Of course not. We will give him the finest care, to ensure his speedy recovery."

"And then what?"

A slow-spreading smile curved across the Macqueen's face. "And then, we will kill the bastard."

Across the bay the next day, Lady Anne Crofton sat before her embroidery frame, her face pale, her eyes glistening with tears, as she listened to the words of Captain Singleton.

"The dead have all been accounted for, but your father's body has not been found. More than likely, it was swept out to sea."

Anne barely looked at the splendid uniform, the gleaming medals, awarded to only the bravest of English soldiers, that the captain sported. Her father's ship was lost, and her father was dead. It was too soon, she thought. Too soon after the death of her mother. Too soon for her to get to know him. "Where did the wreck occur?"

"Not far from here. It seems the *Albatross* was blown off course and broke up on the rocks near Blackness Castle."

"On the island?"

"Yes, just below the castle… At least, that is where the bodies were pulled from the water."

"And my father was not among them?"

Captain Singleton looked down. "No, I regret to say he was not."

"And he is the only passenger not accounted for?"

"Yes."

Anne was silent for a moment. Then she put her embroidery away, and rose to her feet. "Would you be so kind, Captain, as to take me to the place where you found the wreckage?"

"A lady such as yourself should not be going to such a rough place. It is quite difficult to reach, especially with a small boat."

"I do not mind. I am not afraid of a small boat. I often went out alone in England."

"It is a difficult journey. The way is treacherous… covered with boulders and many large rocks."

"I would like to see the wreckage, Captain. If you will not accompany me, then I will go alone."

Captain Singleton's face turned red. His expression said he was quite put out at her request, but he clicked his heels together with true military dispatch, and said, "As an English gentleman and an officer, I cannot allow you to make such a journey alone. I will, of course, accompany you. When would you like to go?"

"Now."

This time, all the color drained from Captain Singleton's face. His mustache drooped with obvious disappointment. "Now?" he sputtered. "You wish to go now?"

Anne nodded her head. "If you please."

"As you wish," he replied, but this time he did not click his heels.

Lady Anne walked from the room, pausing momentarily at the door. "I will only be a moment, Captain. I will change clothes and meet you down at the boat."

Chapter Six

The Macqueen paced the floor back and forth in front of the enormous fireplace in the library. He was waiting for Dr. Burris to finish his examination of the murdering English bastard. Only an hour ago, he had come from the chapel, where he had gone down upon his knees in supplication as he prayed to God for the sparing of Sir John Crofton's life. He did not feel one whit of remorse in asking for Sir John's healing so that he could have the satisfaction of killing him. And why should he?

The Macqueen cursed and turned to brace his hands upon the mantel. As he stared into the flames, the face of his dead wife took shape, and he saw Ailis as he had seen her last, standing upon the walls of Ravenscrag Castle, with their three-year-old son, Colin, in her arms, the two of them waving goodbye as he rode off to fight the British, leading ''the mighty clan Macqueen'' toward a rendezvous with death.

In the hallway, just outside the room, Marta and Grizel passed by, their arms loaded with laundry. Seeing the Macqueen standing before the fire, his broad back turned toward her, Marta stopped and peered at Grizel over a stack of neatly folded laundry.

"He is such a handsome man, and yet so sad. Why is it that no one here will speak of the tragedy that struck him? Everyone I ask tells me to tend my own flock."

"It is wise to heed good advice."

"You can say that, because you know what happened. Why can't you tell me?"

"No one loyal to the Macqueen enjoys talking about his sorrow."

"Yet everyone here knows the story, except me. Someone must have told them."

Grizel stared down at the stack of laundry in her arms for several seconds before she turned to look at Marta. With a resigned sigh, she said, "I can see by the fire in your eye that you will not rest until you have heard it all. Very well. Go and find Manus Finlay. He knows the story best. Let the burden of telling you be upon him."

Marta's face brightened, and she thrust her stack of laundry on top of the stack Grizel carried. While Grizel muttered something about not being able to see, Marta went to find Manus.

She found him cleaning guns in the armory. When she told him why Grizel had sent her to find him, he was reluctant to speak of the Macqueen's misery, but, as she had been with Grizel, Marta was persistent.

"I will have Grizel's head for sending you here," he grumbled, "but I ken you will not let this rest until you have heard the whole story."

"No, I will not. I think I have a right to know. I have already proven my loyalty by coming to work here...even when I know there isn't another lass in the village who would do so."

Manus turned his faded eyes upon Marta, his resigned sigh telling her that she would learn, at last, of the death of the Macqueen's wife and son, the slaughter of the members of the clan Macqueen, and the curse upon the Macqueen's head.

She took a seat beside Manus and listened quietly as he told the tragic story of the clan Macqueen.

"You mean they were all murdered? Every last one of them?"

Manus nodded. "Down to a man, they were butchered...all of them, save the laird himself, and now he is cursed with the memory of seeing his men cut down right before his eyes, their blood mingling with that of a hundred clans, to stain the fields of Culloden scarlet."

"And the Macqueen was the only member of the clan to survive?"

"Aye, he was the sole survivor, although he was gravely wounded. When I found him, I feared he had lost too much blood to live."

"But he didn't die." Marta's tone possessed a hint of optimism.

"No, but it wasn't because he did not pray for death. He cursed the English with every painful breath he drew, and he cursed his own inability to end his own life. It would have been much easier, and far more noble to die there, just like the other Macqueens. But it was his fate not to join the clan he led to their deaths."

"So you saved him and brought him home?"

"I could not bring him home straightaway. He was at death's door. I took him to an abandoned crofter's hut and nursed him back to health. When he was well enough to return home, some three months later, I went with him. It was on our journey to Ravenscrag that the Macqueen made a vow to raise the sons and daughters of the slain Macqueens, and to make the clan as great and mighty as it had once been."

"But you said they were all dead."

"Aye, it was a vow he could not keep. From the moment we first set foot upon the Shetlands, the Macqueen had a premonition that something dreadful had taken place. He fully expected to see Ravenscrag torn apart, stone by stone."

"And it wasn't."

"To his surprise, Ravenscrag was as strong and splendid as it had been the day he left. It was only when we rode closer that he saw just how the British deal with those they call enemy."

Marta shivered. When she spoke again, her words came slowly, and her tone was low. "They were all dead."

"Aye. Down to the lowliest servant. As we passed by the graves, he dropped to his knees beside his horse and cursed God for making the innocent pay. He struck his chest and cried out in anguish, but it was when he discovered the graves of his wife and son that I feared he had lost his mind."

"What did he do?"

"He was overcome with grief, ye ken. That is what made him wish for death. He remounted and rode his horse at a dead run, right up to the gates of Ravenscrag, praying all the while that someone would slay him. From high upon the walls above us came the sound of mocking laughter, and he looked up to see the flaming scarlet coats of the English soldiers. He stood up in his stirrups and held his arms out, making himself a bold target, but not one of his tormentors fired a shot.''

"Why?"

"Because they were told to hold their fire. Sir John preferred to let the Macqueen live, rather than to end his suffering by allowing him to join those he loved in death.''

"A fate worse than death," she whispered.

"Aye," he said, "a fate worse than death. So, now you know." Manus looked tired and worn. He sighed wearily, and it reminded her that he was an old man. "Go back to your work, now, and speak no more of this to anyone.''

Marta turned away, then paused to look at Manus over her shoulder. "But what about the curse?''

"That *is* the curse... to remember when you want to forget. To seek death over and over again, and each time be denied.''

"No wonder the Macqueen hates the Englishman. It was Sir John who brought the curse upon him.''

"Night after night he has walked the castle walls, praying for a way to seek his revenge. And now, after five long years, his prayers have been answered...."

Chapter Seven

Manus came into the kitchen, where Robert sat, hunched over a bowl of soup. "The English captain is snooping around the wreckage. He has a lady with him."

Robert tossed the spoon to the table and stood. A moment later, he yanked his cape from a hook. "Who is the lady? Did you get a good look at her?"

"I was quite a distance away and could not see her face. Perhaps it was Sir John's daughter."

"His daughter? I didn't know he had a daughter. How did you learn of her?"

"I only heard about her. Apparently the mother died, so the girl came to live with her father."

That had a strangely familiar ring to it, and Robert could not help thinking of the girl who had walked out of the water like a silkie and onto his island that day. It wasn't the same girl, he assured himself. He could never be attracted to a daughter of that English pig. "How old is she? What does she look like?"

"Old enough to be wed, and from what I hear, she is comely enough to turn a man's head. Other than that, I do not know. I have yet to see her, ye ken."

"Old enough to be wed . . . She is English, and the spawn of a murdering Englishman. No right-minded Scot would come within a mile of her."

Manus said nothing.

"If it is his daughter with the captain, what would she be doing here?"

"It could be that she is curious about her father's disappearance . . . or it could be that the woman I saw wasn't the Crofton wench."

"It doesn't matter. Let them snoop. They will find nothing."

"What if they find out he's not dead?"

"Finding out he is alive is one thing. Taking him from us is another."

"You cannot fight the English and win. You, of all people, should know that."

"I don't intend to fight the English. I have what I want."

"If they learn he is here, they will come after him."

"Let them come."

"Are you not afraid . . . even after what you've seen them do?"

"What can they do to me, that they have not already done?"

"They could take your life."

At that, Robert gave a shout of mocking laughter. "You cannot kill someone who is already dead." He turned away and made his way to the castle wall. He wanted to see for himself.

He stood on the wall, the wind whipping his hair and cloak as he looked down at the English captain and the woman. Even from where he stood, he could see that she was quite small, and when the wind blew her cape from her head, he saw that her hair was as black as her father's heart.

As he watched them, he kept thinking of the girl who had come here that day. He did not want to think of her, but his mind had a habit of getting its own way. He narrowed his eyes and watched the two snooping around below. Soon, the girl he tried to forget was out of his mind.

But he knew that was not where she would stay.

Lady Anne pulled her wool cape more closely about her, to ward off the penetrating wind. She stepped over shattered boards and bits of rope left from the wreckage, and paused a moment to look at the broken remains of the ship that lay scattered over the rocks. From what she could see, it was easy to understand how all lives aboard the *Albatross* had been lost. It was not easy to understand why her father's body had been the only one not recovered. Not unless one figured that the beast had had something to do with it.

"Where were the bodies found?" she asked the captain who followed closely behind her.

"We don't know for certain, since Macqueen's men discovered the wreckage. They could have been moved, but they were all lying among the rocks that line the shore, or in shallow water."

"All but my father."

"Yes."

She stood amid the wreckage and stared out over the water. "It would be a horrible death, I think, to drown."

"Horrible, but it's a quick death, I am told."

"Then I can be thankful for that, at least."

Captain Singleton glanced at the sky overhead. "It grows dark, and you are cold. We should be returning."

"Yes, I suppose there is nothing further for me to do here." She paused, looking around her. "I don't know what I expected to find here."

"Sometimes it helps the grieving to see the place where a loved one was seen last."

She called her father's wolfhound, Pharaoh to her side, and waited for him to appear from beneath the rocks. Suddenly, she felt someone watching them, and she turned to stare up at the walls of Blackness Castle.

She drew in her breath. He was there, just as the rumors said, a figure of a man, black against the purpling close of day, the wind whipping his hair and clothes, making him look every inch the beast he was reported to be.

"Don't be alarmed. They say his mind is not right. He is a sort of legend in these parts."

"I have heard of him. They say he is a beast, Captain . . . the Beast of Blackness Castle."

"The Scots are a superstitious lot. Don't believe all their supernatural drivel."

"Of course I don't," she said, and turned away, stepping lightly over the stones that lay wet and glistening beneath her feet. Captain Singleton held out his hand to help her into the boat. Just as she took his hand, she caught a glimpse of something shining in the water.

"Just a moment, Captain." She bent down and put her hand into the icy water. She could see now that it was a golden chain, catching the last of the sun's rays as it lay among the black rocks in the sand. She caught the chain between her fingers and lifted it, but as she raised the chain, she realized it was connected to something. A second later, she pulled a gold watch out of the sand.

Paralyzed, she stood there, looking at the watch in her hand.

"What is it?"

"A watch." She opened the case and saw the inscription: *To my beloved John, on the occasion of our marriage. Elizabeth.*

Elizabeth. It was her mother's name, and although Anne had only seen her father's watch a few times, and from a distance, she knew this watch was his.

"Whomever the watch belonged to, it is of no value to them now. Come, my lady, let us be off."

She took the captain's hand and climbed into the boat. She called Pharaoh, and he came running out of the rocks, his nose to the ground. Suddenly, he veered off to the left, sniffing in earnest now, and she knew he had picked up a scent.

A scent of what?

The thought had no more than formed when Pharaoh stopped. He began to whine and bark. A moment later, he began to dig, unearthing a bit of white cloth.

"Pharaoh! Come!" she called, and waited patiently for Pharaoh to return to her, a white scrap of linen still in his mouth.

Captain Singleton laughed. "Seems he found a bit of treasure. It's a pity you cannot train him to sniff for gold. There might be more where that watch came from."

"Yes," she said absently as she took the cloth from Pharaoh's mouth.

She looked down at the linen square, which she realized was a man's handkerchief. There, in one corner, embroidered in white, were the initials *J.C.C.* Her father's name was John Charles Crofton, and this was his handkerchief. She knew it was his, because he had given her one just like it to use one evening when she was telling him about her mother's death and she started to cry.

Her father had been here. She was certain of it. The question was, if he were dead when he came ashore, why would someone go to the trouble to bury his handkerchief? It did not make sense. What made sense was that her father must have been alive, and whoever rescued him had buried the handkerchief in order to fake his death. And who had a better reason to do that than the man who owned this island?

Pharaoh began to whine.

"You have taken his plaything, my lady."

Anne smiled sweetly, "Why, so I have." Then, with a laugh that was a bit higher-pitched than she would have liked, she gave the handkerchief back to Pharaoh.

A moment later, she was staring solemnly into the water, her hand in her pocket and stroking the cold gold casing of her father's watch. As they rowed past the point, she took one last look back at Blackness Castle.

The beast was gone.

Chapter Eight

As his prisoner grew steadily stronger, Robert felt himself coming alive.

He had lived for this moment for five years—waiting and watching, learning a patience he had not known he possessed. And now it had come to pass. At last, he had Sir John Crofton where he wanted him: in the dungeons of Blackness Castle.

Gavin McDougal put the key in the lock. The iron door creaked open. He stepped back and handed the Macqueen the lamp.

"Shall I accompany you?"

"No. Wait here. I won't be long."

Robert ducked his head as he stepped into the small, damp cell. On a straw pallet in the corner lay Sir John. Unaccustomed to the light, Sir John put his hands up and turned his head away. "Have you come to let me go?"

The Macqueen laughed. "I will make a bargain with you."

"One you do not intend to keep, I'll wager. Well, let's hear it. What do you want in exchange for me?"

"I will let you go, when you return my wife and son to me."

"I told you before that I had nothing to do with their deaths...or the deaths of anyone at Ravenscrag. They were all in their graves when I arrived."

"They were murdered to make room for you. Not that it matters, for I don't believe you, anyway. Your hands are as red as your scarlet coats, and nothing will wash it out. Certainly not lying."

"I am not lying. How can I convince you?"

"You cannot, so don't waste what little energy you have left in trying to do so."

"Then I beg you, as one human being to another, let me go. I will petition the king and request that all your possessions be returned to you, including Ravenscrag."

"All my possessions? Save the ones I desire the most. What will you do about my wife and son?"

"You can marry again, and have many children. You are still young."

"It isn't as easy as that. You took something priceless from me. I intend to do the same to you."

"Please. Let me go."

The Macqueen laughed. "You will never leave here."

"What do you intend to do with me?"

"I will keep you here. Forever. And each day you will die a little more than you did the day before, and each night you will pray for death, but it will not come. I will be as merciful as you were. I will not kill you. I will let you live. I will let you live so that you will regret until your dying day that you reaped the profits of another's suffering."

"I have told you—I did not have anything to do with the death of your wife and child. There was no one here when I arrived."

"I do not believe you."

"What would make you believe me?"

"This conversation is finished." The Macqueen turned and started toward the door.

Sir John ran after him and grabbed his hand, going down on his knees before him. "Please. Tell me what I can do. I will do anything . . . give you anything it is in my power to do."

"I want my wife back."

Sir John's eyes were wild, rolling from side to side, as if he were searching for something he could say, something that would change his fate.

The Macqueen shoved his hand away and stepped through the door. He handed Gavin the lamp. "Lock him up."

"Aye."

"No!" Sir John screamed. "Wait! I have a daughter. . . ." Sir John seemed to catch himself. "I am a family man, and although my wife is dead, I understand how a man feels about his family. I would not do anything to deprive a man of his family."

"As I said before, I do not believe you, just as I will never believe anything you say. You are English. It is in your blood to lie."

"You bloody bastard! You are the devil incarnate!"

The Macqueen walked off. The iron gate creaked heavily behind him.

Sir John's shrill voice cut through the dungeon's damp air. "Do you hear me? You are a devil!"

A muscle in Robert Macqueen's jaw flexed. "Then you would do well to remember one thing—you cannot bargain with the devil."

Chapter Nine

Lady Anne knew this was the day she would go to the island again. There were too many questions that remained unanswered, and the island was the only place to answer them.

She was exhausted by the time she had rowed around the point that blocked Ravenscrag from view. Although she had often gone out alone at home, she was not as familiar with these waters as she was with those of Cornwall. As a precaution, she hugged the shore, knowing she must keep it in sight. It would make the trip longer, but that could not be helped.

The waves here were higher, the currents stronger, than she was accustomed to, and the weather was bitterly cold. Already, her gloves were stiff and crusted with ice. Inside, her fingers were numb. Beneath her soaked clothes her body felt warm, and yet her teeth chattered from the cold. Her throat was dry and scratchy. Her eyes teared and made it difficult for her to see.

She had to go on. She had gone too far to turn back, and there was no place along this rugged, lonely coast for her to seek shelter. She realized her foolishness and her overconfidence. She was too headstrong, and she possessed too much pride, and now that pride was asking her to pay a dear, dear price.

How she wished she could go back to Ravenscrag, turn back the clock and be standing in her bedroom, faced with the same decision she had been faced with this morning. Only this time, she would choose to stay home.

From out of the stormy grayness ahead of her, she could make out the dim outline of the island, but she knew her strength would be gone long before she reached its shore. Her head felt light, and she had difficulty focusing. She stared down at her aching arms and realized that the oars were gone, and yet she had no recollection of having let them go. She was doomed now. Without the oars, she was completely at the mercy of the sea, and well she knew that the sea had no mercy.

She was tired…so tired that even the knowledge of her own approaching death did little to shake her. Her only thought now was to lie down, to rest, to close her eyes and to feel warm again.

Dying wasn't so bad. You lay down and you went to sleep. She felt herself slipping downward. Her head struck the seat behind her, and a stabbing, blinding pain shot through her skull.

Robert had been watching the boat for some time now, unable to fathom what kind of fool would set out in a small rowboat at the onset of such a violent storm. One moment he was watching the occupant of the boat battle his way forward. The next, the boat was unmanned and drifting wildly. Whoever the fool was, he had either gone overboard, or had succumbed to the cold and lay frozen in the bottom of the boat. It served the half-wit right if he was carried out to sea.

It was only when the boat drifted toward his island that the Macqueen turned and went inside, calling to Manus and Gavin as he went.

It was almost dark by the time they reached the point where the battered boat was being shoved closer to shore by each pounding wave. The Macqueen held the lamp aloft as he stood on the rocks and watched Gavin wade out into water up to his knees.

Gavin grabbed at the rope tied to the bow, and missed. He caught it on the second try, then turned and put the rope over his shoulder, tugging the boat forward until it rested upon solid ground.

Robert saw the dark cloak covering the man who lay unmoving in the bottom of the boat. He called out to Gavin. "Is he dead?"

"I don't know, but if he isn't, he should be! His cloak is frozen stiff!"

Manus moved forward. "Let me help!"

Together they lifted the body from the boat. "Light as a feather!" Manus shouted. "'Tis but a lad."

"Is he alive?" the Macqueen called back.

Manus shook his head. "I can't tell!"

"Bring him up to the house, then, and be quick about it!"

They carried the lad up the stairs to the Macqueen's chamber, for there was a warm fire going there, and his bed was covered, appropriately, with wolf furs. When Gavin and Manus had placed the lad on the bed, the Macqueen sent them to find Grizel and

Marta. "And bring a bottle of warm brandy and a jar of honey."

As soon as they left the room, Robert turned and placed his hand on the pale skin of the lad lying so silently before him. He had seen this lad before. He was certain of it, but he could not recollect where.

The lad's face was icy-cold—too cold for Robert to tell if he was dead or alive. With a sudden movement, he grabbed the two sides of the lad's shirt to rip it apart, so that he could place his ear to his chest to listen for a heartbeat.

The fabric had barely been ripped apart when Robert sucked in his breath. Transfixed, he could only stare. The sound of the door opening behind him shook him out of his stupor. He cursed.

Marta let out a shriek. "'Tis a girl! Oh, my Lord... 'Tis a girl, and the Macqueen has bared her to the waist!"

"Stop yapping and get out of the way," Grizel said, giving Marta a bump with her hip. She stopped next to Robert and looked down at the girl. "Is she still alive?"

"I...I don't know. I was going to listen for a heartbeat. That is why I... Oh, hell. I'm no good at this. You see what you think."

Grizel nodded. Placing the bottle of brandy and the honey on the chest by the bed, she leaned forward and put her ear to the girl's chest. She remained that way for so long that Robert thought the girl must be dead. Grizel finally pulled her head back and covered the girl. "Her heart beats, but faintly. We must get her out of these clothes. Marta, help me."

Marta scampered around to the other side of the bed and looked at Grizel.

Grizel turned to the Macqueen. "If you would lift her, Marta and I will pull the cloak from under her. The rest we can manage."

Robert lifted the girl off the bed. Even soaking wet, she did not weigh as much as one of his hounds. But when they pulled the cape from her, a long, curly mass of black hair fell to the bed like glossy ropes of wet seaweed. Somehow appropriate, for a creature plucked from the sea.

This was the woman who haunted his dreams at night. Had she come back here on purpose? Or was her appearance an accident, a result of the storm?

Grizel placed a dry, folded blanket beneath the girl, and Robert lowered her onto the bed again. He turned away and saw Manus and Gavin standing nearby. "Send someone to build up the fire," he said to Gavin. "Tell them to keep it going all night."

Gavin nodded and left. Silently Robert and Manus followed him from the room leaving the women behind to minister to the girl.

Anne moaned and stirred in her sleep. she was dreaming again—strange dreams, in which the familiar and the unknown seemed to melt together into a whole. She could hear the crashing force of waves against her boat, and felt the rocking motion as surely as she tasted the tang of the sea on her lips, heavy with salt. She knew she was dying, and yet, when she looked on the other side of the boat, the sea was as calm and as smooth as glass.

Then, from out of the darkness, he came, a creature not quite man and yet not completely beast. Grotesque though he was, she felt no fear of him as he lifted her and carried her over the water toward the darkness that lay beyond, a darkness she feared she could never leave.

She couldn't let him take her there, for once she was within the walls of his lair, there would be no escape. Not ever.

She moaned again, thrashing the bed wildly, repeating the same word. "No... No... No..."

From out of the darkness, a voice came to her—a strange voice filled with reassurance. "There, there. You are safe now. Sleep, and do not fret."

But she wasn't safe. She must leave. Now. Before it was too late. If only she weren't so weak. If only her body would obey. Her throat was dry and swollen, her chest burned as if filled with hot coals. One moment she felt as though she was being boiled alive. The next, she was shivering from the cold.

Someone was trying to kill her. She had to escape. She had to...

The soft voice spoke to her again, but the words seemed too far away for her to comprehend. Someone lifted her head. She felt a sweet, burning liquid slide down her throat, and felt the sharp stab of pain when she swallowed. She turned her head from side to side. She did not want any more. It hurt too much. "Noooo..."

"Just a little more, child. It will help you rest, and keep the bad dreams away."

Three more times she swallowed, each time fighting against the pain. Then she felt her body relax as she drifted off to sleep.

They had lied to her. The dreams came again, only this time they were worse than before. She was lying in a great bed in an unfamiliar room. She was not bound, but she could not move. It was as if she were held to the bed by some invisible binding. She heard a key turn in the lock. Her heart beat wildly in her chest. Then the door opened, and she saw him standing in a pool of pale white light.

His eyes were yellow, his nose was long, and his teeth were pointed and sharp. It was the face of a predator, a wolf. The sight of him terrified her. And yet she felt a craving, a thirst, for him that she could not have explained. She wanted to feel the heat of his skin and the strength of his arms around her, wanted to know the things he could teach her, things for which she had no name.

She felt her arms lift, stretching out to him in a beseeching manner. The thought that she had done it frightened her, and yet she could not stop herself.

He was beside her now, and she felt the weight of him on the bed beside her, felt, too, the warm caress of words spoken softly against her throat. "I am yours, my beautiful one, my lovely creature from the sea."

She wanted to rebuke him, to scream and keep on screaming until he went away, but the words, the resistance, fell away from her, as shed skin falls from a snake.

"Come to me, my beloved...."

Tears spilled down her cheeks. Her body shook with heaving sobs. And yet not a sound came from her lips. *This is a dream. Soon I will awake, and I will be home. This is only a dream. Nothing is real....*

Her fingers spread outward. The bed was solid beneath her. Her eyes fluttered open for a mere second, just long enough for her to see the candle that burned next to her bed. It was real. She took a deep breath, and the scent of the wax filled her nostrils, and she knew then that this, too, was real.

"No," she whispered. "You aren't real. This isn't happening to me."

"I am real, and your body knows it. It is only your mind that won't accept the truth."

She lay still, unmoving, attempting to focus all her energy into her mind. She was trying to understand how something unreal could appear so real, how the imagined could interplay with reality. Her mind swirled in a mist of confusion.

She felt his mouth on hers. Such a beautiful feeling it was—one that sent a ripple of sensation cascading through her. Was this real, or was she dreaming it as well? His hands caressed her body, touching her intimately. It couldn't be a dream. Not this mouth. Not these hands.

She was surrounded by his warmth, his nearness, and bewildered by her unrestrained desire for him. She fought against him, against herself. She could not give in. She had to resist. But whatever it was that consumed her, it was stronger than she. At last, she lay passive, her body drenched in sweat.

Need. Wanting. Desire. They coiled around her like a sweet perfume, seducing her with promises of the exotic, the unknown. And still his hands were upon her, coaxing, leading, persuading, seducing. . . .

She gave in to the aching need, the incredible pleasure. Paralyzed with wanting, she felt herself relax and open to him. She moaned and stirred restlessly.

"You belong to me. You will always be mine."

His voice seemed to come to her from far away.

"You are tired. Rest. Rest and regain your strength. Then I will return, to give you the pleasure you want. Wait for me, little beauty. Wait, until it is time for me to come."

His words flowed out of him like a song. The words were familiar to her, but the melody was one she had never heard. He kissed her again, and her heart fluttered inside her like a trapped bird.

"Rest, my love, my adorable one, my gift from the sea. I will be back. . . ."

His words sounded faint and distant. She willed her eyes to open, and she saw him, standing far away, nothing more than a specter, cursed and wicked, a vague shadow against the night. With his midnight hair and great black cape, he was almost impossible to see.

I will be back. . . .

A gloomy hopelessness swept over her. She knew what she must do. She had to get away from him, from this place. She could not stay here to be consumed by this beast, this creature of darkness and despair.

She was so sick. She could not lift her head. How could she even think she could get away? She tried to reason with herself, to plump up her spirits with a shot of courage, but it was no use. Her mind was empty, all her thoughts sucked away by her gripping fear. No wonder he was so understanding, so kind in telling her to rest, so magnanimous in giving her time to heal.

He knew she was trapped here, trapped by her own pride and foolishness. She understood now why animals sometimes froze when they stared into the face of death.

She closed her eyes and wept.

When she awoke, the room was filled with a soft, diffuse light, and Anne knew it was early morning. She had no idea how long she had slept—whether a few hours or a few days. Yet the need to flee, to get away from this dark, demented place, was still strong within her.

"You cannot stay here," she whispered, forcing herself to a sitting position. "You must leave. Immediately. It may be your only chance."

She raised her head. Dizziness gripped her. The warmth of the bed beckoned. "Get up, Anne. You must get up."

She could not give in. Her life was at stake. "Be strong, Anne. Do not weaken."

She felt the smooth coldness of the stone floor beneath her feet. She looked down and saw she was in a flannel nightgown, one much too large, and miles too long.

She had no idea where her clothes were, or her shoes, for that matter. But she could not waste precious time searching for them. Not if she was to take them by surprise. "They do not expect you to try anything so foolish when you are so ill. If you are to escape this place you must go now. Go, and don't look back.''

The halls were deserted, yet she had no idea how to get out of the half-destroyed shell of the castle. Her instincts told her that as long as she was going downward, she was getting closer to the sea.

Her body ached and trembled from exhaustion and she had almost given up hope of ever finding her way when a cold waft of air washed over her. A moment later, she heard the shrieking of seabirds.

She came to an iron gate made of closely set bars. She gripped the bars and pushed. The gate did not give. Her head was swimming and she was so nauseated and dizzy that she felt she might faint. "Please, God, show me the way. Grant me strength...."

She began to search the gate for a lock. Running her hands over each of the bars, she found nothing. There had to be one someplace.

She braced herself against another wave of dizziness by placing her hand on the wall beside her. Her hand closed around something sticking out of the wall. She knew without looking that it was a key.

One turn, and she was outside.

Though the storm had passed, the weather was cloudy and still quite cold. The threat of rain, or perhaps snow, was in the clouds. Already the wind was up, bitter and bringing a burning sting to her cheeks. The flannel nightgown she wore was drafty. "Don't think about the cold," she told herself out loud, needing the comfort of a voice, even if it was her own. "Think about how wonderful it feels to be free, to be away from that moldy and crumbling old castle, away from the creature who dwells there. Think about how warm you will be when you reach home.''

Chapter Ten

Robert spotted her as he walked along the wall. As he watched her stumble and fall over the rocks below, he knew she was heading for her rowboat, foolish enough to think she could make it to Ravenscrag. At death's door. Weak as a kitten. Barefoot, and—"God's teeth! She is wearing nothing but a flimsy nightgown."

He whirled around and disappeared through the turret door. A dozen flights of stairs later, he found Manus.

Manus listened to the Macqueen. His weathered face registered disbelief. "Escaped? She was out of her head with fever for five days. Where did she get the energy to climb out of bed, much less make it down to the rocks?"

"How the hell do I know? All I know is, she is down there, barefoot and wearing a nightgown big enough for you and I together. Of all the idiotic—" he caught himself. "We had better go after her. If she gets in that damn leaky boat, she will be nothing but bait for the fish."

"I can bring her back by myself. There is no need for you to go. She doesn't weigh any more than a clump of wet seaweed."

"I'll come with you."

"I think perhaps the lass is afraid of you."

His words turned Robert's face hard, and he knew the expression in his eyes was bitter. He did not understand why it painted him so deeply to think the lass was so afraid that she would risk her life to escape his very presence. Perhaps the gossip was right. Perhaps he had turned into a beast—a raging wolf who walked the Shetlands at night, seeking those whom he might devour. It was obvious that she believed that to be the truth of it.

He saw Manus was looking at him strangely. "You cannot mean to leave her out there, to let her try to reach Ravenscrag alone. It would be sentencing her to death."

"I am aware of that."

"Give me the word, and I'll have her back here before she grows any colder."

"It has been my intention all along to go after her. My indecision comes from my inability to decide what would be best for her once we've caught up with her."

"We should bring her back here. She will need looking after."

"True, but she will also try to escape again. And again, if necessary. She will try until she succeeds, or kills herself."

"Then what should we do? Take her home?"

"Yes," Robert called back to him, for Manus was already headed down the narrow passageway that led to the caves below. He went after him.

With a grim set to his jaw, Robert hurried through the ancient caves that he knew like an old friend. There was little doubt in his mind that he and Manus would reach her before she found her boat. What concerned him was whether or not he could let her go.

She was not alone. Anne could feel someone, or something, behind her, moving across the rocks that led down to the water's edge. She knew she was being followed, even before she stumbled and fell.

The frigid wind had taken the last of her strength. She was too weak to get up, too weak even to move. She could do little more than lie there, watching them silently, as she waited to see what they would do to her.

There were two of them, but neither of them was a creature, some half-human form of life that lived in the darkness. They were two men she had seen before, but that did nothing but frighten her more.

The older of the two was short and bent, and he walked with a painful gait. He had rowed her to the big island that day when she first came here. The other she remembered vividly, for how could she forget the way he moved, as gracefully as water over rocks? His torso was lean and long, and his stride covered a great distance. Like that of the beast who walked the castle walls at night, his hair was unbelievably long and black, but, unlike the wild hair of the beast, his was tied back. To her relief, this time he wore no great, swirling cape.

Thankfully, the creature himself had not followed her. She had been wise to flee in the daylight, while he lurked behind the castle walls, afraid of the light.

The powerful one reached her first, and stopped a few feet away to look down at her, irritation and anger gripping his face. How she remembered that look.

She was shivering uncontrollably now. She was tired. Too tired to fight. Too tired to care what they did to her. Not even the thought of being served as the creature's next meal frightened her. It wouldn't be so bad ... as long as she was a *warm* meal.

In spite of her weakness, and the intense burning in her lungs, she began to laugh at the direction of her thoughts. Was she demented, or had her fever reached her brain? Once she started laughing, she could not stop. She laughed until her heart felt as if it would explode, and the fire burning in her lungs seemed to suck away each breath she drew.

She was barely mindful as the man swore, then leaned over and scooped her up as easily as if he were skimming a leaf from the surface of a limpid pool.

His voice was deep and rich. "Her skin is like ice. Give me your cape."

"Is she laughing or crying?" the old one asked.

"Both. She is delirious, and in spite of her icy skin, her breath is hot and feverish. Perhaps our lass wasn't so foolish after all. Coming out here just might have saved her life."

"By freezing her to death?"

"We could not have brought her fever down like this, and certainly not this quickly."

"You aren't going to leave her out here, are you?"

"No, I thought I'd do something more cruel, like rowing her out further and tossing her into the water."

She might be delirious, but there was nothing wrong with her hearing. She could not seem to make the words in her head come out her lips. All she could do was to struggle weakly against the strong band of arms that held her and mutter incoherently.

"I think you've frightened her," the old man said.

"Something I should have done sooner."

"Shall we take her back with us?"

"Only long enough to cover her warmly. Then you and Gavin can take her home."

Manus eyed him speculatively. "Are you certain you want to send her back?"

The Macqueen's body stiffened. "Why wouldn't I? I have no need for a woman underfoot." Without another word, he turned and carried her back to the castle.

Anne opened her eyes only once, but it was enough to burn the imprint of his features into her memory. His face was like a mountain sculpted by the harshness of the elements, yet possessing a raw and breathtaking presence. Like the mountain, he was both beautiful and mysterious, and yet there was something seductive there, despite the threat of danger.

He looked down at her, and for a moment their gazes met and held. His eyes were not the glowing yellow eyes of the creature that had come to her during the night, but a cold, frigid blue that looked as fathomless as the sea that battered the coast.

He might not be the beast, but still he frightened her. "Don't throw me in the water."

He cursed. His body jerked to a stop. When he spoke, his voice was as cold and biting as the wind. He turned toward the old man. "Here. Take her."

She felt herself thrust into another pair of arms. She blinked and looked up into a pair of gray eyes that were gentle and warm. His ancient face wore the weathering of time, and his look was full of wisdom. Somehow she knew he would understand. She lifted her hand and tried to touch his face. She desperately wanted to say something, but her effort came out nothing more than a dry hiss. Her eyes closed. Her hand fell away.

When she awoke again, she was home.

Since her recovery, Anne had returned to the window each night, to stare out at the grotesque outline of Blackness Castle, at those broken towers and jagged walls that were as black as the name they bore.

He was there, she knew, walking the walls, as the village folk said, with his hair wild and flying about him. A madman. A beast. The creature who had come to her. She would never forget his glowing amber eyes. Who was he? Did he really exist? Or was he something that had stepped out of her illness, a phantom of her delirium?

Behind her, the door opened and Fanny came rushing in. As was her custom, she dropped the drapery and let it fall back into place, then turned to see that Fanny was fixing her bed.

"Are ye still starin' at that devil, milady?"

"There is little else to occupy my time during such bitter cold and deep snows." She shivered and drew her shawl higher as she moved to stand before the fire. She held out her hands to warm them.

"Someone ought to go to that island and find the beast. A creature what devours human flesh is not to be pitied. He should be chained in a dungeon ... or shot."

Fanny smoothed the top blanket and removed the last of the wrinkles. "There," she announced, pausing to look at her mistress. "It is wonderfully pleasurable to see the bloom in your cheeks again, Lady Anne. I don't mind admitting I doubted your ability to recover when they brought you home. You looked quite dead, milady. Pale as a gutted fish, and talkin' out of your head."

The corners of Anne's mouth turned up at Fanny's vivid description.

Fanny went on with her work for a few seconds, then paused and looked up to direct her stare in Anne's direction. "Milady, were you afraid you were going to die?"

Anne shook her head. "No. I felt too awful to die."

Fanny's eyes gleamed with amusement. "Sometimes living is worse than dying."

"Yes..." Anne did not know why her thoughts took off suddenly in the direction of the tall, black-haired man, but her reply was interrupted by her recollection of the cold emptiness in his eyes.

Sometimes living is worse than dying....

She remembered the way he had stood there, looking down at her, wrapped in the silent manliness of grief.

"Will there be anything else, milady?"

The sound of Fanny's voice startled her and broke her concentration. "What?"

"Will there be anything else?"

"No...thank you, Fanny." Anne put her fingers to her temples.

"Are you all right, milady? Do you have a headache?"

"No headache, just troubling thoughts."

"I suppose that comes because you haven't quite given up on finding your father alive. It will go much easier for you, once you have learned to accept his death."

"I don't think my father is dead at all."

Fanny gaped at her. "You don't think he is dead? But how could you think that, milady?"

"I have my reasons, Fanny. But I think he is being held prisoner on that island . . . by that madman."

Fanny made a clucking sound. "If he is in the clutches of that devil, then he is worse than dead."

"I know. That's why I have to find a way to go back, a way to discover if my father is alive."

"I would not risk my life again, if I were you. Besides, if the beast has him, he would never turn him over to you. There is too much hatred in his heart."

Anne sighed and sat down in the rocking chair next to the fire. "I know. That is what worries me. But I can't leave my father there. Although I hardly know him, he is the only living relative I have. His health is poor. The doctor did not think he had a long time to live, even in the best of conditions. He had tried to persuade him to seek a warmer climate."

"You cannot sacrifice your life, milady, for that of your father. He has lived his life. You are just starting yours. You will marry one day, and raise a peck of little ones. Your husband and your children will be your family. You will not be alone."

Although Anne heard Fanny talking, she was not taking in what she said. Her thoughts were trapped a few sentences back, as she heard Fanny's words repeated in her head, over and over.

You cannot sacrifice your life for that of your father....

How ironic it was, that what Fanny said she could not do was the very thing she knew she *must* do. When the idea came to her, it seemed so perfect, she was amazed she had not thought of it before.

"Are you feeling unwell, milady?"

Anne leaped from her chair and hurried toward Fanny, who took a step backward. Anne laughed and took Fanny's hands in hers. "Dear, dear Fanny, I did not mean to alarm you."

"You gave me a fright, milady, coming out of that chair like the devil himself were nippin' at your heels."

"I know . . . I could hear your knees knocking."

Fanny blushed and looked down. "I am sorry, milady."

"Don't be. You have no idea how much you have helped me."

"Me, milady? How?"

"You have just given me the answer to this dilemma."

Fanny looked at her with a puzzled look in her eyes. "I have?"

"Yes, you have."

"What was it, exactly, that I gave you, milady?"

"The perfect plan to bring my father home."

A bit of Anne's excitement was stolen by the look of pity on Fanny's face. "Oh, milady, don't you understand? If your father is there, the beast will never, ever, allow your father to leave Blackness Castle, much less that evil island."

"I understand the beast would never set my father free, of course, but he might be persuaded to exchange him for another prisoner."

Fanny's brows arched with surprise. "Another prisoner? Who might that be, milady?"

"Me."

Chapter Eleven

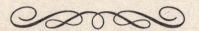

Manus heard the roar of the Macqueen, and stopped just outside the door. He gave Gavin a questioning look. "Do you think we were a wee bit hasty in telling the Macqueen who the girl was?"

"Aye. He has been in the devil's own black mood since we told him she wanted to go home to Ravenscrag. Though I think his mood would have been worse if we hadn't told him and then he'd learned she was Sir John's daughter."

"I can't imagine how it could be worse. One minute he is raving, and the next he is sullen and quiet. He lashes out in a fury at anyone who disturbs him, and then he goes through the castle bellowing because he is alone. There doesn't seem to be an end in sight."

"Dare we go in?" Gavin whispered.

"Aye. We all need companionship during our sufferings."

"What if he doesn't want companionship?"

"He doesn't know what he wants. The pain is too sharp. He cannot think. He is like a lion with a thorn in his paw. He doesn't know how to get it out, yet to walk on it causes more pain." Manus took a step, then paused, looking back at Gavin, whose feet seemed embedded in the stone floor. "Are you coming in, or not?"

"Aye . . . if you are."

Manus opened the door, and the two of them stepped into the great hall, just as they heard a splintering crash, followed by the clang of metal. They looked toward the table and saw eating utensils rolling across the floor.

"He's been drinking again," Gavin said, stopping behind Manus, as if the old man offered some sort of protection.

"Aye, drinking and brooding. He is always this way when the devils go to tormenting him. When the pain becomes unbearable, he strikes out at the first thing he sees. Tonight, it was the dishes on the table."

"Yesterday, it was Marta's mop bucket, which he kicked down the stairs."

"And two days before that, he put his hand through a glass. That particular display cost him nine stitches in his arm."

"And now he's at it again," Gavin whispered, "acting as ornery as a penned stallion."

The Macqueen's voice seemed to explode within the room. "If the two of you have anything to say, you can say it to my face. You don't have to whisper behind my back."

Manus winked at Gavin, who grinned at him through his rusty red beard. "I was just wondering if you had changed your mind about letting the lass go," Manus said, "because if you have, it would be easy enough to go after her and haul her back."

"Why would I want her back? I've more important things on my mind than nursing some kelpie that beached herself on my island."

"Better things? Like torturing her father?"

Robert threw down his tankard and crossed the room in a few long strides. He stopped a hairsbreadth away from Manus.

Gavin swallowed loudly and stepped farther back, his tall form seeming to shrink, but the old man stood his ground, never flinching or looking away. His gaze was steady as he looked the Macqueen in the eye.

"What I do with her father is my own business, and you of all people should know the bastard deserves much more pain and suffering than I could ever hope to give him. He should be down on his knees and praying that locking him up is all I do. I have not tortured him . . . yet."

"Keeping him chained in that hole is torture enough. Why don't you kill the poor bastard and go on with your life?"

"I am warning you, Manus. Stay out of this. I make my own decisions. When I want your opinion, I will ask for it."

"I hear your warning, but I cannot remain silent any longer. You have suffered much, but you have allowed your loss to turn you into a bitter man. Look at what you've become. You are so tormented by the past that you come dangerously close to being the beast you are rumored to be. Your only pleasure is indulging your grief."

"My grief is just that—*my* grief." The words came out like a snarl.

"You cannot stop the birds of sorrow from flying over your head, but you can prevent them from nesting in your hair. What is gone, and what is past help, should be past grief. Time passes, and so does our grieving. You need to let it go. It has been over five years. Even the sea has its ebbings."

"Are you finished?"

"Almost."

"And what is left? The thrust of the final blow? A knife between my ribs . . . or is it to be my back?"

"If I were younger, I would never let you remain standing for saying that."

"If you were younger, we wouldn't have gotten that far. I would have flattened you at the beginning of this conversation."

Manus did not say anything, and the room grew tomb quiet.

Robert looked at the old man who had saved his life, the man who had been like a father to him. He did not want to have words with Manus...or Gavin...or Grizel . . . or even Marta. He did not want to have words with anyone. He wanted to be alone—to be away from them all. He wanted to leave—now—and take his sorrow and his bottle of whisky with him. His grief was too heavy to share.

His insides were on fire from drinking too much. His head ached abominably. Ever since that English witch had beached herself on his island, his life had been in torment. It was bad enough that she was as lovely as a sunlit loch. Did she have to remind him of everything he had lost? The soft feel of a woman lying next to him. The beckoning look of desire. The feeling that what he did, what he thought and where he went mattered, mattered to someone who cared about him, not because of who he was, or what he could provide, but because he was her sun and moon and stars.

Ailis . . . His heart wrenched. When she was taken from him, the world had turned suddenly dark and cold. Grief had changed him and made him hard. There was no gentleness in his life now, no softness, no woman's loving caress. There was only torment and nagging guilt, and always the vivid red stain of innocent blood on his hands.

Blood that he could never wash out.

As if Manus were privy to his thoughts, his next words hit him with a broadside. "As your friend, as someone who has watched you suffer, I have only one word of advice, one warning. Take a careful look at yourself. Vengeance follows close on the heels of guilt. Are you certain that is not what you are feeling, what has caused you to harden your heart?"

Plain and unvarnished came the words of truth, striking him sharply. "And if it is?"

"There are times when a hard heart is worse than a bloody hand."

"Advice that comes too late. It has been too long. I don't know how to undo my hate. I have nursed this cub, and now it will eat me."

"Perhaps that is why *she* came. She seems to be a quiet, gentle sort . . . the kind to teach you the power of forgiveness."

Robert scoffed at that. "The power of forgiveness would turn to hate in a heartbeat. The moment she learned I held her father . . .

"We often hate what we fear."

"If she is afraid of every blade of grass, then she should not sleep in a meadow. She came here of her own accord. I did not invite her."

"I was wrong to try to make you see reason. The fires of hate burn too strong within you. You have lost all feeling."

"Perhaps that is because you are knocking at the door of a deserted house. I am empty inside, Manus. It is only my body that perseveres. There is, I fear, nothing more stubborn than a dead man." He turned abruptly, and walked back to the table. "Go to bed. I want to be alone."

Gavin, who needed no further encouragement, hurried from the room.

Robert saw the look of both hurt and pity in his friend's eyes, saw the way his old body seemed to go stiff. He owed Manus more than a liberal dose of his own bitterness.

Manus gave a curt nod, then turned and walked from the room, taking his hurt, his pity with him. Once he was gone, there was nothing left behind but the haunting sound of his last words. "I pray that you are not lashed by your own stubborn tail."

Robert filled his tankard, then took his chair before the huge fireplace. He was soon lost in reflection . . . upon the words Manus had spoken.

How could he change? How could he give up the thing he had lived with for so long? How could he forgive, rather than hate? He could sooner change squares to circles.

He had waited so long. For years he had thought of nothing but the time when he would have Sir John Crofton at his mercy. And yet, when that moment came, he had not felt the elation, the sense of triumph, he had imagined. He hated his inability to feel anymore. Hated the weakening of his thirst for revenge, the need to strike out and hurt because he hurt. Even as he thought these things, he knew, deep down in the most secret part of him, that the thing he hated most was what he had become.

It had taken a tiny slip of a girl, delirious and out of her head, to show him just how far down he had gone. He could not remember a woman ever being frightened of him, and certainly not to the point that she would prefer death to his presence. And yet her act of desperation had proven one thing: Her driving need to escape him had been greater than her fear of death.

He did not known how long he sat there, but it was long enough for him to down the last bit of whisky.

Grizel's voice announced her presence. "It grows late, and you do not need anything more to drink."

He picked up the empty tankard and tipped it toward her. "There is nothing inside." He laughed. "It bears a striking resemblance to me and my life, does it not?"

"It is only your eyes that cannot see. If you were truly dead inside, you would not feel so much pain. Your heart is heavy. Take it out on sleep. Things will not seem so grim on the morrow."

"Too many devils chase me tonight, Grizel. I cannot sleep. There are many decisions to be made."

"It is always better to sleep on things than to lie awake thinking."

"When I am bedeviled, I cannot sleep. Sleep then becomes my enemy."

"Aye, I know. I have heard your cries in the night, when you are tormented by dreams. Perhaps tonight will be different. Perhaps the whisky has dulled the memory. Sleep is what you need."

"Sleep," he said, staggering to his feet. "A beautiful fruit . . . such a bitter taste."

Grizel walked with him to his room and removed his boots when he fell across the bed. She drew the furs over him, then doused the candle and crept quietly from the room, leaving him to seek the counsel of his pillow.

He dreamed of Ailis again.

Beautiful Ailis, with the musical voice and the fair, fair skin. Only, when he reached for her as he always did, hungry to take her in his arms, her long golden hair turned an inky black, and the face that leaned into his kiss was not the face of his dead wife, but the face of the spawn of the devil who took her life.

He talked in his sleep. He tossed and turned in the bed, then awoke with a start. He sat upright, his body drenched in sweat. The black-haired witch had robbed him of his dreams again. As she had done nightly since she had first come to his island. She who managed to cover his wife's pale golden image with her devilish black one.

Even in his sleep, she mocked him, tormented him. He wanted to put his hand to each side of his head and press until he crushed the image of her lying pale and cold in front of him. Even now, he could not rid himself of the memory of her that burned within him like a red-hot brand.

He wanted her—had wanted her since the first moment he had looked down at her. He climbed out of bed and threw his cloak about him. He needed the cold shock of the wind upon him tonight to clear his jumbled thoughts.

He walked the wall, willing his thoughts to remain on his dead wife. He stopped and braced his hands against the wall and stared out over the sea that stretched endlessly before him. Her soul, her sweet, sweet spirit, was out there . . . somewhere just beyond his reach. "Ailis, my love, my life. How can I bear it?"

He dropped his head down between his shoulders. "I will never be at peace. I will know only torment for the rest of my days." He threw his head back then, and cried out in agony. The mournful sound of his wail drifted over water that lay as dark and cold as death.

A sharp, stabbing pain cut into his chest. Hot tears scalded his face. Consumed by grief and abject loneliness, he cried out again, his tears mingling with the sound of anguish, as he repeated, "Why? Why? Why?"

His heart stilled. A cold, cold chill passed over him. He felt the warm touch of Ailis's hand upon his cheek. She did not speak. She did not have to. He knew why she had come.

She wanted to be free of the chains that bound her to him, even in death. She wanted him to release her, to let her go, so that she could rest in peace. The thought terrified him. She was the only link to sanity he had, just as his hatred of the man who had killed her was the only thing that kept him alive. Without either of them, he would go as mad as the wolf they reported him to be.

"No! Do not ask this of me. Do not ask for what I cannot give!" He could not let her go. What would become of him, of his hatred, if she left? "Don't go, Ailis. You promised to be with me always."

The warm hand upon his face turned suddenly cold. The shimmering image of her moved over the wall, then began to slowly drift away from him and out over the water, growing fainter.

"Hate me!" he cried. "I left you alone and unprotected. I caused your death. I murdered you! Haunt me! Haunt me, and don't let me forget!"

She hovered in one place for a moment, as if she were undecided, as if his words had reached her, but then she held out her hand.

He leaned over the wall and stretched out his hand toward her, begging her to return to him, to bring her memory back. But the specter of Ailis, the love of his life, moved away. Gradually the image grew dimmer and dimmer, until she was gone completely from his sight.

He dropped down to his knees, overwhelmed by anguish, and grieving over his loss so completely that he did not feel any pain when he began to beat his head against the stones of the wall.

It was only when Grizel and Manus came for him and drew him to his feet that he realized he was bleeding.

Chapter Twelve

This time, Anne rowed herself toward the island with ease. Even before she reached there, she knew the beast was watching her. She could feel his presence, the debilitating power of his gaze. The strangest feeling crept over her, and she knew the castle, the island itself, was drawing her, as if it had dominion over her will.

Come. Come to me, it seemed to say. This is where you were meant to be. This is where you belong. I am waiting... waiting... waiting...

The day was clear and not too cold. The sun seemed to favor the island—especially the castle itself—with its light and warmth. It must have been something in its day, for there was a magnificence to it even now, when more than half of it lay in crumbling and tumbled ruin.

She reached the edge of the island just below the point where the battlement towers of the castle seemed to rise out of thick stone, like a fist reaching toward heaven. It was at least an hour later when she stood beneath a Norman archway and knocked on the studded oak door.

A young woman with belligerent red hair tied in a kerchief answered the door. "Come in, Lady Crofton. We were expecting you."

"You saw me coming."

"Aye, 'twas the master himself who saw you."

"The master—?"

"The Macqueen, milady, the last laird. If you will follow me, I will take you to him. This way, please."

Anne followed her. "I did not come here to see the Macqueen. It is the bea— It is the man they call the Beast of Blackness Castle that I wish to speak with."

The girl said nothing. She continued down a long, dim passageway, lit intermittently by burning torches. They passed many doors, all closed. The warm, accepting feeling Anne had in the boat earlier was gone. She felt an uneasiness creep over her, as if this immense castle were empty and she were here alone, without another living soul on the entire island—none, that is, save this girl, and the creature.

They went up a narrow, winding staircase and stepped into a sparsely furnished medieval gallery. Sunlight squeezed through the cracks in the drapes to provide the only light. Suddenly, the girl stopped before a door that was much larger than the doors they had passed.

"*He* awaits you in there." She paused, then stepped to one side.

The castle was abnormally quiet. Not even the usual sound of wind blowing around the merlons and through the embrasures could be heard. The girl turned the handle. Anne felt a shiver creep over her, and she almost cried out for the girl to stop.

The door creaked, then swung open. With a fast-beating heart, Anne looked down, her gaze fastened upon the folds of her cape, where a slice of the dark green gown beneath was exposed.

"You may go in, Lady Crofton."

With a deep, steadying breath, Anne lifted her head. A moment later, she stepped through the doorway, understanding at last what was required of those unfortunate queens who faced the headsman's ax. She knew now how they felt, knowing they took the last steps they would ever take upon this earth.

The moment she was inside, the door closed behind her. Instinctively Anne flinched and looked behind her.

"It is not locked."

Her head whipped around.

He stood unmoving, a somber black figure in a dark, poorly lit room, supernaturally tall, imperially slim. One solitary candle burned low on the massive carved table that stood next to him. The light caught, and illuminated his face—just enough for her to make out his features.

He was staring intently at her.

She felt herself trembling, and realized that she was gripping the soft wool of her cape almost savagely. Her stomach cramped violently. He narrowed his eyes, as if to see her better in the dim light, and she recalled the golden-yellow eyes of the beast she had seen during her illness here. There was something strange about her attraction to him, an attraction laced with fear. He reminded her of a cat waiting at a mouse-hole. Foolish, foolish, she called herself, and that was what she had been, to allow this evil place to seduce her with a feeling of welcome and well-being. She wondered now just how dear a price she would pay for her foolishness.

"What are you doing here?"

His voice was smooth and seductive, with an undertone of authority. All the life, all the vitality, seemed to have drained from her body, for she trembled when she heard his voice. "I will state my purpose to the... That is, I wish to speak to the...the other man."

His sensual mouth curved slowly into a smile. "There are many men here."

He was the cat, and he was toying with her. She took a deep breath. She would end the game now, with an act that went beyond the brazen, to border on stupidity. "I wish to see the one they call the Wolf of Blackness Castle." There. She had said it. At least the floor had not opened up to throw her into a bottomless pit.

"You are very bold to use such rashness. He despises that name."

She was really trembling now, and she prayed her voice did not quiver. She knew she must speak with conviction. "It was the only way I had to identify him. I could not afford to lose the opportunity. It is imperative that I speak with him...a matter of life and death. I meant no disrespect."

"Whatever the reason, rashness is not always fortunate. Why did you take such a grave risk? Was it impudence? Stupidity? Or simply to hide your fear?"

"It is said that boldness wins the favor of the gods."

"And what is the favor you seek?" His gaze swept over her. "I admit you have a great deal to bargain with, but it remains to be seen whether he will be interested in what you offer.''

She gasped. ''I am afraid you have mistaken my intentions.''

''Have I?''

''Yes.''

''Then why are you trembling?''

She realized she could not get anywhere with a man whose very presence drained all the strength from her. Hoping to quell her trembling, she took a step back and came flat against the door. Held by his relentless gaze, she felt trapped, like a flower pressed between two transparent pieces of paper.

''Perhaps it is time for you to tell me why, exactly, you are here. And no lies this time. I *know* who you are.''

''What I have to say must be said to *him.*''

''Him? You mean the beast?''

Wringing her hands, she looked around her, hoping *he* had not heard. ''I thought you said he abhorred being called that.''

''He does, but only when it is used by others.''

''Others? You mean strangers?''

''I mean others . . . beings other than himself.''

''But you just called him the b— Oh, God!''

He took a step toward her.

''You! All along, it was you!'' Blind with fear, she stretched her hand out and felt her way along the wall until she came to a table. She stepped behind it and realized her mistake. In her effort to put something solid between them, she had placed herself away from the door and farther into the room.

He must have read her mind, for she thought she saw a flash of amusement cross his face. He continued coming toward her.

Instinctively she reached behind her and, finding her way by groping with her hands, she retreated, like an animal being stalked.

He closed the distance between them.

Unable to take her eyes off of him, she bumped up against a window. She had no choice now but to stay here, for to turn would give him cause to grab her. She was terrified of what he could do...what he might do. After all, she had, as he had said, lied to him. That thought caused her to press backward. She did not care if she broke the glass and fell through. It was a way to escape.

She pressed harder. The glass did not give.

"You tried this once before, if I remember. I cannot help but find you interesting. If you are so frightened as to risk death in order to escape, why did you choose to come here in the first place?"

Never had she been this frightened. She knew he sensed her fear, knew, too, that it amused him. His lips curled and his eyes seemed to glow with a light from within. She felt a tingling sensation of both horror and amazement that traveled the length of her spine. How long, she wondered, before he turned into the beast she knew him to be?

This was her own foolish fault. It was her boldness that both challenged and attracted him. She had played right into his hands. What was left but to admit it? "I—I am not sure. I have a history of making bad choices."

"Yes, I seem to remember. And this you consider a bad choice?"

"Yes. A very bad choice. I realize that now. I should not have come here. I should not have allowed my idiotic curiosity to bring me here again. My actions were rash and foolish. I have interrupted you and your household. My only choice is to admit it, to beg your pardon, and leave."

"There are other choices."

He was so close now, she could hear him breathing. "I don't want to hear them."

"Then tell me why you are here."

"I would rather not."

"I will ask you one more time. Why are you here?"

Was this how one died? By suffocating with fear? What would he do if she did not tell him? The possibilities were too awful for her to imagine. "I have a proposition to make."

"Go on."

"I am Sir John Crofton's daughter."

"I have known that for quite some time. Now, go on."

This was it. She drew in a deep, deep breath—perhaps her last. "I know my father was not lost at sea. I know he reached your island with the others, and that he was alive. If you did not murder him, then he is here, now, being held as your prisoner."

"And what makes you certain he was here? How can you think that I would let the bastard set foot upon this island?"

"The day after I received word of his death, I came over here, to your island."

"Why?"

"I found it strange that my father's body was the only one lost. I had heard stories about the quarrel between you. I wanted to see for myself."

"And did you?"

"Yes. My father's dog accompanied me. It was Pharaoh who found my father's handkerchief, buried in the sand."

"It could have washed up and been covered in the storm."

"But my father's watch could not. Gold is quite heavy. The moment it slipped out of his pocket, it would have gone straight down, instead of washing up on the beach."

"You found a watch...."

She reached into her pocket and withdrew her father's watch. "I found this lying in the shallows, near the shore. I know he was here."

"And if he was?"

"I want to know where he is...what happened to him...."

"You think I killed him?"

"I know you hate him enough to take his life."

"What if I didn't?"

"Then he is here."

"And what will you do if he is?"

"If he is here and alive, then I have a proposition to make."

"Now we get back to the *proposition*. I take it I am supposed to release your father in exchange for a few favors. What's it to be? A sampling of your body?"

Anne clenched her jaw, afraid that if she said anything, she would say too much.

"Don't tell me you are offering me your sacred and treasured virginity?"

She turned her head away and closed her eyes. He was a master at humiliation. She would not let this coldhearted monster have the satisfaction of reducing her to tears.

When his fingers touched her face, her body jerked in response. She had no fight left in her, and that made it easy for him to turn her toward him. She could not help looking up into his eyes.

"Tell me the truth. I hate lies even more than I hate being called the beast. If you discovered your father was alive, what were you going to propose?"

She was shamed to the depths of her soul when a tear slipped down her cheek. "To exchange my life for my father's."

The Macqueen swore. "The bastard is not worth saving. He is a murderer. He deserves whatever happens to him."

"I would take his punishment."

With an oath, his hands came around her and, grabbing the drapes in each hand, he gave a mighty jerk. Sunlight flooded into the room.

He stared down into her face.

She could see him clearly. The face of the beast was a mystery no more. She stared at him in confusion. He did not resemble in the least the beast she had seen during her illness. His eyes were not yellow, or anything close to it. They were blue. Such a deep blue that they were almost black—and so cold that she shivered. He looked more like Lucifer than the beast . . . Lucifer, the fallen angel, with his beguiling, tempting ways.

"You must love him a great deal, if you are willing to give your life in exchange for his."

"I do not know him well enough to love him in the way you mean. I was raised by my mother in Cornwall. She died a few months ago. I have no other relatives. That is why I came here. We had been together only a short time when my father disappeared."

"I seem to have heard this story before...only a different version. Are there more?"

"No, only this one, for it is the truth."

"Why would you make such an offer?"

"He is my father. I owe him my respect."

"You don't owe the bastard your life!"

"My father has lung fever. He is dying. I can do nothing to help. I would not want that on my conscience."

"I am tempted to take your offer, if for no reason other than to call your bluff. I know what you are thinking. You believe in the basic goodness of mankind, therefore you think I would not stoop to do a woman harm. You do not know how wrong you are."

"It does not matter. That is not why I came here."

"Then come, little captive, for I am giving you the opportunity to prove it."

"You will spare my father's life?"

"Only if you remain here, as my prisoner."

"I will remain. You have my word."

"Then God help you, for you have no idea what you have done."

Chapter Thirteen

The next morning, Robert paced back and forth across the solar. He was in a foul mood, angry at himself. He had allowed a woman—a woman who was the daughter of his sworn enemy—to distract him. It was something he had never done before, and because of it, he had made a foolish bargain.

He realized now that keeping her and releasing her father was not enough. The crux of the matter was that Sir John would go free and unscathed. Yet how could he punish Crofton without bringing dishonor to himself? Like it or not, he had made a bargain. There had to be some way to drive a nail into that murderer's heart, and still keep his word.

He stopped abruptly, giving thought to an idea. It might work. It just might work. He grunted his satisfaction at the idea, then left the solar.

A short while later, Robert walked into the dungeon and ordered the guard to unlock Sir John's door. The moment it creaked open, he picked up the lamp and stepped inside.

Sir John was sitting on a stool, shielding the light

from his eyes. "Have you come to gloat, or have you decided it is time to kill me?"

"Neither. I have come to tell you that your daughter is here."

Sir John sprang to his feet and wobbled a bit, then reached out to steady himself by bracing his hand against the damp stone wall. "Why did you involve my daughter in this? There was no reason to bring her here. I'm the one you want. What do you want with her? What do you intend to do with her? She is not part of this thing between us. She is innocent."

"Your daughter came of her own accord. She has come to bargain for your life...something that is a surprise, if what she said is true."

Sir John's face was like stone, and his eyes blazed, but he did not speak.

"Tell me, is it true that she has just come to Ravenscrag, that the two of you hardly know each other?"

The hardness in his face softened somewhat. "It's true. My wife left me when Anne was three weeks old. She took her to her family in Cornwall, and raised her there. It was only after Bess died that she came to me."

"Interesting. I wonder where she has learned to have such love and devotion for a father she had never seen."

"What do you mean?"

The muscles in Robert's face tightened, but his hard expression did not change. "She has come like an angel of mercy, and offered herself as my prisoner...in exchange for your miserable life."

Sir John paled. "You cannot accept such an offer. I will not allow her to settle my debts."

This was going better than he had expected. His appetite was whetted by his first taste of blood. He went for the throat. It was only a matter of time before he closed in for the kill. "My, my, such fatherly love and devotion for a child you never saw until she was a grown woman. I had no idea the protective paternal instinct ran so deep. Of course, I have no experience in such matters, seeing as how you murdered my only child."

As the Macqueen had known he would, Sir John ignored his last comment. "She is young. She has much to look forward to. I am an old man..."

"And you are dying."

Sir John's expression was a startled one. "She told you..."

"Something interesting you chose not to reveal."

"You are not a man of compassion. I knew it would do no good."

"Oh, but I am a man of compassion. I am compassionate enough to accept her sacrifice. I will spare your life."

"God's blood, I hope you suffer for this," Sir John said, and his eyes blazed with a rage of utter frustration and bitterness. Without warning, he sprang to his feet. His hands went for the Macqueen's throat.

Robert easily subdued him and shoved him back against the wall. "I would suggest that you refrain from becoming physical. You might tempt me to keep your daughter and end your miserable life, as well."

Obviously weakened, Sir John's legs gave way, and he slid down the wall to sit on the floor, his breathing heavy and rasping. He coughed violently. When the coughing subsided, he rested his head back against the wall. "What do you want of me?"

A slow smile curved the corners of the Macqueen's mouth. He had his man. And he had his answer. Now he knew the way to drive the stake through Sir John's evil heart.

"It is a little late for fatherly intervention, I'm afraid. Your life is spared. The girl is mine. However, it would suit my purpose to have your blessing."

"You fool. Do you honestly think I would ever accept you as a suitable mate for my daughter?"

The Macqueen regarded him impassively. "Did I mention marriage? There are ways to enjoy the fruit without buying the tree."

"I will not agree to it. I will never agree to it. Take my life. Take it now, and be done with this thing. I grow weary."

"What is done cannot be undone. I have given my word. Your daughter will remain here."

"You cannot do this."

"I did not come here to ask your permission. The deed is already done. You are free to go. You will be returned to Ravenscrag on the morrow."

"You miserable fiend. I will return, and I will have my daughter back, if I have to start a bloody war. And when it's over, I'll see my daughter properly wed."

"I'm afraid there is one major flaw in your plans. Lady Anne has agreed to become my wife. Even the king doesn't have the authority to take a woman from her lawful husband. The matter is out of your hands."

Sir John closed his eyes and threw back his head, a tormented scream ripped from his throat. *"Noooo..."*

But the Macqueen was already gone.

* * *

Manus looked up when the Macqueen entered the gallery, but he said nothing.

"Bring Lady Anne to me in the chapel."

Manus gave him a strange look, but chose not to reveal what he was thinking. With a nod, he departed.

The Macqueen was waiting in the chapel, near the altar, when the door opened and Lady Anne stepped inside.

Manus closed the door behind her.

The Macqueen did not miss the way Anne's gaze darted toward the door, or her look of panic when she saw that Manus had gone.

"Why have you brought me here, to the chapel?"

"You do not like chapels?"

"I do not think the chapel an appropriate place for the plotting of wickedness."

"And here I thought we understood each other. You are expecting wickedness, when in truth, I have a proposition to present to you. One that will make you very happy, I am certain."

"What is your proposition?"

"I am prepared to offer you your father's freedom ... the chance to walk out of these gates a free man, with this thing between us settled forever."

Her expression was confused. "Are you jesting with me, or is it your turn to play the simpleton? We agreed to that last evening."

He feigned a surprised look. "Beg pardon, Lady Anne, but we did not."

She gasped. "We did!" she said, her tone loud and angry. "You granted me my father's freedom in exchange for my remaining here. You gave me your word."

He feigned indifference. "Obviously you have read something into the bargain that was not there. What I granted you was your father's *life*. Not his freedom."

"By all that's holy! You tricked me!"

His jaw clenched. He spaced his words evenly, and kept his tone low. "On the contrary. I gave you precisely what you asked for. Your exact words were 'I came to offer my life in exchange for my father's.'

Anne paled, as if she realized the blunder in her choice of words. "But, in the end, I asked you if you would set my father free, and you agreed. I remember what you said—'Only if you remain here, as my prisoner.'"

"You err again, little captive. What you asked was, 'You will spare my father's life?'"

"They were right to call you the devil. You are the prince of deception."

"The error was yours, mistress, not mine. Direct your anger, and your poetic names, where they belong."

"You knew I was asking for his freedom. There could have been no misunderstanding, no matter what words I used."

"You would do well to learn a man can only agree to what is stated. He cannot be held accountable for another's thinking or logic. If you intended to trade yourself for your father's release, then you should have asked for it."

"But I—"

"A bargain is a bargain. You gave your word, as did I. Your father's life will be spared, and you will remain here."

She winced at his words. One pale, slim hand came up to her forehead.

Silent as a sunrise, he waited . . . for her to make her next move.

It did not take long. Her hand dropped away from her face. When she turned her face up to his, the expression he saw was wary. She was ready to do battle. She would be cautious now. She would not make the same mistake twice. She learned fast, clever girl. How could he ever have thought her a simpleton?

"What happens now?"

He raised his brows. "Why, nothing. We will go on with our lives. You will take up residence here. You will be free to come and go . . . as long as you remain on the island. If you should try to escape, you will be placed under guard."

"And my father?"

"Will remain alive."

"Where?"

"In the dungeon, where he is now." Her lower lip quivered, and he wondered if she was going to cry. She did not. It pleased him to learn that she possessed such strength of control.

"And if I want my father to be free . . . free to leave the dungeon, free to leave this castle and this island, free to return to Ravenscrag to live in peace for the rest of his *natural* life?"

"Then you will have to come to me with another proposition, or accept the one I offered you."

"I am your prisoner already. I have nothing further to give you...nothing I can exchange for his freedom."

Her sadness touched him. He would have done anything in his power to end the sadness he saw in her face and in her eyes. He would have, save for the fact that he wanted her, so much that he was willing to risk it all for the chance to have her. He picked up her hand. It trembled in his. "I beg to disagree with you, lass, but you are not as impoverished as you think." He brought her hand to his lips and pressed a kiss there.

His move plainly surprised her, and her expression was startled. Her eyes were large and round with surprise, but she said nothing.

He did not release her hand, but went on to say, "You have overlooked something...something rare and priceless that you can only give once."

She jerked her hand back. "I will not be your whore!"

"I have not asked you to be."

She spun around and walked angrily across the room. She stopped in front of the altar and stared down at it, hugging her middle with her arms. She trembled—whether from frustration or anger, he was not certain. He only knew she was trying to get control of herself.

He heard her release a long sigh. She stopped trembling, but she did not turn around. "What were you suggesting? If you were not thinking of my becoming your...your harlot, then what is this rare and priceless thing you were thinking I could offer?"

"You could become my wife."

She whirled around. "Your wife?"

He narrowed his eyes. "The only way you will gain your father's freedom is to give me your hand in marriage."

"I cannot."

He came to stand next to her. She turned to face him as he spoke. "The decision is yours. In either case, you will remain here."

Her eyes filled with tears, but she did not cry. "Why would you want to marry the daughter of a man you despise, a woman you do not love?" she asked, with a lost look that stabbed into the heart of him.

"It is the only way to give you what you ask for. The only way to settle an old debt."

"An eye for an eye," she whispered. "My father was responsible for your wife's death, so you force me to become your wife."

"I will not force you. The decision is yours."

She seemed to grow smaller before his eyes. When she looked at him, her entire being seemed consumed with sadness. "You have my word."

"I am not an easy man to dupe. The words are short, but the possibilities are endless. I am a man of precise definition. I have your word...on what?"

"You have my word that I will become your wife, but only when you have released my father and agreed to let him live in peace for as long as he lives...without being murdered."

"You will have to learn to trust your husband."

"When he becomes king of England."

He was amused, but he did not show it. It would not do for him to reveal that now. She wanted her father released before they wed. He could not trust her any more than she trusted him. "You will become my wife, then I will release your father."

He saw by the expression on her face that she realized she had no leverage to use to gain her way. It amused him to see her fury at being forced to yield. She would make a fine wife ... someday.

"You will never be satisfied with this arrangement. Never!"

His eyes bored into hers. This time he allowed the desire he felt to warm in his look. "On the contrary, little captive, I plan to be quite satisfied on our wedding night."

Chapter Fourteen

The Macqueen did not keep his word.

It wasn't that he did not marry Anne Crofton, for he did, some three months later, and he changed her name, as he said, "from that vile, evil name, Crofton, to one more suitable—and honorable, as well."

And it wasn't that he did not release her father as he had promised, for he had kept his word on that, as well.

The sad truth was that when it came to fulfilling his claim to be satisfied on his wedding night, Robert Macqueen had told a lie. He had not come to her since they married, not even to consummate the union.

There had been a few times, Anne would have to admit, when she thought they came dangerously close. One time in particular stood out in her mind. It had happened when he wanted her to tell him about herself, about her life. Apprehensive and nervous around him still, she had been quite reluctant to tell him the things he wished to know.

"Why the continued shyness? I want you to tell me."

"No."

"We will start with your mother. What was her name?"

"Bess . . . Elizabeth."

"Tell me about her."

"She was born a little girl. I didn't know her then. She grew up to be a lady. She was betrothed to my father, whom she had never met. They were married. They had a daughter. They named her Anne. A few weeks later . . ."

He started laughing. "We seem to be back where we started, with you playing the simpleton."

"And you the ogre."

He shrugged. "It is a role that comes naturally to me, I suppose, but that doesn't mean I can't change."

"It doesn't mean you will."

"No, it doesn't, but we can talk about it—perhaps even reach a compromise."

"I have made bargains with you before, milord. You will have to forgive me if I am reluctant to stick my hand into that same fire. I am still recovering from the last time."

He looked as if he had decided to let things ride a bit. As she expected, he turned the conversation back to her. "All right. Tell me more about your mother. How did she look?"

"She looked average."

He lost his temper at that point, and actually had the audacity to *command* her to tell him everything.

She would have died first, but she knew better than to give him any ideas. So she remained willfully mute.

He stared at her, as if trying to smother the flames of anger that burned hotly within him.

"What are you going to do to me? Lock me in the dungeon, or have me whipped for disobedience?"

She had never seen anger disappear so quickly in anyone. There must have been something in her defiance, her manner or her words that penetrated his harsh exterior, something that was able to go through all the layers of pain and hurt to the core of the man inside, for he did something she had never heard him do before.

"I have offended you and caused you pain by my callous disregard. For that, I apologize. My manner, I know, is abrupt, and my way exacting. I cannot promise it will change. You are ten-and-seven, while I will see my thirtieth summer soon. My age has given me more of life's experiences—most of them unpleasant—which have made me demanding, critical, and difficult to live with. I can only ask you to try and understand . . . to be patient."

Since he had given a mile, Anne felt charitable. She gave an inch. "I will work on not being offended."

He did not smile—he rarely did—but amusement lit up his eyes. "I find myself sitting here looking at you, and trying to remember what it was like to be your age."

"You make me sound like a child, while you portray yourself to be positively creeping with age."

"I am a man of many years and great regrets. I became laird of my clan at a very young age...too young to shoulder such a responsibility. Times were hard. Life was harder. My life seemed to be building up to some sort of climax, and when it came, it was more than I could handle. I was surrounded by suffering and consumed by darkness. My pain was so great that there were times I thought God had handed me over to Satan.

"I was convinced my life was over, until I saw the darkness penetrated by the thinnest beam of light, and I saw something there, something I envied, something I wanted. I knew longing, but saw no way to have what I longed for. I had been out of touch with myself for too long, and life had gone on around me. They say God works in mysterious ways, and I have proof of that. I saw hope coming toward me with her arms outstretched, an angel of mercy and light."

He paused to study her face, as if he were looking for something. He smiled softly, then leaned his face toward hers and kissed her firmly on the lips. The power of it almost knocked her off her perch. When he spoke, she could barely hear what he said over the loud hammering of her heart in her ears.

"The Arabs have a saying—'When the angels appear, the devils vanish.' I never understood that until now."

She did not understand, exactly, what he was trying to say, but that did not matter. What did matter was that after that night, she knew she would never be afraid of him again.

It was a sad state of affairs to have to admit it, but she was still a virgin after three months of marriage. Anne remembered what Grizel had said to her a few weeks back. "I have a feeling, lass, that you have decided being married to a beast isn't so bad after all."

That was at least partly true. Aside from her continued state of maidenhood, it wasn't so bad. In fact, her only displeasure was her husband's lack of interest in making her his wife in the truest sense. She would have never believed that she would come to feel this way. But how could she not?

Since the day of their marriage, she had not seen the beastly side of him at all—if, indeed, there was one. She saw only pain. And, through his suffering, she had begun to understand the man he was.

She did not, however, understand his unbelievable self-restraint. For she knew he desired her.

That should have pleased her. It did not. What it did was make her furious.

How dare he humiliate her by leaving her a virgin....

Suddenly it occurred to her: What if he had intended from the beginning not to consummate the marriage? It would be the perfect revenge, for what better way to torment her father than to marry her, letting her wither on the vine like an old maid, with no love and no children?

She took back everything—no, just the things that were kind and in his defense—that she had thought. He was a beast. He had tricked her into this marriage, and now he was going to trick her out of it. How easy she had made it, playing into his hands like a simpleton.

Anne could not remember ever being so angry. Well, she wasn't ready to give up yet. What she wanted and intended to have was desire gratified, and that meant everything that went with it. She had some thinking to do, and a walk was the best way to do it.

In order to make her way outside from her room, she went through the keep, which lay mostly in ruins. Only the forge, weaving room and laundry were still in use, the laundry having the best access to the bailey.

The fragrant, steamy smell of soap and water greeted her when she stepped into the laundry. Although it was Wednesday, the day Grizel and Marta did the laundry, it appeared to be empty. She ducked under the drying clothes, and was about to walk between the wooden tubs when she heard Marta talking.

"I swear on my grandmother's grave that the sheets have not shown any proof of it. If you ask me, I'd say she was still a virgin. Now, I ask you, why would that be? It was his idea to marry her in the first place, wasn't it? So, why did he marry her, if he did not intend for them to live together as man and wife?"

Anne paused and crossed her arms in front of her and nodded in agreement. Perhaps she would get the answers she sought here, in the laundry, and the walk outside would not be necessary.

"You must be mistaken about the sheets, lass. Whatever the reasons the Macqueen had for taking the lass to wife, I would wager my best cotton drawers that remaining celibate was not one of them."

"I am not wrong about the sheets, Grizel. There has been no consummation. In fact, I don't think they have slept together at all. Not once. At least, their beds don't show the proof of it."

"Perhaps they went someplace else."

"And where would that be? The stables? The pigsty? Strapped to the porticullis? Floating in the dye vats? Even if the Macqueen were so disposed, I cannot imagine Lady Anne accepting such conditions."

Anne nodded her head vigorously at that. She peeped through a pair of drawers and saw Grizel twist the sheet in her hands.

"No, I cannot imagine it, either," Grizel said. "If what you say is true, then there must be a reason."

"But what? Lady Anne is more than comely."

Lady Anne puffed up, then smiled as she thought, I never suspected Grizel had such wisdom.

Grizel went on. "We both know what a devil he was to live with when he let her go... after she tried to run away. He was in love with her then, if you ask me."

Anne's head snapped up in surprise. In love with her? She narrowed her eyes. *Piffle! A man does not avoid a woman he is in love with.*

"Aye, she has tormented him since the first time she came here," Grizel said. "I think he wanted her, even then."

"You don't suppose he is angry now, because he let his heart rule his head, do you? He waited a long, long time to have Sir John in his lair, and then when he had him, he allowed his desire for Lady Anne to change all that."

"He did not have to let him go," Grizel said. "He could have taken what he wanted."

"He had to let him go if he wanted her as his wife. He could not marry her and hold her father prisoner."

"He could have, but he is not the sort of man to do such a thing. He may be a beast at times, but he is an honorable one." She paused. "Perhaps he is sorry he let her father go. I have never seen anyone so tormented. If he makes a go of it with Lady Anne, he will have to turn his back on his past. If he continued his pursuit of Sir John, then he will lose his wife.''

''That must be it—'' Marta paused.

Anne started to turn away.

Marta went on. ''Unless something happened to change the way he felt about her.''

Anne jerked to a stop.

''What do you mean, something happened?'' Grizel asked.

''You remember the way Lady Anne was in the beginning? A regular shrew she was, independent and headstrong. Outspoken, too, and using her wit to bait him, playing the dimwit when it pleased her. She rowed herself to this island more than once, and when things did not suit her, she was ready to row herself away. She would have made good her escape, too, if she had not been so ill.''

''So what has changed?''

''*She* has changed. She is meek and docile now.''

Grizel chuckled. ''That is because she is in love with him. Love will turn the biggest shrew into a sheep.''

Anne gasped. *A sheep? How dare they call her a sheep!*

She had heard enough. . . .

She left, going back into the keep, where she wandered around aimlessly for most of the afternoon. She had no idea where Robert was, nor had she seen Gavin or Manus. Not that it mattered. She did not feel like talking to anyone right now. She wanted to be alone.

Somehow, she found herself in the solar that led to her husband's chambers. She opened the door and went inside. She had never been here before, and she was shocked at the spareness of it. Except for the bed and a large chest, the room was entirely bare.

Something about the meager furnishings touched her. It also reminded her that the rest of the castle did not look much better. There were not the usual trappings—tapestries, fine carpets, beautifully carved furniture, or anything that would even hint at luxury or wealth. She had not fully realized the extent of his losses until now.

"He has nothing," she said, her gaze resting on the large chest at the foot of his bed. Curiosity got the best of her.

She went to the chest and opened it. His clothing was as scarce as the furnishings. As she touched the fabrics, she realized they were of very fine quality, but they were old and worn and sadly in need of replacement.

She sat down on the floor and looked through the chest, learning more about him than she had before. There was little here, and certainly nothing of great value, save for an ornate silver dirk and a leather bag that contained a few silver coins. Mostly, it was a collection of relics from the past—a family Bible, a child's spinning top, a blue silk ribband, and a journal of some sort.

Anne removed the journal and opened the lock, not knowing that inside lay a horror of great darkness.

The journal's first entry was filled with suffering and anguish, for it told of the Battle of Culloden, the loss of his entire clan. The next entry was as harrowing, as pain-racked, as the first. Page after page, she read the outpourings of his agony, his aching pain, the grief he had felt when he returned to Ravenscrag and discovered his wife and son were dead, along with all the women and children of the clan.

On and on she read, page after page of his suffering—his spirit somber, his words moving and powerful, touching her and bringing tears to her eyes. And then she read about the dreams, the horrible dreams that had such a profound influence upon him.

She shivered when reading of the grinding influence of nocturnal scenes chillingly, fearfully and vividly described—scenes that were relentless and cruel, scenes of ghosts and visitations, of lost souls and fallen beings. It was little wonder that this poor, desperate man was forced to banish sleep by night, why he was destined to suffer disturbed and distorted mental peace by day.

And yet, underlying it all was a message from a man of true benevolence; a man who had once believed in fidelity and home life; a man of constancy, tenderness and loving kindness; a man who had once held with the concepts of forgiveness and mercy; a man who had changed because of the acts of man's inhumanity, from a man of passion and feeling, into an ever-suffering soul of violence, a beast of ceaseless and unquenchable rages, a man of great emotion, as well as cruelty; a creature unredeemed, who carried his hell with him, and never once strayed from his arrow-straight course toward his own destruction.

And then she read about herself, learning of his true feelings for her, his delight in her beauty, her kindness that was sometimes at war with her defiant manner.

She has come into my life bringing goodness, flooding the darkness with light, and giving me hope. She is my salvation, my restoration, the healer of the past, the promise of tomorrow, my angel of mercy, my guiding light.

She paused. Those words had a strange ring of familiarity, and she tried to recall where she had heard them before. And then she remembered the time he had told her about himself, the time she had not understood what he was trying to say.

I saw hope coming toward me with her arms outstretched, an angel of mercy and light.

She closed the journal and replaced it in the trunk. Just before she closed the lid, she removed a soft, worn linen shirt. She went to his bed and lay across it, tucking his shirt against her chest, feeling his nearness, his presence, assured of it by his scent.

She looked around his room, with its meager furnishings, its bare floors. The windows were covered with old, faded drapes that were more holes and tears than fabric. She thought about his pitiful collection of clothes, the few mementos and possessions he had in his trunk to show for a life that had mainly been losses. And then she thought about his home, his castle, and how much it reminded her of him.

Like Blackness Castle, he was a tall and solid mass of crags, once mighty and strong, a place of refuge, shelter and protection that was now nothing more than a burned-out hull, lonely and abandoned, battered by the elements and lying in ruins.

It was all there, in his journal. Past and present, dream and reality, hopes and disappointments, all blended into one credible whole. There, too, lay the explanation of how a man of strength and compassion, a beloved laird with a fine mind, could turn into a brooding, sullen man capable of vindictiveness and given to black moods.

Nothing and no one had ever touched her this deeply. Never could she remember feeling such anguish for another human being. She had judged him, when he needed understanding. When he sought kindness, she had given him hate. She grieved that she had been cold and indifferent. He was a man grievously wronged and greatly misunderstood, and she was as guilty of it as anyone.

His pain, his suffering, and the unfairness of it all, were more than she could contain. She buried her face in his shirt, feeling as if he were here, with her, and began to cry. Once she started, she could not seem to quit. She cried in a tortured way, her sobbing wretched and passionate, her heart full of regret.

She did not cry for a man who had set out to destroy himself, a man who wanted desperately to forget.

She cried for a man who could find no reason on earth to go on—or enough joy in life to make him want to live.

Her last thoughts were a reminder that she would stay here, waiting for him in his bed. That way, she could tell him she understood now what he had tried to say to her, the pain he wanted to forget. Knowing she truly loved him, she waited, crying herself to sleep, thinking about all the things she wanted to say.

She did not get the chance to tell him.

For before her husband could return, her father's men stormed the castle and took Lady Anne Macqueen away.

Chapter Fifteen

The Macqueen exploded with rage when he returned and discovered his wife was gone. Not even Manus and Grizel together could soothe the ranting, the madness, the passion of his anger. "Get out of here! All of you! I don't want your sympathy, or your pity, damn you!"

They all agreed the Macqueen was like a wild man, completely out of touch. He destroyed everything in his path, roared at anyone who got in his way.

Grizel and Manus watched helplessly until he went for his gun, returning with the intent to go to Ravenscrag. Alone. He was determined to bring her back. That was when Manus picked up a piece of firewood and knocked him unconscious.

For two days, they kept him drugged and tied to his bed.

On the third day, he was calm, and acting like himself again, rational, yet determined as ever to get back what was his, the part of him that had been stolen. But even then, they would not untie him, until he promised to wait one more day.

* * *

After she was brought home, Anne sequestered herself in her room for two days, refusing any food that was brought to her and every entreaty that was made. Her father would not talk to her. And she vowed to starve herself until he relented, or the undertaker carried her away.

On the third day, Sir John sent for her. He was ready to talk.

"I want to go back. You had no right to take me from my husband."

"I had every right. You are my daughter, and the bastard forced you to marry him."

"He did not force me to marry. It was my idea."

"Regardless, I am having the marriage annulled."

"You cannot have a consummated marriage annulled."

"I can, because you will swear that the marriage was not consummated, or you will never see daylight again. I would rather see you dead than sacrificing your life to a monster to save mine."

"Father, you cannot have this marriage annulled."

"It is already being done."

"Then you will have to stop it." She was surprised at her own calmness, in spite of her father's wrath. "I will not tell them the marriage was not consummated. They would soon know it for a lie."

"What are you talking about? What lie?"

"I am with child. That is something I cannot lie about, or hide. Before long, it will be obvious, and then they will realize the truth."

Her father suddenly looked older, his body more bent, his forcefulness turning to wistful regret. With a weary sigh, he said, "Anne, I do not have long to live. I have never done anything for you. I saw this as a way to make amends for all the years I was not there."

She went to her father and put her arms around him. "Don't you understand? You don't have to make amends for anything. And certainly not by destroying a marriage I want very much."

"You are in love with him?"

"Painfully so." She did not expect him to understand, so she was not surprised when he didn't.

"Of all the men, why this one?"

"Perhaps it was God's way of righting a wrong that was done a long time ago."

Her father did not say anything, but after a while, he patted her hand and told her to go. "I am tired now. I would like to rest."

She came to her feet and, after kissing him on the head, started toward the door. Just before she walked out, she turned and said, "When may I return? I am most anxious to see my husband."

Her father's voice was soft. It sounded weary. "Send Joseph to me. I will send him to Blackness Castle with an invitation for your husband to come after you."

"No tricks. I will have your word."

"No tricks," he said, putting a spark of life into his voice. "You have my word."

When Robert Macqueen arrived at his former home, he paused at the front door, uncertain he would be able to go inside. He could not help wondering if all the agony he had once felt here would be waiting for him. He could not step back into the memories, the pain.

When he thought about the reason he was here, what he stood to lose if he did not, it was enough. He knocked. Loud.

He was shown into the library, where he found Sir John waiting for him. He was offered a seat.

"No, thank you, I prefer to stand."

"How about a glass of port...or brandy?"

"This is not a social call. I came for my wife."

"Anne will be down shortly. In the meantime, I have something I have been needing to say to you for a long, long time."

"I have no interest in hearing anything you have to say. Whatever it is, it has no bearing on anything now. You waited too long. Do not think you can ease your evil conscience just before you die."

"I met with my solicitor this morning. I have deeded Ravenscrag back to you. The signed documents are on their way to London. I have included a letter to the king, which confesses my wrongdoings, and explains my desire to set things right. You may have noticed my carriage is packed and waiting. As soon as you are reunited with my daughter, I will be leaving for Italy. The weather is dry there, and better for my health."

Robert's expression remained hard and unmoved. He did not trust this man. And for good reason. The last decent thing he had done was to bring Anne into the world.

Sir John rose unsteadily to his feet. "I know it is difficult for you to trust me, or to believe anything I say. Only time will prove the truth. Unfortunately, time is the one thing I do not have. Before I go, I have one more thing I wish to say. It is not something I find easy, but it is necessary. Although I did not kill those you loved, I am guilty, because I was the one who stood to benefit the most from it. For that, I am eternally sorry. I do not expect you to accept my apology, any more than I can change what happened. My only hope is that perhaps I can, in some way, atone for it."

With a slow, obviously painful gait, he walked to a door on the opposite side of the room. When he opened it, Anne stood behind it.

Sir John motioned for her to come forward.

Anne walked silently into the room, and paused beside her father.

Sir John took her arm and walked her to where Robert stood. He took her hand and held it out.

Robert was so emotionally charged at the sight of her, looking lovelier than he had ever seen her, that it took him a minute to comprehend just what was happening.

When he reached out and took Anne's hand in his, and drew her to him to rest against his side, Sir John said, "What I took, I give back. A wife for a wife."

Anne turned to her father and kissed him, thanking him for giving her back her happiness.

Then she put her arm through Robert's, and together they stepped out into a sun-filled world. Her thoughts were of the future, with her husband at her side. When her father's carriage drove off, she waved until it was out of sight, until Robert took her in his arms and kissed her soundly.

Breathless and a bit giddy, she looked into his face, knowing the question he was going to ask.

"What did you do to make him change?"

"I talked to him."

"You *talked*? Or did you plant some little seed, and leave it to sprout? Was it something you told him that made him see things differently enough to apologize?"

"How did you know?"

"I know how you are."

She began to laugh. "All this talk about seeds and sprouting is uncanny... and so near the truth. I must confess, I told a small lie."

Up went his brows. "You?"

"Only a wee little one."

"What was this insignificant lie?"

She poked him in the chest. "I did not say it was insignificant, only tiny. In truth, it was very significant, I think."

"Are you going to tell me, or leave me hanging in suspense?"

"When I first arrived, my father was completely unreasonable. He already had his solicitor working on an annulment."

"The bastard."

"Please, I am speaking of the way he was, in the past."

"All right—the erstwhile bastard. Now, tell me what you said to change his mind."

"I told him I was going to have your child."

Robert grinned at her and kissed her again, even more soundly this time. While she was still reeling from that, he swung her up into his arms and carried her up the stairs.

"Where are you taking me?"

"To your room. Which one is it?"

"The last one...on the right." She began kissing his face, his throat, his ear.

"If you don't stop that, we may not make it to your bed."

"My bed? Why, Robert Macqueen, whatever are you thinking?"

"I am thinking it is time to make an honest woman out of you."

"An honest woman? But we are married."

"True, but my wife has a bad habit. She does not always tell the truth. The only way I can help is by turning fiction into fact, and I better start working on it now."

"Oh, Robert, I thought this moment would never come."

He kissed her. "I must admit I was beginning to wonder a bit, myself. You are a hard woman to convince. I was running out of devices."

"Do you mean you were contriving?"

"A man does what he has to do." She was laughing when he carried her into the room and kicked the door shut.

A moment later, he lowered her to the bed, and then he followed her, covering her body with his own. She had never experienced such delicious weight. She had wanted this for so long. She was eager to have him know how much she wanted this, and she was eager to explore every part of him.

"Kiss me," he whispered, his lips brushing hers.

She needed no further invitation. His mouth against hers was warm, inviting. She wondered how anything could ever be any better than this. How had she done without it? If only she had known. She realized, then, that the time was not right, that if she had known earlier, she might not have waited, that she would have missed the one true and great love of her life. It wasn't just a matter of enjoying the things he did to her when he kissed her, or the things he was doing to her body now. It was not the ritual. It was the man.

She knew that she would love this man until the day she died, and then, if it was possible, she would love him longer, stronger, for all eternity.

He removed the last of her clothing. She did not realize he had done so until she felt the cool brush of air against her skin. He warmed her, bringing his body against her, aligning himself perfectly with her. She felt a sudden and urgent craving for him, and her arms went around his back to press him closer. He groaned, and then she felt his hand as it smoothed over the skin of her legs, across the flat surface of her belly, then lower, to where she ached.

He smothered her face with kisses, then took her mouth as swiftly as he had captured her heart. This kiss was different from the others, more intense, more demanding, and it made her want something that she could not have named.

Her hands came down, learning the texture, the shape, of his back, then dropping lower. He lifted his body slightly, then brought his knees between her legs. Willingly, she let them part. She could feel him against her now, touching her in a way that made her arch her back. With a gasp, she realized her movement brought him inside her.

It was all the invitation he needed. She heard her own intake of breath, then felt him come into her with a driving swiftness. A sharp pain caused her to cry out softly, and he paused, even though she knew what it cost him to do so.

She decided the pain was worth the wait. Something inside her was building with such intensity that she was star struck. She wanted more of him, all of him, everything he could show her, all he could teach her about her own body, and his, as well. "Love me, Macqueen," she whispered. "Love me as much as I love you."

"God help me, but I already do," he said, and he began to move, taking her with him. It was a ride, a journey that she would remember even when she was old, for she realized then that there was something magical between them, something that opened like a secret cave, and when they stepped inside they found a room filled with treasure.

She was rich. Rich with loving and being loved. Rich in the joy of knowing she had found not a husband, but her lifelong mate. "Hold me," she whispered, her arms going around him. "Hold me until I ache. I love you, Robert Macqueen. So much it frightens me."

A breeze stirred, and blew through the window. She felt the cool chill of it, the ripple of goose bumps left behind. She rubbed his arms and felt the chills there. "An angel just went through the room," she said.

Robert chuckled and rolled over, his body partly covering hers, and then he kissed her. "Don't think this is going to cool the heat of the moment. Inside, I still burn for you. I have since the moment I first saw you. I love you, little captive."

She smiled at his choice of words, finding them somehow appropriate. "I am your captive," she said, biting his ear. "Forever."

"Forever isn't long enough."

She kissed him and thought how beautiful it was . . . whenever they agreed.

* * * * *

Maverick Hearts

Ruth Langan

Chapter One

Texas, 1880

"What in blue blazes—?" The stagecoach driver squinted against the glare of the late-afternoon sun and let out a string of oaths. "Whoa!" he shouted as he pulled frantically on the reins.

Standing directly in the path of the horses was a tall, lean young man, waving his hat, flapping his arms like a rooster. The team came to an abrupt halt just inches from the stranger, jostling the passengers as they scrambled to keep from falling off their seats.

"Wasn't sure you'd spotted me" came a friendly voice.

"Good thing I did, stranger. Otherwise, these horses' hooves would have ground you into dust." The driver watched as the cowboy picked up a saddle from the dirt and balanced it easily on his shoulder.

"Sorry to startle you like that. But my horse went lame, and I had to shoot him. Been walking for miles. Then I spotted your stage." He pulled a coin from his pocket and flipped it to the driver. "Think there's room for me until you reach the next town?"

The driver examined the coin. For this much, he'd make room.

"Sure thing. Hand me up your saddle," he said, reaching down and retrieving it from the cowboy's hands. He secured it on top with the assorted trunks and carpet bags, then leaped down and pulled open the door with a friendly command, "Climb aboard."

As the door was yanked open, the passengers began grumbling among themselves. There were already four bodies crowded into a very small, dust-choked compartment.

"We paid good money for this trip, Wylie," called a stocky man in a dark blue suit and hat. "I don't see why we should have to share it with a trail bum."

"Sorry I look so bad," the cowboy said with an easy smile. He good-naturedly brushed the trail dust from his clothes and slapped his hat against his thigh, sending up another cloud of dust.

"This stranger was willing to pay more'n you, Mr. Ellsworth. Besides," the driver said around the stump of a pipe in his stained yellow teeth, "it's near ten miles or more to the nearest town. You wouldn't want him to have to walk, would you?" Without waiting for the scowling man to reply, he turned to the cowboy. "Climb in. It isn't safe to be in these parts after dark."

The man called Ellsworth, and the plump woman beside him, refused to move, forcing the stranger to turn to the passengers who sat across from them. At once a thin, nervous-looking man in a faded brown suit slid toward the small window. The young woman beside him barely glanced up from the book in her lap before moving aside, allowing the stranger to take the seat between them.

"Afternoon," the cowboy said to one and all. "Sorry for the inconvenience, folks. I may be dusty, but I assure you I bathed just this morning, so I don't smell too bad." He breathed in, then turned slightly toward the young woman beside him. "But I sure don't smell as good as you, ma'am. Lilac water, is it?"

She barely nodded her head before returning her attention to her book.

He hung his hat on one knee and glanced around like a friendly pup. "My name's Montana. And who are you good people?"

"I am Rodney Ellsworth," the stocky man said, with an air of importance. When Montana made no reply, the man continued, "If you were from these parts, you would have heard of me. I own banks in Hollow Junction, and several more towns."

"Tried banking once," Montana said with a smile. "Didn't last."

"And why is that?" the banker asked.

"Kept helping myself to samples." He chuckled at his joke, while the others merely stared at him. "'Course, you wouldn't do that, would you, Mr. Ellsworth? You say you own banks? That must mean you have the use of a lot of people's money. Hope you're investing it wisely."

"My investments over the past couple of years have done very nicely indeed," Ellsworth assured him, puffing up his chest just a little.

Montana gave a sly wink. "A few failed ranchers, a few down-on-their-luck farmers, and you can afford to open another bank. Right, Mr. Ellsworth?"

The banker merely looked smug.

"And who is the lovely lady beside you?" Montana asked.

"This is my wife, Harriet."

"Howdy, ma'am."

The plump woman beside him managed a curt nod, but it was obvious that she considered this dusty cowboy unworthy of her time. She lifted her nose in the air, as though she'd just been assaulted by an obnoxious odor.

Undaunted, Montana turned to the man beside him. "And who might you be?"

The man muttered, "I'm Jasper Thompkins."

"Howdy, Mr. Thompkins. What do you do?" Montana asked.

"I own a shop in Hollow Junction. I trade. With the Indians, mostly. In fact, I'm just returning from a trading trip with the Cheyenne."

"I hear those Cheyenne are tough customers," Montana said.

"Don't know where you heard that." The shopkeeper couldn't help boasting just a little. "I consider them easy pickings. They'd rather spend their money on cheap beads, trinkets, bolts of colorful fabric, than buy quality goods that cost me money, like food and sturdy blankets. Those fools are my best customers."

"So, it looks like trading with the Indians has made you a wealthy man." Montana studied the heavy sack held tightly in Jasper's hands. "Unsold goods? Or money?"

"What do you think?" The man's hands tightened just a fraction as he gave a knowing smile.

Montana turned his attention to the young woman beside him. He'd been pressing his knee to hers ever since he'd sat down, and she still hadn't given any sign that she noticed him. He wasn't accustomed to being ignored by the fairer sex. Most women found him downright irresistible. Especially when he set his mind to being charming.

She sat ramrod-straight. Her hair was pulled back in a severe bun, but a few wisps had managed to pry loose and fell in little corkscrew curls around a small, oval face. Perched on her head was a traveling hat with a pink ribbon tied primly under her chin. She wore a nondescript gown of faded pink calico, with a high, modest neckline and long sleeves, and over that a simple shawl. But the shawl had slipped off her shoulders, and Montana could make out the shape of softly rounded breasts and a tiny waist.

"Name's Montana," he said, turning the full force of his smile on her. "What's yours?"

She glanced up from her book. He had a quick impression of amber eyes, drawn together in the slightest frown at his impertinence. "Virgin—" she said.

He blinked. "Did you say Virgin, ma'am?"

She seemed to sit even straighter. "I said Virginia." Her voice was just a bit over a whisper, with a shy, tremulous quality to it.

Montana had the idea that if he were to holler, "boo!" she would run like a rabbit. "Virginia. That's a nice name, miss," he said, still smiling.

"It's Mrs.—Mrs. Virginia Merle."

If she'd hoped to discourage him from further conversation, it didn't work.

"That book must be interesting." He glanced at the dog-eared pages. "It's had your attention since I came aboard."

"I'm reading the Bible, Mr. Montana. I find it a source of great inspiration."

"That's real nice, ma'am." The Bible. He was beginning to think he could rub his knee against this little sparrow's knee all day and all he'd get for his trouble was a sore knee. He reminded himself that at least she'd remembered his name. He must have made some kind of impression on her. "And what does Mr. Merle do?"

"My husband, Charles, is a newly ordained minister. We intend to travel across the West, preaching and converting sinners." She gave him a stern appraisal, as though she knew he fit into that category. "Charles left shortly after our wedding to begin his ministry, and I agreed to join him as soon as I could manage to save enough money for the journey."

Montana figured he'd be gone right after the wedding, too, if he found himself married to a female that spent all her time reading.

She returned her attention to her Bible.

The cowboy turned to the couple across from him.

Seeing his gaze fixed on her bosom, Harriet Ellsworth flushed slightly. It wasn't that she minded men looking at her feminine attributes. But this young man was nothing more than a lowly cowboy. Even if he was extremely handsome. And bold. She touched a hand to her throat. It wasn't that her gown was immodest, she reminded herself. But there was so much of her bosom, it was difficult to cover it completely.

Montana continued staring at her as though mesmerized. Pasty-white flesh jiggled with every bump and movement of the stage.

Seeing the way she was staring daggers at him, Montana said, with his most ingratiating smile, "Those are mighty fine jewels, ma'am."

For a moment, everyone in the stagecoach went rigid with shock at the audacity of his statement. The young woman beside him coughed discreetly, and covered her mouth with a crisp white handkerchief. Harriet Ellsworth's face flamed. Her husband's head swiveled, and his scowl deepened. Jasper Thompkins sucked in his breath on a quick gasp.

Montana quickly recovered his composure. "I meant your necklace, ma'am."

Everyone seemed to sigh in relief.

"Family heirloom?" he asked.

The woman's face softened into a smile as she fingered the heavy gold chain from which dangled a series of glittering rubies surrounded by diamonds. "No. It's new. Rodney bought it for me in St. Louis."

"I guess the banking business has been very good this year." Montana shot an admiring smile at her husband.

Harriet Ellsworth settled her hands on her lap in such a manner that her rings caught and reflected the slanting rays of the sun. It was plain that she took great pride in her jewelry. She had even pinned a gaudy brooch of gold and assorted sparkling jewels to the lapel of her traveling cloak.

"You probably shouldn't display all that wealth while you're traveling, ma'am," the cowboy said.

"You mean because of the Indians?" she asked.

"No, ma'am. Thieves. Outlaws. Highwaymen." His smile was as lazy as his drawl. "There are a lot of men out there who would just love to get their hands on your jewels."

Again he'd misspoken. Sweat beaded his forehead as Rodney Ellsworth fixed him with a challenging look.

The young woman beside him quickly covered her face with her handkerchief and let out a series of coughs. If she wasn't so shy, he'd have sworn she was laughing behind that handkerchief. But when she looked up, her face was composed.

Montana saw the scowl on Rodney Ellsworth's face deepen, but he chose to ignore it, rather than say more and possibly dig himself even deeper into trouble. He turned to glance out the window. Spotting a familiar towering butte just off to the right, he fell silent and watched for several more minutes before letting out a moan and clutching his stomach.

"What is it?" Ellsworth demanded.

"Pain. Ooh...." The cowboy suddenly doubled over and clapped a hand to his mouth. "I'm going to...be sick."

"Good heavens," Harriet Ellsworth clutched the hem of her gown and cowered against the seat. "I believe he's going to— Oh, Rodney! Get him out of here at once, before he soils my gown!"

"Wylie!" Ellsworth banged on the roof of the stagecoach and shouted at the top of his lungs. "Stop this coach, man!"

A minute later, the coach came to a hiccuping stop as the driver brought the galloping team under control. At once he jumped down and threw open the door to the stage. "What's going on in here?" he demanded.

"This cowboy is sick," Ellsworth said. "And we certainly don't want him to be sick all over us."

The driver helped Montana from the stage and deposited him in the grass beside the trail. The others followed, and stood to one side as the cowboy lay with his back to them.

The driver leaned over and touched a hand to Montana's shoulder. "Think you can go on?"

"I don't know. Give me a minute."

The others watched as he got slowly to his feet, then turned. Their mouths dropped open in shock and surprise when they saw what he held in his hand.

A small, deadly pistol glinted in the sunlight.

"I guess I'll be fine," he said in that lazy drawl, "as long as you good people hand over all your valuables."

The men swore, loudly, fiercely. The women gasped.

"You first, Jasper," the cowboy said, holding out a hand toward the shopkeeper's sack.

When he opened it, his smile bloomed. "Why, Jasper, you sly fox. You're even better at stealing from the Cheyenne than you admitted."

The man turned a ghastly shade of white as he thought of all the money he'd just bilked from the unsuspecting Indians.

Montana turned to the banker and his wife. "I'll take your money, Rodney, that you've earned by the sweat of other people's brows. And your jewelry, Harriet."

"No," she whimpered. "Not my new necklace."

"Especially the necklace," he said. "It will fetch a very pretty price."

As she dropped her jewelry into the sack, she muttered, "You are a dirty, despicable, low-down, good-for-nothing..."

"Why, Harriet..." he said with a smile. "And I thought you were such a lady."

"If I weren't such a lady, I would—"

Montana cut her off. "I tried to warn you about outlaws, didn't I?"

He turned to the younger woman. "Your turn, Mrs. Merle. I'll take your valuables, if you please."

She looked stricken as she reached into her pocket and withdrew a couple of bills. "This is all the money I have, Mr. Montana." Her lips quivered, and she bit them in an effort to control the trembling. Very deliberately, she took several deep breaths before adding, "It took me almost a year to save up." She held the money out to him. "It's only enough for a bed and meals until I am reunited with my...new husband." At that her voice wavered, and she very nearly cried.

He closed his hand over hers, crumpling the bills. Her hand lay in his, soft and warm. He tried to ignore the little tingle along his arm, but it was impossible. Just touching this innocent, he felt a fire starting deep inside him. He was surprised by his reaction to this woman. She wasn't his type. He'd always been attracted to earthy, volatile women. Women willing to live on the edge of danger. Besides, he reminded himself, she was married. A newlywed. A traveling preacher's wife, who preferred the Bible to the marriage bed. Still, he couldn't ignore the feelings her touch aroused.

"Keep your money, Mrs. Merle." His tone was gruff. "You need it more than I do."

She blinked. Her eyes widened in surprise. "Oh, thank you, Mr. Montana." She thrust the bills into the pocket of her gown.

"Just give me that ring on your finger, and I'll be on my way."

At his words, her head came up. A single tear slipped from the corner of her eye and trickled down her cheek. "This ring belonged to my husband's mother." Her voice was wavering again, and it appeared that at any moment she would break down and begin weeping. "She was killed during the war. And this is all he has left of her. It meant so much to Charles to slip it on my finger on our wedding day.'' Another tear trickled down her cheek, and she blinked furiously. "It hasn't been off my finger since. Not...once.''

He felt like the lowest kind of animal. Lower than a snake in the grass. All he'd wanted was a quick infusion of cash. And these people had been perfect marks. No weapons. No one wanting to be a hero. Just nice, wealthy pigeons sitting on a fence rail, waiting to be plucked. He hadn't counted on a little missionary spoiling all his fun.

"You keep your money and your ring, ma'am.'' On an impulse, he lifted both her hands to his lips and pressed a kiss over her knuckles in a courtly, dashing gesture. At once he felt the jolt. And once again resented it. What the hell was the matter with him? He'd better get himself to the nearest saloon, as quickly as possible.

"Oh, thank you Mr. Montana.'' She lowered her eyes demurely and stared at the ground.

But for just one tiny moment, he'd caught a spark of something in her eyes. A glint of triumph, he thought. Or suppressed laughter. He studied her. Her head was bowed, and tears still slid down her cheeks. His gaze took in the shapeless gown, the sturdy, sensible shoes, the hideous bonnet. Impossible. He must have imagined it. There wasn't a single spark of fire alive in this dull, drab little sparrow.

He gave a whistle, and a horse emerged from the woods. "Wylie, would you mind tossing down that saddle?'' he called, in that same cheerful, polite tone.

With a muttered oath, the driver climbed on top of the coach and did as he was told.

Minutes later, Montana waved his pistol, herding the passengers inside the coach once more. "Come on now," he called. "Wouldn't want you good people to be out in these parts after dark. It isn't safe."

As the driver cracked the whip and the team took off, the four people watched through the small window as he pulled himself into the saddle and, with a gallant wave of his hat, took off in the opposite direction.

"I've been fleeced by outlaws before," Rodney Ellsworth said through clenched teeth. "But this one takes the prize. Sweet-talked his way into learning all he could about us before he robbed us. Walked into his trap like blind men, we did."

"You must admit," Harriet Ellsworth breathed, touching a hand to her naked throat, "he was the most charming outlaw we've ever encountered."

"Charming or not," Jasper Thompkins muttered, "I spent the last month accumulating that money."

"I thought you said you practically stole it from the Cheyenne," Ellsworth said, with a trace of sarcasm.

"Maybe." Now that he realized what a fool he'd been to brag in front of the others, he was even more furious. "But it was my money." Jasper's eyes glittered with unconcealed frustration. "Besides, I'm no worse than you, Ellsworth. And I resent that cowboy taking what's mine."

They glanced over at the young woman, who had opened her Bible and was busy reading.

"It would seem, Mrs. Merle," the banker's wife said, with a trace of anger, "that you are the only one who hasn't given over all your wealth to that outlaw."

"I would hope," the young woman said shyly, "it's because my only true wealth lies in my faith."

The others flushed and looked away, to hide the emotions that swept through them. Anger at having been taken in by a charming outlaw. A burning desire for revenge. And a twinge of shame at the resentment they felt toward this modest young woman. After all, it wasn't her fault that the cowboy had softened his heart and allowed her to retain her meager funds.

The remainder of the journey to Hollow Junction was endured in stony silence.

Chapter Two

The town of Wood Creek looked like dozens of other small towns scattered across Texas. And its saloon smelled like hundreds of others. Montana figured he'd seen them all. And been run out of most of them. He picked up the cards and glanced at the faces of the men around the table before saying, "I'll open."

He tossed a coin on the growing pile in the center of the table and paused so that the others could do the same. While he waited, he fished an expensive cigar out of the pocket of his new suit and struck a match. A cloud of richly scented smoke curled in a wreath above his head.

His hair was freshly cut, and he'd paid an extra dollar to have a tub of hot water brought up to his room. It was a luxury he intended to enjoy as often as possible. He'd even indulged in a new saddle for his horse, tied behind the saloon, in case he needed to make a fast getaway. Best of all, he'd been winning for over two hours. All in all, a very good day.

Of course, he kept glancing toward the swinging doors of the saloon each time someone entered. He figured Sheriff Otis Pain, from the nearby town of

Whistling Creek, might be looking for him soon. How was he to know the outlaws he'd robbed over there were working for the crooked sheriff? Pain was a cruel, sadistic lawman who signed all his documents O. Pain. And meant it.

When the bets had been made and the cards dealt, Montana set his hand down with a flourish. "I doubt that anyone can beat three ladies."

The others shook their heads while he dragged the pile of coins close.

A gray-haired rancher scraped back his chair and stood.

"Where're you going?" Montana asked. "The evening is still young." Besides, he'd spotted the wad of bills in the man's pocket, and he was eager to relieve him of such a burden.

"Sorry, gentlemen." The rancher picked up his hat. "I promised my wife I'd accompany her to a revival at the edge of town."

"A revival?" One of the men chuckled. "Now that beats all. You mean you'd rather watch some Bible-thumper than enjoy our company?"

The man shrugged. "From what I hear, this preacher, Sister Goodness, is a lovely young thing who could sweet-talk the devil himself."

Montana sat up straighter.

"That's so," said another. He looked slightly embarrassed as he admitted, "I had to take my wife and mother-in-law there last night. I tell you, that sweet little lady made me think I was in the presence of an angel." He shoved back his chair. "And I'm glad you reminded me. I promised to take my wife back there tonight. I'll see you gentlemen tomorrow night."

"If the preacher's that good," said another man, "maybe I'll go, too. Been promising my wife I'd go along, but I figured it was just another fire-and-brimstone service."

Montana watched as his well-orchestrated poker game fell apart. In no time, the others had drifted away, some to their homes, some to the revival, and a couple to the bar.

Alone with his cards, he shuffled them, playing a solitary game that tested his ability to read each card before turning it over. He filled a tumbler from the bottle on the table. As the whiskey burned a path down his throat, he mulled over what he'd heard. Could it be? he wondered. Could this...could this Sister Goodness be the young woman from the stage-coach?

He filled the tumbler a second time, and downed it more slowly. There was only one way to find out.

Curiosity had the better of him. He had to know. That prickly little female had been on his mind ever since that day he'd robbed the stagecoach. Not that he wanted to see her again, he thought morosely. But he just wanted to see if she was the traveling preacher they were all talking about.

He shoved the deck of cards in his pocket. Picking up his brand-new hat, he jammed it on his head and made his way out back of the saloon to retrieve his horse.

It was easy to figure out where the revival was being held. All he had to do was follow the crowd.

It was the-same-by-God female. Montana stood on the fringes of the assembly, watching and listening. If he hadn't seen it with his own eyes, he still wouldn't believe it. This fiery little preacher had the crowd weeping one minute, leaping to its feet, clapping, singing, cheering, the next. And she was the same drab little sparrow he'd seen in the stagecoach. But now she called herself Sister Goodness. And the sparrow had turned herself into a lark.

In order to be seen, she stood on the highest step of a shiny new wooden Gypsy wagon, which bore the name Sister Goodness on its side in neat, even letters. A horse was tethered nearby.

She was dressed in a prim white high-necked blouse and a simple dark skirt. The hemline brushed the tops of shiny leather boots. Her hair had been pulled back in a neat knot at her nape. As she preached, little tendrils drifted around her cheeks and clung damply. Her eyes gleamed with a fiery zeal. And her voice, which had sounded so soft and quivery on the stagecoach, was now rolling over the crowd with a commanding tone that would rival any tent preacher Montana had ever heard.

As the crowd settled down on the grass for another sermon, Montana leaned back against the trunk of a tree and crossed his arms over his chest, watching and listening. Damn, she was good. It was just as that rancher had said. She did rival the angels. Sweet. Modest. Sincere. Zealous. She held the entire crowd in the palm of her hand. With just a slight inflection of her voice, she had them smiling or frowning, laughing or weeping. She told a sad, uplifting story about how the Lord had lifted her out of the depths of despair. By the time she'd finished speaking, there wasn't a dry eye in the crowd. Not even Montana's.

Almost at once, she began to pass among them with a basket. The men couldn't get to their pockets fast enough. And many a housewife was seen digging into her egg money before the basket moved on.

Montana grinned. Wouldn't he like to help himself to some of that?

Just then his thoughts were interrupted as the young preacher paused directly in front of him and shook the basket under his nose. He looked up to find her staring at him with a challenging light in those amber eyes.

"It appears the Lord has been good to you," she said, allowing her gaze to roam him from head to toe. "I hope you can find it in your heart to show a proper gratitude."

"Oh, I'm grateful, all right." A slow, lazy grin touched his lips as he reached into his pocket and removed a roll of bills. Peeling one off, he tossed it into the basket.

Instead of the thanks he expected, she rattled the basket again. Her frown grew. "You call that gratitude? I call that cheap, sir. And so does the Lord."

He saw several heads swivel his way. His armpits grew damp at the thought of everyone watching and listening. The last thing he wanted was to draw attention to himself in a crowd this size. With a sigh of exasperation, he peeled off another bill, and then a third, and dropped them into the basket.

With a curt nod of her head, she moved on, making her way through the throng. And all the while, his admiring gaze followed her. She was bold, he thought. Most women, confronted by a thief, would have begun trembling or weeping, or would have called for the law. But Sister Goodness, cool as you please, had simply demanded more money.

As the crowd began to drift away, she stood beside her wagon, shaking hands, smiling, listening. Because of her charming manner, several of the ranchers pressed even more money into her hands and insisted she take it, even though she appeared most reluctant to do so.

Montana waited until everyone was gone before leading his horse across the clearing toward her wagon. Once there, he tied his mount to the back, then climbed the crude wooden steps and lifted aside the blanket that served as a door. He found her inside, eagerly counting money.

"Well, well, Sister Goodness. The Lord's work seems to be quite profitable."

She spun around. Seeing him, her eyes narrowed. "I would have thought someone would have hanged you by now."

"I rarely stay around long enough to get caught."

"I hope you were paying attention tonight. If you want the Lord's forgiveness, you'd better mend your ways."

He eyed the bills in her hand. "It isn't the Lord's forgiveness I want, ma'am. I'm more interested in his money." In one smooth movement, he snatched the bills from her hand. "I can see that I've been in the wrong business, Sister. I'm sure you won't mind helping a poor, unfortunate soul like me."

She gave a gasp of outrage, but before she could say anything, he handed back half the money. "There. You see? I can be very generous when I want to. And right now, after all the work you've done, I don't want to appear greedy. So I'll let you keep half. But the other half is mine, to make up for the poker game you cost me." Wearing that same charming smile, he turned away.

An instant later, he felt the unmistakable press of a pistol against his back. And the soft purr of her voice as she muttered, "Find your own con, cowboy. This one's all mine."

It took Montana a full minute to recover from the shock. He hadn't believed it possible for him to be taken in by a con artist. After all, he'd practically invented the word. He turned. And found himself staring at a small silver derringer held in her hands. The same hands that had held a Bible so lovingly.

"I believe you have something of mine," she said. Even her voice had changed. Gone were the soft, sweet-spoken words that fairly trembled from her lips. Now her voice was strong, commanding. And the only tremor came from anger. She reached out and took the money from his hands.

"Who'd have thought?" he muttered. "Why, Sister Goodness, you're a bigger thief than I am."

"I am not a thief," she said, with righteous indignation.

"What would you call someone who relieved these poor ranchers of their hard-earned money? Whether you do it at gunpoint or in the name of the Lord, you're still a thief."

She brandished the gun at him. "I bring drama into their drab lives. I take them away from the misery of their humble existence."

"What you do is lie."

"What I do is entertain," she said firmly. "And by the time the evening's over, I've given them more than their money's worth."

Montana glanced around. "What happened to your husband?"

A hint of a smile touched her lips. "There is none. I have no use for a man."

He stared at the gold band on the third finger of her left hand. "What about that?"

She held it up admiringly. "A repentant widow had nothing else to put in the basket. I assured her the Lord would accept jewelry. When I saw that it fit, I decided to wear it. I thought it added a nice touch to my story. Don't you agree?"

He shot her a look of respect. "I can't believe I didn't see through you. You're just about the best actress I've ever met. You had everyone on that stage, including me, believing that you were a poor, helpless missionary's bride. Why, you even cried on cue." His eyes narrowed, his tone hardened. "But the game's over, Sister Goodness."

His hand swung out in a wide arc, knocking the pistol to the floor. With a cry of distress, she dropped to her knees to retrieve it. But before she could, he pounced on her in an effort to stop her.

"Get off me, you oaf!" She writhed around, pummeling him with her fists, but she was no match for his strength. The more she struggled, the more determined he became to subdue her.

"I didn't come here to hurt you," he said, just as she landed her fist on his nose. He let loose with a string of oaths.

"Oh, no?" She drew back, prepared to hit him again. "You just want to take what is rightfully mine."

"Not all of it." Gingerly rubbing his nose, he caught her by the wrists and dragged her arms up over her head to keep her from attacking again. "Just my half."

"Your half?" She was effectively pinned and unable to strike out, but she continued twisting and turning in an effort to break free. "When did you become my partner?"

"When you conned me into returning your money on the stage. You even managed to keep your ring with those phony tears. And today you cost me a poker game. You owe me, Sister Goodness."

Her chest was heaving from the exertion of battle. Lying over her, struggling to hold her still, he became acutely aware of the press of her breasts against his chest, the warmth of her thighs pinned beneath his. Her dark hair had pried loose from its neat knot and tumbled wildly around her shoulders. The hem of her skirt was caught beneath her hip, revealing a length of shapely ankle.

She saw his gaze fasten on her lips, which had parted as she dragged air into her lungs. She felt a tingle of fear at the dangerous light that came into his eyes.

"Why, Sister Goodness. That mouth of yours is just made for kissing."

"Don't you dare—"

He cut off her protest with a quick, light kiss. It was the merest brushing of mouth against mouth, but it had her heart racing and her breath backing up in her lungs.

His hands tightened on her wrists, and he pressed himself to the length of her as he ran one hand down her side. Then he kissed her again.

Fire and ice danced along her spine. She couldn't move. Couldn't fight him. She felt frozen to the spot. All she could do was moan softly as he moved his mouth over hers, drawing out the kiss until she thought her lungs would burst. And all the while his hand continued its lazy exploration, causing a rush of heat deep within her.

At last he lifted his head and stared down at her. What he saw disturbed him more than he cared to admit. Her lips were moist and swollen, and incredibly tempting. The thought of losing himself in another kiss had his blood heating, his heart galloping. Her body was lean and slender, and softly rounded in all the right places. The mere touch of her had him inflamed.

"What's your name?" he whispered.

"I told you—"

"Your real name," he said more firmly. His roguish smile had vanished.

She ran a tongue over her lips, and saw his eyes darken. The fear was back, making her heart skip a beat. "Summer."

"Summer." He spoke the name like a caress, and for a moment she thought he was going to kiss her again. "Summer what?"

"Summer Chambers." She swallowed. "Let me up."

"In a minute." He continued studying her. "You intrigue me, Summer Chambers. I've never met a woman quite like you."

Her temper was back, and she seized it, hoping to hide whatever other feelings had surfaced. "And you never will again. Now let go of me."

He picked up her pistol and scrambled to his feet, then helped her to stand. Her body still tingled from his touch. Her lips were still warm from his kiss. A kiss that had shattered all her composure. As she dusted off her backside, he counted out the money and thrust half in his pocket. The other half, he handed to her.

"You have no right—" she began.

But a sound outside had both their heads coming up sharply.

"Shh…" he commanded, pressing a hand over her mouth. "Are you expecting anyone?"

She shook her head.

"Whoever it is," he whispered, "get rid of them."

She strode to the entrance of the wagon and peered out. Three pairs of frightened eyes stared back at her from the gathering darkness.

"Who are you?" she asked a dirty little girl of about eight.

"My name is Pansy," the girl said. "Pansy Miller. And this is my brother, Ned, and my baby sister, Hannah."

"It's awfully late," Summer said. "Don't you think you should be home?"

"We don't have a home anymore," the little boy said.

"No home?" Hearing that, Montana strode to the entrance and peered out from behind Summer.

At first he'd been annoyed at this interruption. Now he was intrigued by the sight of these three. Their feet were bare, their clothes ragged and torn. Their arms and legs were bloody and scratched from brambles. "What happened to your home?"

"Our ma and pa died," Pansy said. "And the banker came and said we couldn't live there anymore."

"Don't you have any kin who will take you in?" Summer asked.

The little girl shook her head.

"Friends of your folks?" Montana asked, though he already knew the answer. It was written on their forlorn little faces.

. "Nobody wants three more mouths to feed," Pansy said. "But the banker's wife wants to take Hannah, and send Ned and me to an orphanage in St. Louis. That's why we came here tonight."

"I don't understand." Summer could already feel her heart breaking for these three innocents.

"We heard about the revival and decided to ask the Lord to help us stay together. And now that we've found you and your husband, Sister Goodness, we know our prayers have been answered."

"Now, wait a minute . . ." Montana began.

Just then he heard the sound of hoofbeats. At the same moment, the children swiveled their heads to glance nervously over their shoulder at the shadowy figure approaching on horseback. The brother and sister began to cry, and the baby followed suit.

"Now what?" Montana asked. "Who's that?"

"The sheriff," Pansy said.

Both Montana and Summer stiffened.

Montana's mind raced. Had someone in the crowd spotted him and summoned the law? He should have been more careful. But there was still time to make it to his horse and get away.

Summer blanched, and wondered if one of the ranchers had begun to regret his generous donation to Sister Goodness. Was the sheriff about to call her bluff and confiscate all her money?

The children's weeping grew louder.

"The sheriff's coming to take us!" Pansy cried.

Both Summer and Montana reacted at the same moment. If their fear was this great, how much greater must be the children's?

"What's this sheriff's name?" Montana demanded.

"Sheriff Lacy," the little girl said.

Montana whispered, "Quick. Hide these three."

"What are you going to do?" Summer demanded.

He shot her a dangerous smile. "What I do best, Sister Goodness."

Chapter Three

"Quick. Come inside," Summer called, drawing the three children into the wagon. "Lie down under that blanket. And don't make a sound."

She watched as Montana strode into the shadows and greeted the sheriff with a hearty handshake. She could hear the deep rumble of his voice, and the sheriff's deeper response. But she couldn't make out their words. She experienced a sudden rush of fear. What had ever possessed her to trust this outlaw? What if he decided to set her up in order to save himself? At this very moment, he could be telling the sheriff that she was an impostor. While the sheriff was busy arresting her, Montana would have time to make his own escape.

Or he could be telling the sheriff about the children. Her gaze flew to the bunk in the corner of the wagon, where the three little ones huddled. There was really no safe place to hide in such a small space.

Cursing her carelessness, Summer looked around for a weapon. Montana still had her derringer. All she had left to use in her own defense was a knife. Still, she thought as she picked it up and held it behind her back, it was better than nothing. Her heart began beating overtime. She wouldn't let the sheriff take her without a fight. At the sound of masculine laughter, she drew back, ready to strike. But as she peered around the blanket in the doorway, she saw Montana hitching her horse to the wagon, with the sheriff's help.

Now what was he up to? she wondered.

The baby whimpered, and the sheriff's head came up. Summer could hear his question. "What was that?"

"Night bird," Montana said. "You're mighty jumpy tonight." He slapped the sheriff on the back, and the two men chuckled as they returned to their chore.

Thinking fast, Summer tore off a piece of her petticoat and dipped a corner of the fabric into a bucket of water, then into sugar. She knelt beside the children and handed it to Pansy, who in turn offered it to Hannah. The baby sucked greedily.

Everyone breathed a sigh of relief. But only for a moment.

The sound of the men's voices was even closer. Was that fool cowboy planning on bringing the sheriff inside? Summer flew to the doorway and peered around the edge of the blanket. While she watched, the two men shook hands.

"Goodbye," Sheriff Lacy called. "Be sure you tell your wife how grateful the folks of Wood Creek are for her uplifting message."

"Yes, sir. I will."

While the sheriff stood by, Montana climbed aboard the seat and flicked the reins. The horse leaned into the harness, and the wagon began swaying as it rolled away. The sudden movement had the infant squalling. Terrified, Pansy leaped up, hugging the baby to her shoulder to still her cries.

Summer raced to the back of the wagon and watched through a crack in the boards as the sheriff continued staring after them with a look of intense concentration. At last he climbed into the saddle. And headed in the opposite direction.

Summer leaned weakly against the wagon's frame and let out a long, slow breath. Then, when her heart had resumed its normal pace, she climbed out onto the seat beside Montana.

"What did you tell him?" she demanded.

Montana glanced at her, then returned his attention to the trail. "I told my good friend Sheriff Lacy that my wife and I were heading on up to Poplar to give another revival."

Wife. The word rankled. But, for the moment, she had no choice but to accept it. "Did he believe you?"

He chuckled. "Now, Sister Goodness, you've seen me in action, so you know what I'm capable of while managing to remain utterly charming."

"I wouldn't go that far. You're a liar, I'll give you that. But charming?" She gave a short laugh. "That day on the stage, I could see right through that phony charm."

"Phony? I'll have you know I've charmed ladies from Amarillo to Laredo. They'll tell you there's nothing phony about this cowboy's charm. It's all true. Why, I'm practically a legend."

She decided not to debate the issue. "I'll take back my gun, if you don't mind."

He handed it to her. After checking it, she turned on him. "It's empty. What happened to the bullets?"

"You don't think I'm going to give you a chance to shoot me in the back, do you?"

"I'll restrain myself. For the moment." She tucked the pistol in her pocket and lowered her voice. "What about those three back there?"

Instantly his smile faded. "They were telling the truth. The sheriff said he was looking for three little kids who were running because a certain fine, upstanding lady, a banker's wife from the town of Hollow Junction, wants to adopt their baby sister."

"Hollow Junction?" Summer's eyes widened in suspicion. "What's the lady's name?"

"Harriet Ellsworth," Montana said through gritted teeth.

"That nasty woman from the stage?"

"The same." Montana nodded. "The sheriff seemed to think that uppity snob would make a real fine mother."

"Oh, poor Hannah," Summer whispered. "No wonder they're all so afraid. What are we going to do with them?"

"If you'll recall," Montana said dryly, "I just got rid of the sheriff for you. I'll let you worry about what to do with the extra baggage."

"Well, I can't just dump them along the trail. Especially not with the sheriff looking for them."

"I've been thinking." His mind had been working overtime ever since the sheriff had told him that Sheriff Otis Pain and his gang were mad as hornets and searching for an outlaw who'd been robbing stages in these parts. It was time to go under cover for a while.

And what better cover than a couple of traveling preachers and their children? "Maybe those kids would have a better chance of evading the sheriff if they looked like they belonged to a family."

"That's what I intend to find them. A family. But you heard Pansy. How many people are willing to take on the care and feeding of three extra mouths? What if I can't find them a home?"

He shrugged. "Then I guess, Sister Goodness, you'll just have to let the Lord provide. In the meantime, we could pretend to be their parents. That way, no one will suspect them of being runaways." And after a while the law might forget about him, Montana thought.

She gave a snort of disgust. All this cowboy wanted was her money. And when he had it, he'd be gone. Still, it might work to her advantage to have a husband and children.

When she heard a whimper from inside her wagon, she put aside her troubling thoughts and climbed over the seat. "I'd better see if I can fix them something to eat."

"I'll have whatever they're having," he called to her retreating back.

It occurred to Summer that she had just acquired four extra mouths to feed.

It wasn't much of a meal. Beans, biscuits, and some strips of dried meat. But there was a full moon, and Montana had built a roaring fire, over which coffee bubbled invitingly. It made the evening seem festive. As the children gathered around, Pansy and Ned joined hands and bowed their heads. There was a moment of awkward silence.

"Well?" Montana inquired. "Aren't you going to eat?"

Pansy glanced toward Summer. "Mama said we should never take our blessings for granted. Aren't you going to pray, Sister Goodness?"

"Pray? Yes. Of course." Summer offered her hand, then shot Montana a look. At once he doffed his hat and did the same.

Summer's mind raced. "Why don't you lead us, Pansy?"

"Bless this food," the little girl said. "And thank you for sending us these good people who are going to keep us together. Amen."

"Amen," Summer and Montana intoned together, avoiding each other's eyes.

The children were ravenous. They ate everything, then proceeded to lick their plates. The sight of it made Summer's heart ache. Maybe, she thought, they would be better off in an orphanage. At least there they'd be assured of food and shelter.

Pansy mashed the food for little Hannah, and saw to it that she ate every bite, before washing it down with half a cup of water. By the time the chubby infant had finished eating, her little body was covered with the remnants of her meal.

"I'm sorry I don't have any milk." Feeling somewhat awkward, Summer dipped a towel in a bucket of water warming over the fire and proceeded to wash Hannah's hands and face and strip away her soiled clothes. At once, the infant set up a wail.

With great tenderness, Pansy picked up her little sister and managed to soothe her.

"Maybe tomorrow we can persuade a rancher to sell us some milk," Summer muttered.

"It doesn't matter." Pansy continued cuddling the baby. "Don't fret on our account, Sister Goodness. Hannah hasn't had milk for more than a week now." She glanced over to where her little brother sat by the fire, eyes closing, head bobbing, as he struggled to remain awake. "Neither has Ned. This is the most food we've had since Mama and Papa died."

Summer and Montana exchanged a glance.

"Well—" Summer kept her tone crisp, to hide the feelings that were beginning to churn inside her "—let's see about a place for you to sleep."

"We've been sleeping in the woods." Pansy scratched at an insect bite. "We were afraid to go back to our cabin, 'cause we knew the sheriff was looking for us."

That did it. Summer made up her mind quickly. "Well, tonight you're going to sleep indoors."

The inside of the little wagon was as neat and tidy as the woman who occupied it. Summer decided that if she removed the narrow bunk and spread blankets on the wooden floor, the three children would be able to sleep side by side.

"This will have to do for now," Summer said, indicating the blankets.

"Thank you, Sister Goodness." Pansy laid the sleeping infant down, then led her little brother toward the bed and stripped off his dirty clothes.

"Thank you, Sis..." was all little Ned managed before his eyes closed.

The eight-year-old girl stepped out of her dress and crawled between Ned and Hannah, drawing the blankets over them, before closing her eyes.

By the time Summer had pulled on a modest night shift and climbed down from the wagon, the three children were fast asleep.

Outside, Montana sat with his back against a stump. On his face was a pensive look. He held a flaming stick to his cigar and drew smoke into his lungs before glancing up.

Seeing the blanket over her arm, he asked, "Where are you going to sleep?"

She shrugged, uncomfortable beneath his scrutiny. There was something there, just below that charming surface, that worried her. Something tantalizingly dangerous that both repelled and attracted her. "Under the wagon, I guess. As soon as I wash these things." She dropped the filthy clothes in the bucket of hot water and scrubbed them until the worst of the soil was gone. "What about you?" She noted that he'd unsaddled his horse and turned it loose to graze. "I . . . wasn't expecting you to stay on. Wouldn't you be more comfortable in a saloon somewhere?"

"If I'm going to pretend to be the father of this brood, I'd better stay the night," he said, studying the glowing tip of his cigar to keep from staring at her. In the moonlight, as she hung the children's clothing on low branches, her slender body was clearly outlined beneath the opaque fabric of her night shift. His throat was as dry as if he'd just ridden across the desert. "For the sake of the kids," he added lamely. "Just to see that the sheriff doesn't change his mind and follow their trail."

"Oh." Part of her mind was protesting, eager to be rid of him. But another part of her felt a rush of relief that she wouldn't have to deal with the problem alone. When it came to children, she felt completely helpless. "I...don't have another blanket."

"Don't worry. I've got a bedroll. I've made do plenty of nights under the stars."

Summer draped the blanket around her shoulders and turned away, feeling suddenly self-conscious. Montana's presence caused her much more discomfort than she cared to admit. She could still recall the way his lips had felt, pressed to hers. And the way she'd responded to his kiss. "I'll say good-night then. And, Montana..." She turned her head and called over her shoulder, "Thanks for getting rid of that sheriff."

"Don't bother thanking me," he said with a lazy smile. "I'll just take my reward out in profits....partner."

She should have known. There was nothing noble about this clever outlaw. With a scowl, she crawled under the wagon and wrapped herself in the blanket. And fell asleep reciting a litany of reasons why she had to get rid of this cowboy as soon as she found a home for the children. Before he managed to relieve her of everything she'd been working for.

Morning sunlight slanted warm against Summer's back. She sighed and snuggled deeper into her blanket. Nearby, she heard the splash of water spilling over rocks in the stream. And from within the wagon came the sound of a baby crying. It took several seconds before the strange sound registered on Summer's brain. Instantly she was awake and racing up the steps. She shoved aside the covering at the entrance and stepped inside.

"What's wrong?" she whispered as her eyes adjusted to the gloom.

"Nothing. Hannah's just hungry, that's all," the little girl replied.

Beside her, Ned stirred and rubbed his eyes, looking thoroughly confused, as he glanced around at the unfamiliar surroundings.

"I'll fix something to eat." Summer fumbled with her night shift and slipped into a simple cotton gown.

When she was dressed, she tied her hair back with a ribbon and said, "If you'd like, Pansy, I'll take Hannah outside with me, and you and Ned can wash up down by the stream before breakfast."

The little girl reluctantly handed over her baby sister. It was plain that she didn't like the idea of giving her up for even a few minutes. Especially to a woman who held Hannah out stiffly in front of her like a piece of fragile crystal.

Taking Ned's hand, Pansy gathered up their clean, dry clothes and led him toward the stream.

As Summer emerged from the wagon, Montana was standing nearby, shaving. He was naked to the waist, and little drops of water glistened in his hair, indicating that he'd just bathed in the stream. He looked up from the mirror he'd nailed to a tree. "What's wrong with the baby?" he asked.

"Wrong? Nothing." Summer took a few steps toward the fire, still holding Hannah stiffly in front of her.

The infant started to cry.

"You don't hold a baby like that." Montana tossed his razor into a bucket of water and dried his face on a towel before crossing the distance between them. He took Hannah from Summer's hands and cradled the baby against his chest. At once her cries were stilled. With murmured words, he began to circle the fire, all the while patting the infant's back.

Summer was assaulted by a wave of strange emotions. His shoulders were wide, his arms corded with muscles. The dark pants emphasized his flat stomach and narrow hips. The sight of this big, strong outlaw cradling an infant in his arms was so unexpected, all she could do was stare. This seemed a far different man from the one she'd first met.

His hand moved lower, to Hannah's bottom. "Here's the problem," he muttered.

"What?" Summer brought her hand to her throat in a gesture of fear.

"She's wet. Do you have any linen?"

Relieved that there was nothing seriously wrong with the infant, Summer stepped into the wagon and emerged a minute later carrying a piece of clean linen. Montana had settled the baby on his saddle blanket beside the fire, where Hannah was cooing and smiling up into his face.

"Well?" he asked as she approached.

She stared down at the tiny figure, and felt a rising panic. She held the linen out to Montana. "You change her."

His eyes narrowed. "What's the matter, Sister Goodness? Afraid of a little baby?"

"I...don't know what to do with her. I've never even held a baby before, let alone changed one. I'm afraid I'll do something wrong."

"She won't break, if that's what you're afraid of." He took the cloth from her hands and patted the blanket. "Come on. It's time you learned. I'm not going to show you this twice."

Summer knelt beside him, acutely aware of his state of undress. The muscles of his shoulders bunched and tightened as he folded the square into a triangle. His arm brushed hers, causing a sudden tingle along her spine, as he smoothed the fabric and placed it beneath the baby.

"Now all you have to do is remove the soiled linen from her and replace it with this clean one. Tie the two corners into a knot, and you're all done."

He got to his feet and walked back to the tree, where he resumed shaving.

Summer watched him for a moment, then looked down at the smiling baby. He'd made it sound so simple. Gingerly she plucked at the knot that held the soiled linen. As she removed it, she wrinkled her nose. "Good heavens! Who'd have thought one little baby could—"

She wiped frantically at the mess and managed, after several clumsy attempts, to get the baby's bottom cleaned and the fresh linen in place. By that time, Hannah had started to wail again.

Montana watched in the mirror as Summer scooped up the little one and pressed her awkwardly to her shoulder. He kept his face averted until he managed to stop laughing. But the laughter faded at the sight of

Summer soothing the infant with murmured words and nervous kisses. Despite her awkwardness, she displayed a tender side that, until now, she'd kept carefully hidden from view. While he finished shaving, Montana continued to watch in the mirror.

Within minutes, Pansy and Ned returned from the stream, their faces gleaming, their hair slicked back.

Pansy held out her arms for her baby sister. Summer was happy to relinquish her.

"What's this?" Ned asked as he poked at a covered bucket near the wagon.

"Milk," Montana said casually as he pulled on his shirt.

Seeing Summer's startled look, he explained, "There was a ranch nearby. I didn't think anyone would mind if I milked one of the cows. And I happened upon a couple of eggs, as well."

Summer arched a brow. "You just happened upon them?"

"I've always been lucky that way," he said with a wink.

Summer felt her heart tumble, and quickly turned away. She filled three mugs with milk and handed them to the children. With a delighted laugh, Pansy sat down and settled her little sister on her lap, holding the rim of the cup to her lips. The baby drank eagerly.

Soon Summer had prepared a breakfast of eggs and biscuits and dried meat, while the wonderful aroma of coffee filled the air. Montana and Summer were brought up short when Pansy and Ned clasped hands and bowed their heads. Reluctantly they, too, joined hands.

After a moment of silence, Summer said, "Ned, I think you should lead us in prayer this time."

"Yes, ma'am." The little boy thought a moment, then said, "Bless this food. And all of us." His voice wavered. "And especially Mama and Papa."

Summer had to stifle an almost overpowering urge to take the little boy in her arms and soothe his fears. Instead, she woodenly began to eat.

When he was finished, Montana leaned his back against his saddle and sipped a cup of hot coffee. "This was a tasty meal."

Summer blushed, though she had no idea why she should feel so pleased by such an offhanded compliment.

"You're almost as good a cook as Mama," Ned declared.

Summer smiled. "Why, thank you, Ned. Tell me about your mother."

The little boy's eyes took on a faraway look. "Mama had yellow hair. It was as soft as corn silk. She used to hug me a lot. And she smelled good." He breathed in. "She smelled like—" he struggled to think of a comparison "—biscuits." He popped one into his mouth.

"She sounds wonderful." Montana sipped his coffee. "I'll bet you miss her. How'd your folks die?"

"They were shot. Out in the fields." Pansy's voice was tight with unspoken emotion.

Montana went very still. "Who shot them?"

The little girl shrugged. "I didn't see anybody. I was in the cabin with Hannah. Ned came in crying and led me out to the field and . . ." Her lips quivered, but she forced herself to go on. "I found them lying by the plow horse. We walked all the way to town and reported it to the sheriff. He brought us back to the cabin and left us there while he buried Mama and Papa." Tears pooled and began to run down her cheeks. She brushed them fiercely away. "Next day, the banker came and said we couldn't stay there anymore, because Papa still owed the bank money. Then the sheriff came and said the banker's wife wanted Hannah, and that Ned and I would be sent to an orphanage in St. Louis. That's when we ran away and hid in the woods. We've been running ever since."

Ned began to whimper, but Pansy dropped an arm over his shoulder and drew him close. "Everything's going to be just fine now," she whispered against his cheek. "Sister Goodness and Montana are going to take care of us from now on. And we don't ever have to be afraid again."

Montana took a gulp of coffee and burned his tongue. A string of oaths flitted through his mind, but because of the children, he managed to keep from uttering them aloud. On his face was a look both dark and frightening.

Summer abruptly looked away. The food she'd eaten lay like a rock in her stomach. How was she going to make these innocents understand that she intended to leave them as soon as she found them a home? They were sweet children. And they'd been through the horrors of hell. But they had no place in her plans. And neither did Montana. If she allowed this outlaw to hang around too long, he would surely bring the law down on all of them. Before the day ended, she vowed, she would make certain that these three orphans had a home. And that her unwanted partner was out of her life.

Chapter Four

Montana doused the fire, then took a last sip of coffee before tossing the rest on the coals. Summer had loaded the wagon and was preparing to break camp. Beneath the shade of a tree, Pansy sat rocking her little sister. Ned was throwing pebbles in the stream and watching the ripples.

"Come on, children," Summer called.

Montana saddled his horse, then, on an impulse, called to Ned, "I'm going to ride ahead and scout the trail. Want to ride along?"

"You mean it?" The little boy shot a glance at his sister. "Can I go?"

Pansy seemed to be weighing the offer very seriously, and it was plain that she was reluctant to let him out of her sight. But the pleading look in Ned's eyes convinced her. "I guess so."

He opened his arms, and Montana leaned down, lifting him with ease. He placed the little boy behind him and said, "Hold on tight now. I wouldn't want to lose you along the way."

The little boy wrapped his thin arms around Montana's waist and pressed his cheek to the big man's back. As the two rode away, he waved triumphantly to his sister.

Summer climbed up to the wagon seat, then reached down to hold Hannah while Pansy climbed up beside her. When they were comfortably seated, Summer flicked the reins and the horse and wagon took off at a leisurely pace.

"It seems funny," Pansy said, cradling her little sister, "that you live in a wagon, and travel from town to town. Don't you miss having a real home, with fields to plow and crops to harvest?"

"You can't miss what you never had," Summer said simply.

"You never had a home?"

Summer smiled, diverting her questions. "This is my home now. And think of it this way—no matter where I travel, it's always here with me." She paused a moment, biting her lip as she considered how to proceed. "About my name," she began. "I don't mind being called Sister Goodness in town, in front of strangers. But when we're alone, call me Summer."

"Summer." Pansy tried out the name. Her smile grew. "Is that your real name, or one your papa gave you?"

"Summer is my real name. Why do you ask?"

"Because," the little girl said proudly, "Pansy isn't my real name. I was given the name Sara. But Papa always said I was as pretty as a pansy, and from the time I was little, he called me that. Now I don't ever want to be called anything but Pansy," she said fiercely. "That way I'll never forget how much Papa loved me."

Summer's heart went out to this little girl who was trying desperately to hang on to her memories. "You're very lucky to have had parents who loved you."

"Yes, ma'am. But what about Ned and Hannah? I'm worried that Ned will soon forget. And Hannah will grow up never knowing Mama and Papa."

Summer clutched the reins tightly. Pansy was so young to have so much responsibility. "Then you'll have to keep the memories alive for them."

She noticed that Hannah had fallen asleep in her sister's arms. "She must be heavy," she murmured. "Would you like to climb back into the wagon and lay her down?"

Pansy pressed a kiss to the infant's cheek. "I don't mind holding her. No matter how heavy she gets."

Summer had to swallow the lump in her throat before she could say, "You might want to get her out of the sun."

"All right." The little girl climbed over the seat and laid the baby down in the cool, shaded wagon, placing a folded blanket on either side of her to keep her from rolling as the wagon swayed.

Alone up front, Summer found herself battling conflicting emotions. These children had already been so wounded. She didn't want to do anything to cause them further pain. But she knew one thing. She wasn't equipped to care for them. They deserved much more than she could ever give them. They deserved a mother and father to love them. And a respectable way of life, with parents who had the esteem of the community. What they didn't need was a phony preacher and an outlaw.

She looked up as Montana and Ned came into view. Ned was wearing Montana's wide-brimmed hat. He lifted it in the air and waved it as they drew near.

"There's a town up ahead," he called as they pulled alongside the wagon. "We rode way up to the top of that butte, and off in the distance we could see a town."

"How soon before we're there?" Summer slowed the horse and lifted a hand to shade the sun from her eyes.

"Couple of hours, I figure." Montana easily swung Ned from the horse to the seat of the wagon.

Ned's face was flushed with excitement. "Montana knows just about everything." His eyes glowed with adoration. "He told me all about the Cheyenne, and how they live, and what they eat. And he said he's been to almost every town in Texas. And—" he paused for breath "—when I get big, I'm going to be just like Montana," he announced with pride.

"You might want to aspire to loftier goals," Summer said dryly.

"What does that mean?" Ned glanced from Montana to Summer.

Montana reached over and lifted his hat from the boy's head. "It means," he said with a wink, "you might want to think about becoming president instead."

"I don't want to be president. I want to be like you," Ned said fiercely.

"I want to be a traveling preacher like Summer," Pansy announced.

Summer glanced at her in surprise. "Now when did you come to that decision?"

"When I heard you preach last night. When you talked about all of us being God's children, and being held in his loving arms, it made me feel so good. I wasn't so afraid after that. I want to be able to share that news with other people, so they won't be afraid, either."

At the little girl's look of adoration, Summer felt a wave of guilt and ducked her head.

She was grateful for the distraction when Montana said, "If you'll stop for a minute, I'll tie my horse to the back of the wagon and hitch a ride."

She drew on the reins and waited in silence until Montana pulled himself up on the seat. Then, with Ned and Pansy between them, they resumed their journey.

"Summer said she never had a home, or fields to plow or crops to harvest," Pansy announced.

Summer felt Montana's sideways glance and kept her gaze firmly on the trail.

"How about you, Montana?" the little girl asked. "Did you ever have a home, and brothers and sisters?"

He kept his smile in place as he tugged on one of her curls. "The whole world is my home, Pansy. That's always been my motto. Just make yourself at home wherever you are."

"Mama and Papa came from Missouri. That's where they were born. But Papa thought they'd have better luck in Texas." Ned stared up into Montana's handsome face. "Where are you from, Montana?"

"Here and there," he said with that same charming grin. "And everywhere, partner."

At the affectionate nickname, the little boy beamed.

Over his head, Summer glanced at Montana's profile. His eyes were fixed on the horizon. But the look in them was far from happy. And, despite the pretense of a smile, his jaw was clenched in a tight, hard line. It was plain that the children's questions had bothered him far more than he cared to admit.

The smooth, gentle rhythm lulled the children until, eyes closed, heads bobbing, Montana carried them into the back of the wagon and settled them among the blankets alongside the baby. When he returned to the seat, he took the reins from Summer's hands. "Tired?"

She shook her head, grateful for the chance to flex her tired muscles. She pressed a hand to the small of her back. "Just a little stiff."

"I spotted a creek up ahead. We could stop there, if you'd like."

"I'd rather keep going. I'll need to get word around town if I want to have anyone show up for a revival tonight. Besides, I'd like to ask around—" she ignored the sudden chill she experienced "—and see if there might be any ranchers in the area who'd be interested in taking in the children."

It was clear that Montana found the subject equally distasteful. A frown furrowed his brow. "I suppose I could ask around the saloon."

For no apparent reason, her temper flared. "Now there's a good place to find hardworking, decent parents for three orphans. Why didn't I think of a saloon?"

His sudden flash of temper matched hers. "I was just trying to be helpful. Don't act so damned righteous, Sister Goodness."

"I will not have you swearing around the children," she said through clenched teeth.

"They're asleep." His voice lowered. "And I'll remind you that you're the one who's in such an all-fired hurry to get rid of them. Not me."

"You're not the one who'll be stuck with feeding them, and keeping them in clothes. Not to mention schooling," she whispered furiously. "Children are a mighty big responsibility. And though I didn't ask for this, I'm willing to shoulder it for the moment. What about you? Anytime you please, you can just ride on out of their lives, without so much as a backward glance."

That barb found its mark. He knew she was right. Still, it hurt. In a softer tone, he said, "Look, I don't intend to just ride away. At least not until you find them a home."

She shot him a look of surprise. "Really?"

"Yeah." He felt a wave of shock at his own admission. Now where had those words come from? It hadn't been his intention to stick around very long. In fact, he'd been thinking of leaving them as soon as they reached Poplar. By then, he figured, Sheriff Otis Pain and his gang would lose the trail.

What the hell was happening to him? He flicked the reins, and the horse and wagon moved out at a faster pace. What had ever possessed him to make such a foolish promise? Now he was stuck. But not for long, he promised himself. Maybe they would get lucky and find a home for the kids tonight.

For some strange reason, that thought thrust him even deeper into gloom.

Poplar wasn't much of a town. A dirt track led past a stable and blacksmith, a saloon, a mercantile, a sheriff's office and jail. At the end of the road was a line of small houses. It had the look of many small towns across Texas. Women bustled in and out of the mercantile. Children and dogs chased each other around wagons or behind buildings. Horses dozed at hitching posts. The surrounding land was dotted with homesteads, ranch houses and barns, and herds of cattle.

The arrival of Summer's wagon caused a considerable stir among the residents. When it rolled to a stop in front of the mercantile, women poked their heads out doors, and children began to gather around in anticipation.

Summer walked into the mercantile to announce to one and all that there would be a revival at the edge of town just after supper. "I promise you a stirring sermon, and a chance to sing some of your favorite old hymns." Seeing the interest on the faces of those around her, she added, "Do you know of any good people in need of children?"

The proprietor of the mercantile arched a brow. "Nobody in these parts looking for more mouths to feed," he stated flatly.

"Thank you. I ... promised I'd ask. I hope you'll pass the word."

As Summer walked from the store, the women set up an eager chatter. This was, after all, a breath of excitement in their otherwise dull routine. A chance to hear a real preacher, and to forget, for a little while, the problems they faced every day in this rugged wilderness. They hurried home to mend their best dresses and iron their husband's Sunday shirts. Soon everyone in the town knew about the arrival of the traveling preacher. And everyone was eager for the entertainment to begin.

When Summer returned to her wagon, she found Pansy standing on the step, speaking to a cluster of children.

"We're having a prayer meeting tonight," she announced in a loud, clear voice. "Be sure to tell your folks."

Summer felt a stirring of strange maternal feelings at the way the little girl faced these strangers. Not every child could do such a thing.

"You going to tell us how you got saved?" a boy shouted.

Pansy gave her most beguiling smile. "I guess you'll just have to come tonight and hear for yourself. After all, everyone needs to be reminded to pray."

"You better pray for some new clothes," a boy taunted.

Summer gasped at the cruel remark.

The other children joined in the laughter.

Pansy's cheeks flamed, and for a moment she looked as though she'd cry. Instead, she lifted her chin and said, "The Bible tells us not to fret over such things. Consider the lilies of the field. Even Solomon in all his glory was not arrayed as one of those. The Lord will provide all that we need."

With that, she grabbed Ned's hand, and, holding tightly to her baby sister, disappeared inside the wagon. The blanket dropped down, effectively shielding them from the world outside.

The crowd of girls and boys continued talking and laughing among themselves before dispersing. Their voices faded away.

But Summer's mind was no longer on tonight's sermon. All she could see was Pansy's face as she'd been taunted. All she could hear was her humble plea for acceptance. Summer's heart nearly broke for the little girl. She glanced at Montana, who was standing off to one side. His hands were clenched into fists, and his face was stiff with fury.

In silence, Montana drove the wagon to a lovely meadow outside of town. A graceful old oak offered shade from the late-afternoon sun. Nearby was a small stream.

"This is the perfect place," Summer declared. "Pansy, gather up all the soiled linen, and we'll wash it in the stream. Montana, I'll need a fire to start supper."

While Montana and Ned went off in search of firewood, she and the little girl carried Hannah and her soiled linen to the stream. The baby played on the banks, under Pansy's watchful eye, and Summer scrubbed the linen squares and hung them over low branches to dry.

"I didn't know one little baby could make so many messes," she muttered.

"You sound just like Mama," Pansy said. The little girl had been quiet ever since the cruel taunts hurled by the children. But, as always, she found solace in the company of her baby sister. "I heard her tell Papa that if babies could go naked for the first year of their life, they'd save everyone a lot of trouble.''

''Your mama was right.'' Summer draped the last linen across a low branch, then turned toward the wagon. ''I'll call you when supper is ready.''

''Yes, ma'am.'' Pansy picked up her little sister and carried her to a grassy knoll, where she soon had her laughing and giggling as she toddled among the wildflowers.

Summer was pleased to note that a fire was already started, and enough wood had been piled beside the wagon to see them through the night.

She glanced at Ned, who was just heading in the direction of his sisters. ''Where's Montana?''

''He said he was going into town,'' Ned called over his shoulder.

Summer felt a wave of disgust. It was as she'd expected. He'd seen to one simple chore. And now he was going to the saloon to see to his own pleasure. She rolled up her sleeves and prepared a batch of biscuit dough. Then, brushing an errant strand of hair from her eyes, she vowed to dismiss the infuriating cowboy from her mind while she tackled more important things.

Summer walked along the banks of the stream until she came to a spot overgrown with brush. Laying out clean clothes, she stripped off her soiled gown and undergarments. Using a cake of homemade soap, she scrubbed first her clothes, then herself. When she was done, she pulled on the prim white blouse and modest dark skirt she'd brought. Running a comb through the dark tangles, she tied her hair back with a simple ribbon, then laid out her wet clothes on branches before making her way back to the wagon.

She was surprised to see Montana's horse tied in its usual place behind the wagon. She was even more surprised when she stepped inside and saw Montana's arms filled with parcels.

"What's this?"

"Things," he said simply.

"Things?"

"For the children. They can't keep walking around in those rags. I'm not going to have the kids in town making fun of them." He poked his head out of the wagon and shouted, "Pansy, Ned! Come in here!"

The children bounded inside and came to a sudden halt at the sight of the colorful clothes spilling out of the parcels.

"This is for you, Pansy." Montana held up a pale blue gown, the color of her eyes, with a high stand-up collar trimmed with lace, and long sleeves cuffed with matching lace. Around the waist was a sash in deeper blue, and there were matching ribbons for her hair. And best of all was a pair of soft calfskin boots.

The little girl's mouth dropped open, and she couldn't seem to find her voice.

"Go ahead and put them on," Montana said, shooing her out of the wagon. He turned to Ned. "I thought it was time you had some long pants, partner. And shoes for your feet."

The little boy gaped at the dark britches and simple white shirt and cowhide boots. "They look—" He swallowed. "They look just like yours, Montana."

"Why, so they do." Montana winked. "Better get dressed. The whole town will be here soon."

Ned and Pansy walked to the creek to wash and dress. Montana turned briskly to Summer, who hadn't yet found her voice. "This is for Hannah." He held up a lacy white gown that looked fit for an angel. "Think you can manage to dress her? Or would you like me to do it?"

"I—I'll manage." She suddenly felt as overwhelmed as Pansy. As she turned away, she fought back tears. "I thought, when I saw you gone—"

He caught her roughly by the shoulder. Surprised, she stiffened. He placed a finger under her chin, tipping her face up. His tone was low, angry. "You thought what? That I'd run out on you?"

She shrugged, embarrassed by the rush of emotions she was experiencing. She didn't know whether to laugh or weep. "Something like that."

"I told you I'd be with you until we found these kids a home." His tone softened, but just barely, and his gaze burned over her. "I may be a thief," he said, bending until his lips hovered just above hers. "And a very good liar when it suits my purpose." He rubbed a thumb over her lips, fighting a sudden flare of heat that left him shaken. Then, giving in to the need, he brushed his mouth over hers. At once he felt the flame, but instead of backing away from it, he dove into it, taking the kiss deeper.

For a moment, the whole world seemed to stop. Her heart forgot to beat. Her mind was wiped clean of thought. Her eyes closed, blotting out all light.

"Just remember. When I give my word," Montana muttered against her lips, "I keep it."

Her first reaction was to push him away. But the instant her hand pressed against his chest, all her good intentions fled. Her fingers curled into the front of his shirt, and a sigh of pure pleasure escaped her lips. She was afraid that at any moment her legs would fail her. She clutched at his shoulder, and his arm encircled her, pressing her firmly to the length of him.

"Why, Sister Goodness," he breathed into her mouth, "if I'd known you'd be this grateful, I'd have spent the whole day in the mercantile."

His tongue tangled with hers, and she found herself lost in the wonders of his kisses. Heat engulfed her, and strange feelings began curling deep inside, leaving her trembling. If he hadn't been holding her so tightly to him, she was certain, she would have fallen.

At the sound of someone entering the wagon, they lifted their heads and took a step back, dragging air into their starving lungs.

The return of Pansy and Ned shattered the moment. Montana straightened, but kept his hand on Summer's shoulder until she seemed steady enough to stand alone. They took another step apart, and then another, feeling dazed and disoriented.

"Look at us!" Pansy cried in excitement. "Oh, I don't think we've ever looked so fine!"

"I don't believe that." Montana watched as Summer turned away and began fumbling awkwardly with the baby's gown. "I'm sure you had new clothes before."

"Never," Pansy said, and Ned nodded his head in agreement. "All my clothes were made over from Mama's. And she made over Papa's torn clothes for Ned." She happily wiggled her toes in the soft boots. "And I never had a pair of shoes before." Her eyes shone as she whispered, "Thank you, Montana. I feel . . . beautiful."

"Me too," Ned said fiercely.

"You're . . . welcome." Montana's voice was gruff as he tousled their hair. "There's more." He held up two slates. "It's time you practiced your sums. And your writing, if you're ever going to be able to read and write Bible verses."

The children's eyes were wide with excitement.

"Are you going to teach us?" Pansy asked.

"I sure am. And so will Summer."

"Come look at your little sister," Summer called as she held the baby aloft.

"Oh, my . . ." was all Pansy could manage when she caught sight of little Hannah, dressed all in white.

"Well." Montana's tone returned to its usual briskness as he surveyed the children. "I think we're ready to face the good people of Poplar. Let's see if anybody scoffs at the way we look now. Come on," he called, sweeping aside the blanket at the doorway. "Let's show them what our family can do."

Summer could hardly believe what she'd heard. But there was no time to analyze Montana's words. Already a crowd was assembling. It was time to do what she did best. And tonight her heart was so light, she could feel love and goodness fairly bursting forth. In fact, she thought, if she wasn't careful, she might even start thinking good things about a certain handsome, charming outlaw.

Chapter Five

"That was a good crowd," Summer said as she finished counting the night's profits.

The children lay asleep beneath their blankets, their clothes neatly hung on hooks along the wall of the little wagon.

"I think we should stay in Poplar for a few more days." She carefully folded half the money and handed the other half to Montana. It wasn't that she was feeling generous. But she wanted to repay him in some way for the kindness he'd shown the children earlier. "These folks are extremely generous. We won't get rich, but maybe if we stay around long enough, we'll be able to set aside a little money."

Montana didn't say a word. He simply shoved the money in his pocket without counting it. He was feeling tense and edgy, for no apparent reason. He should be feeling like a king. After all, the evening had been a smashing success. The children had easily won over the hearts of the crowd. And Summer had preached her finest sermon yet, bringing the cheering crowd to their feet so many times, it would have been easy to believe she'd just dropped from heaven in a cloud lined with gold.

But instead of enjoying the triumph, he was as agitated as a mountain cat caught in a trap. And he didn't know why. All he knew was that he needed to get away for a while. Maybe it was that kiss. Maybe it was the way he'd felt when she was in his arms. Like a warrior. Protective. Like he wanted it to last forever.

He headed for the doorway of the little wagon.

"Where are you going?"

"Out."

"But..."

"Don't worry," he snapped. "I'll be back."

He strode out into the darkness and saddled his horse. Within minutes he was heading toward the lights of town. What he needed was a drink and a relaxing game of poker at the saloon. He wanted to be around men, talking, joking. Cussing without having to apologize. What he didn't want was to spend another night around Summer, watching her. Wanting her. Feeling an itch that was driving him mad.

He walked through the swinging doors and absorbed the familiar sights and sounds. Music from a tinny piano. Men's voices, cursing, laughing.

Two young women, their cheeks heavily rouged, their gaudy gowns cut daringly low, looked up from the bar and started toward him with eager smiles. A cluster of men barely glanced up from their game of poker. One of them, Montana noted, wore a sheriff's badge.

"Aren't you that smooth gambler who took all my money in Amarillo?" a man asked.

Montana froze. His gaze flew to the sheriff, who was staring at him through narrowed eyes. Before he could issue a word of protest, another man called loudly, "Why, that's no gambler. It's Brother Goodness."

Brother Goodness? Montana was taken aback. So were the two saloon women, who stopped in their tracks. And the sheriff, whose hand relaxed once more on top of the table.

"I heard that pretty little wife of yours preach tonight," the man went on. "Damned fine lady—begging your pardon. And those kids of yours are angels, pure and simple."

For a moment, Montana couldn't think of a thing to say.

"I bet you're here to preach on the evils of whiskey, women and gambling," another man said.

Montana's mind worked feverishly. There was no way he could indulge himself now. Not with everyone thinking he was "Brother Goodness." He felt a wave of bitter disappointment. He'd hoped to pass the better part of the night here, where he was safe. Where he wouldn't have to sleep just a few feet away from the most tempting female he'd ever seen.

"Now, I didn't come here to preach," he said with an easy smile. "That's not my way. Fact is, I've even had a sip or two of whiskey myself." Seeing that he had everyone's attention, he went on. "For medicinal purposes, you understand. But I would remind you that the Lord prefers all things in moderation." He bestowed his most charming smile on the two soiled doves, then crossed the room to shake hands with the piano player and the bartender. "I'll say good-night now."

"Just a minute," the sheriff called.

Montana tensed. His hand went to the pistol hidden beneath his jacket.

"You being a traveling preacher and all," the sheriff said, "I'd like you to keep an eye out for a handsome young fellow who's been robbing folks. Sheriff Otis Pain over in Whistling Creek wants him real bad."

Montana relaxed. "Handsome young fellow, huh? Why, I'll be happy to watch out for him."

As he turned toward the door, a voice called, "Hold on."

Montana began to sweat.

The saloon owner crossed the room and handed him a jug. "This is my best whiskey," he said. "I'd be honored if you'd accept it. For medicinal purposes, of course."

Montana was speechless. But only for a moment. He managed to recover quickly. "Why, thank you, brother. I'll accept this in the spirit it was given. And... bless you."

He backed out of the saloon, then pulled himself into the saddle. As soon as he was out of town, he uncorked the jug and took a healthy swig. "Bless you, one and all," he muttered as he lifted it to his lips again.

Summer banked the fire and surveyed her handiwork. She had plied needle and thread to make the children's old clothes suitable for play and chores. That way, they could save their new clothes for prayer services. A batch of biscuit dough had been set aside and covered with a towel to rise. She carried a jug of buttermilk to the creek and knelt to weight the jug down with rocks. After the heat of the day, the water felt soothing against her arms. On a sudden impulse, she returned to the wagon and retrieved her night shift and a cake of soap. Back at the creek, she stripped off her clothes and strode into the water.

A soft sigh escaped her lips as the water lapped against her breasts. She soaped herself, then ducked beneath the waves and came up sputtering. She gave a little laugh of pure pleasure as she floated, weightless, staring up at the stars. Oh, it was heavenly to know that all her chores were done and this special time was all her own. She paddled leisurely to the opposite shore, then turned and swam back. As she climbed the banks, she picked up a linen square and vigorously dried herself. The night air quickly chilled her damp flesh.

As she reached for her night shift, she heard a familiar voice, warm with humor. "Why, Sister Goodness. I do declare, you are truly a vision."

"Montana." She caught sight of him leaning against the trunk of a tree, one foot resting over the other in a lazy pose, his arms crossed over his chest. She held the garment in front of her like a shield. "What are you doing back so soon?"

"So soon? I figured you'd be missing me so much, I'd better hurry back to your side." He uncrossed his arms and stepped closer, forcing her to take several steps backward, until she felt the water lapping at her ankles. "This isn't the warm reception I'd been expecting, ma'am."

Her voice dripped ice. "You will have the decency to turn around until I'm dressed."

"Don't dress on my account." He chuckled. "I like you just the way God made you." He stepped closer, until they were mere inches apart. His gaze moved up and down admiringly. "In fact, I surely do appreciate his work, ma'am. From what I can see, you're just about perfect."

"And you're drunk," she said with a look of disgust.

"No, ma'am. Not yet. But I intend to keep trying till I get there."

Her tone hardened. "It's as I thought. You went to the saloon."

"Yes, ma'am. I did." He reached out a finger to trace the soft white slope of her shoulder.

She flinched, knowing there was nowhere to go. She had backed up as far as she could. The next step would have her floundering in the creek.

"It's a terrible thing," he went on, staring pointedly at the pale column of her throat, "when a man's reputation precedes him."

"Reputation?" She slapped his hand away, but he instantly raised the other hand to brush a damp strand of her hair from her cheek.

He allowed his hand to rest there, loving the feel of her skin against his palm. "Yes, ma'am. It wouldn't do for 'Brother Goodness' to be seen in a den of wickedness."

"Brother Goodness?" She glanced around, hoping to find a way to escape him. But his towering figure blocked any chance of getting by him.

"That's what they called me. 'Brother Goodness.'" He laughed, and the warmth of the sound trickled over her senses like honey. "So I gave them my blessing and left."

"You did?" Without her realizing it, her voice had softened. "I'm glad to hear that you accepted your responsibility."

Responsibility. The word rankled. What he wanted was to forget about responsibility, forget about everything except the press of her body against his.

"If you didn't drink at the saloon, how did you happen to get drunk?"

"A grateful saloon owner gave me a jug of whiskey. For medicinal purposes, of course."

"And you felt in dire need of medicine."

"Uh-huh." His hand closed around the back of her head, and he drew her face close. "Just like I feel the dire need to taste you."

Before she could pull away, he covered her mouth with his in a slow, deliberate kiss that had her head spinning, her bones turning to liquid. A fist seemed to close deep inside her, and strange curling sensations spiraled upward. The gown she'd been holding in front of her fell from her hands and fluttered to the ground. She took no notice as her fingers closed over his wrist.

The kiss seemed to go on and on, draining her, then filling her. His lips were warm and firm and practiced. Her lips trembled beneath the assault. She had no defense against such mastery.

"You taste as good as you look," he whispered against her mouth.

"And you taste like..." She'd almost said *sin*. There was no denying it. What he offered her was the sweetest temptation. Her body strained toward his, hungry for the feel of his rough fingers against her naked flesh. But she knew that if he touched her, she was lost. "You taste like whiskey." She pushed away from him, struggling for breath. Her chest heaved with each gasp of air she dragged into her lungs. Her voice quivered with indignation. "If you hadn't downed half a jug, none of this would have happened."

"If I'd downed the other half, we wouldn't be having this conversation. You'd already be in my bedroll and purring like a kitten."

She picked up the fallen night shift and wrapped herself in it as if it were a mantle of dignity. "You have a very high opinion of your masculine charms."

"If you ever decide to come off that pedestal, Sister Goodness, you can judge for yourself."

She brushed past him and started to stalk away. Then, thinking better of it, she turned and fixed him with an icy stare. Still holding the gown in one hand, she reached out the other and gave him a shove, sending him tumbling backward into the creek.

"This will help you cool off, Brother Goodness."

The night air rang with his curses as she made her way to the wagon.

They stayed in Poplar for two more days, and their revivals were the talk of the town. But, though the money was good and the townspeople were receptive, there was a definite chill in the relationship between Summer and Montana.

Even the children noticed.

"What's wrong with Montana?" Pansy asked as she fashioned a necklace of daisies for Hannah.

"Wrong?" Summer pretended to be busy with dinner, which had become something of a feast, since the women of the town had presented her with a basket of jams and jellies, breads and meats.

"He's grumpy."

Summer shrugged. "Men get that way sometimes. He just needs to be around other men for a while."

"I don't think that's it," the little girl said. "He watches you. Especially when you're preaching."

Summer swallowed. She'd noticed. It was if he were reaching across the crowd, across the darkness, touching her. Sometimes she could actually feel his touch burning her skin. Yet they'd barely spoken a dozen words since the night he'd last kissed her. And every night, as she lay alone beneath the wagon, she'd thought about that kiss. And wondered what would have happened if she hadn't stopped him. And wished...

"Montana looks at you the way Papa used to look at Mama sometimes," the little girl went on innocently. "Mama used to say it was time for her healing touch."

"Healing touch?" Summer paused.

"Uh-huh. I don't know what she meant. But for days after, they'd laugh a lot. And when I'd ask what they were laughing at, they'd just say 'things.'"

A little thrill raced up Summer's spine. "Maybe it's time to move on," she said with a sigh. "A new crowd, a new town, might give us a new outlook."

"I like it here," Pansy said.

"So do I." Summer gave her a gentle smile. "But maybe the next town will be even better."

*   *   *

In the next two weeks, they passed through eight towns. Some were little more than clusters of shabby homesteads. Others were thriving communities, with prosperous ranches and dozens of successful businesses.

It was in the town of Towering Butte that Montana spotted the well-dressed man in the wide-brimmed hat sporting a pair of matching Colt revolvers at each hip. Though the man was surrounded by a throng, his gaze wasn't riveted on Summer, as most of the others' were. Instead, he searched the crowd until he spotted Pansy, Ned and Hannah, standing slightly behind the wagon.

Montana's blood turned to ice. He'd always been able to smell a lawman. He herded the children inside the wagon, then drew the blanket and stepped down. When he looked around, there was no sign of the man.

That evening, at their makeshift camp, Montana sat brooding, his hands wrapped around a steaming cup of coffee. He was a man who always trusted his instincts. And all his instincts were telling him they had to run. It was too bad. He knew they were all enjoying their success in this town. But he'd learned early in life that nothing came easy to him. Nothing except trouble.

Summer stepped from the wagon and watched him for a moment before walking closer. "What's wrong?"

He shrugged. "I'm not sure. But when I figure it out, I'll let you know." He tossed the rest of his coffee on the flames, causing them to sputter. He turned on his heel.

"Now where are you going?"

"To town. Don't worry," he said quickly when she opened her mouth to argue. "I don't intend to get drunk again. I just want to look around."

He saddled his horse, and was soon swallowed up by the darkness.

With a muttered oath, Montana turned his mount away from town. His first stop had been at the sheriff's office. But one look in the window had assured him that the lawman was alone.

He'd stopped next at the only boardinghouse in town, where he was told that no one fitting the description of the stranger had taken a room. Though he was eager to be on his way, the proprietor of the boardinghouse had attended the revival, and had insisted on singing the praises of Sister Goodness. Not wanting to arouse suspicion, Montana had been forced to stand by and listen politely, wasting precious time.

The same thing had happened at the saloon, where he was again disappointed to learn that no one had seen the stranger. But there had been plenty of men who wanted to tell him how much they enjoyed the prayer meeting. When he finally managed to get away, Montana had felt the icy blade of fear scraping along his spine. He'd wasted precious time. And if the stranger wasn't here in town, there was only one place he'd be.

As he pushed his horse to the limit, he cursed himself for his carelessness. And prayed he'd be in time.

Summer looked up at the sound of a horse approaching. When she realized the figure approaching was not Montana, she felt a sudden, shocking jolt of terror. Too late, she remembered that her little derringer was in her bedroll, beneath the wagon. In the past few weeks, with Montana's gun for protection, she'd allowed herself to grow careless.

"Who...are you?" she demanded. Though she was trembling with fear, she struggled to give no outward sign.

"Name's Wade Farmer, ma'am." His eyes were hard as flint, and the pistol in his hand was aimed at her heart.

"What do you want?"

"I think you know. I work for the Pinkerton Agency. Hired by the Ellsworths to get their baby. You're guilty of harboring fugitives. That makes you a criminal." He glanced around the clearing. "Where's your husband?"

Summer's mind raced. "Over by the creek. Cleaning his gun. You'd better go before he spots you. He has a vicious temper."

Though his eyes remained hard, Farmer's lips curved into a chilling smile. "Well, now...I'm real scared." He moved so quickly she had no time to react. Grabbing her by the front of the gown, he dragged her close and grabbed a handful of her hair, yanking her head back until tears sprang to her eyes. "Don't try to be clever, woman. I already scouted your camp. There's no man here. Now, let's get down to business. I came for the kids." His gaze moved beyond her to the little wagon. "Get them out here."

"Please," she pleaded. "They're just babies. You can't take them now, in the night. They'll be so afraid. So...hurt."

"I guess they should have thought about that before they ran away." He shoved her ahead of him, toward the wagon. "Let's go. I have a long ride ahead of me."

Tears stung Summer's eyes as she stumbled toward the wagon. Farmer shoved aside the blanket at the doorway and caught sight of the three children asleep beneath their blankets. "Wake up!" he shouted in thunderous tones.

Pansy and Ned sat up, rubbing their eyes. Little Hannah blinked, then stuffed her thumb in her mouth and rolled over.

"Get dressed," Farmer commanded. "I'm taking you to Hollow Junction."

The children stared in terrified fascination at his pistol, pressed firmly against Summer's temple.

"Don't hurt her!" Pansy cried.

"I'll blow her head off if you don't get moving," the Pinkerton man said through clenched teeth.

The children dutifully began to slip into their clothes, while Farmer watched. When they were done, he commanded, "Now the baby."

Hannah set up a wail when she was awakened from sleep and forced into her clothes.

"Give her to me," he snapped when she was dressed.

"No." With a look of defiance, Pansy held the infant to her shoulder.

"I said—"

"No." Ned, who had been standing beside his sister, caught everyone off guard with his fierce reaction. "You heard Pansy. You're not touching my baby sister." He picked up his slate and threw it at Farmer's head.

"Why, you little . . ." The man ducked. As he did, he was momentarily distracted.

That was all the time Summer needed. Snatching up her Bible, she caught Farmer on the side of the head with a blow that sent him reeling. His pistol slipped from his fingers and clattered on the floor of the wagon. Pansy, balancing the baby on her shoulder, gave the gun a kick that sent it flying out into the darkness.

Before the Pinkerton agent could reach for his other pistol, Ned lunged at his ankle and sank his teeth into the man's flesh. With a cry of pain and rage, Farmer kicked, again and again, trying vainly to dislodge the little boy, who clung to him like a burr.

When he finally managed to toss Ned free, he snarled, "Now you'll all pay for this."

As his hand went to the gun at his waist, he heard Montana's voice, choked with rage. "Go ahead and draw. I'd welcome any excuse to kill you, you bastard."

Summer smothered the fire and moved about the campsite, gathering up their meager belongings. She was aware of Farmer's eyes watching from the tree where he was tied and gagged.

Montana stepped down from the wagon. "They're asleep," he said softly.

"Poor little things must be exhausted," Summer muttered. "Not to mention terrified."

Montana shook his head. "As a matter of fact, they're pretty proud of themselves. And they ought to be. So should you. Ned said he got the inspiration from your story about David and Goliath. It seems you told him that right will always win over might.''

Summer felt tears welling up in her eyes and quickly blinked them away. ''I'll pack up. We can take turns driving through the night.''

He watched as she disappeared inside the wagon. Turning to Farmer, he muttered, ''You'd better be grateful for the lady's powers of persuasion. If it had been up to me, I'd have left your bones for the buzzards. If you're smart, when you work yourself free, you'll head back to Hollow Junction and tell the Ellsworths to find themselves another baby.''

The Pinkerton man mumbled something. Montana stepped closer and removed the gag. ''Was that a promise to leave us alone?''

''It was a promise, all right. To see you hang. There's a certain sheriff, Otis Pain in Whistling Creek, not far behind me, who's going to make sure you dangle from the end of his rope.''

''He has to find me first.'' Roughly Montana stuffed the gag back into Farmer's mouth and checked his bonds, to make certain he wouldn't free himself too soon.

He climbed to the seat of the wagon and offered Summer a hand as she settled herself beside him. At a flick of the reins, the horse started off at a fast clip.

''You were really something back there,'' he muttered.

''It wasn't me. It was the children. They were so brave.'' She felt a welling-up of pride, then suddenly shivered. ''If you don't mind, I'd rather not talk about it. It was too frightening. We came so close to losing them.''

They both fell silent, lost in private thoughts.

''I don't want to lose them.'' She spoke so softly, he wasn't certain at first that he'd heard correctly.

''You mean . . . ever?''

''I mean I want to keep them with me. Always.''

''How could you possibly provide for them?'' he asked.

She shook her head. ''I don't know. I only know that when Farmer tried to take them away, I couldn't bear the pain.'' Her voice trembled with feeling. ''Somehow I'm going to find a way to keep them.''

''All right. I'll help you.''

Though he spoke the words softly, there was an underlying thread of steel that caused a tremor along her spine. ''Thank you, Montana.''

She leaned her head back and studied the path of a falling star. Until now, she'd never had the luxury of allowing someone else to share the burden. Right now, at this very moment, despite all they'd been through, she felt completely at peace.

Her eyes closed. Her breathing became soft and steady. With her head nestled against Montana's shoulder, she slept.

Montana drew her into his arms and held the horse at a smooth, steady gait. It was the sweetest torture to have her snuggled against his chest, while in his mind he was teaching her a hundred different ways to make love.

Chapter Six

They rode for three days, avoiding towns and homesteads. Veering off the usual trails, they traveled until they came to a river. Crossing it, they found themselves in gently rolling hill country. Montana brought the wagon to a halt at the top of a hill. Below lay a graceful little town, and scattered in all directions were large, prosperous-looking ranches.

"What do you think?" He turned to Summer, seated beside him on the wagon seat, holding little Hannah in her arms.

"It looks like a fine place to hold a revival." She glanced at him. "Do you think the Pinkerton agent is behind us?"

"We've been careful," he said, studying the town through narrowed eyes. "We haven't left a trail for him to follow. And we haven't traveled in the direction he'd expect."

"Do you think he'll give up?"

Montana swung his gaze to her. As always, the sight of her took his breath away. And this time, with her dark hair falling in damp tendrils around her cheeks and Hannah snuggled to her heart, she was a classic Madonna.

He couldn't lie to her. "Pinkerton men are like mongrels with a bone. Once they sink in their teeth, they never give up." Seeing the look of fear that came into her eyes, he softened his tone. "But at least we've bought some time. As long as we don't stay more than one night in any town, we should be able to stay ahead of him."

She took a deep breath. "All right, then. Let's find out the name of the town and start announcing tonight's meeting."

"Who's the sweetest baby in the whole world?" Summer asked as she stepped down from the wagon.

Hannah gurgled and cooed and toddled toward her with her arms outstretched. Montana watched in the mirror while wiping the last of the lather from his face. Summer swept up the infant and pressed a kiss to her cheek, then swung her around and around until she was giggling. Seeing the way the children beamed with pleasure, she paused to press a kiss to each of their cheeks.

It occurred to Montana that Summer had become as easy and comfortable with the children as though they'd been born to her.

"Did you do your sums?" she asked.

"Yes, ma'am," Pansy said proudly. "Montana checked them, and I got mine all right. Ned only got two wrong."

"Two?" Summer tousled the little boy's hair. "I'm real proud of you, Ned. Tomorrow, we'll work on the two you got wrong."

"Montana already showed me my mistake. Tomorrow," the boy said with his little chest puffed out, "I'll get them all right."

Montana studied their little assembly. The children were dressed in their finest, their hair shiny, their eyes dancing with unconcealed excitement. Summer, in her simple white blouse and dark skirt, looked every inch the prim and proper preacher. He felt a rare swelling of pride. In his childhood, this was all he'd ever dreamed of. The perfect family. A good woman. Fine healthy children. And himself...

He could picture himself as he traded a life of crime for a way of life above reproach, assuming responsibility for their welfare. He realized wistfully that it was about as foolish as wishing on a star.

He blinked, and realized that Summer had spoken to him.

"...folks from town are on their way. There's the first wagon. You will...keep an eye out?" she said meaningfully.

"You can count on it."

He took one last look at his little brood, then swung away.

Summer tucked the children in and stood studying them for long, silent moments. They had fallen asleep as soon as the last wagon load of townspeople had rolled away.

It had been a memorable night. Her sermon had been greeted with tears, cheers and rousing applause. Pansy, caught up in the fervor, had leaped to her feet to add a few impromptu words of her own, which had left the people begging for more. Ned had led the singing with a voice like an angel, and had earned a penny from a rancher for his efforts. And little Hannah, with her smiles, had won the hearts of the entire crowd. But it was Montana who had been the biggest surprise. He had stood proudly beside Summer while she bade good-night to the ranchers and their wives, shaking hands, learning all their names. One of the men had thrust a handful of bills into Montana's hand, but he had steadfastly refused to accept it, insisting that the man had already given enough.

"The Lord has been very good to us," Montana had said simply. "Our hearts are filled to overflowing."

That was exactly how she felt. At this moment, looking at the faces of these sleeping angels, she felt her heart brimming with love. No one was going to separate them, she vowed. Not even the law.

She slipped into her night shift and stepped down from the wagon. Outside, Montana was standing by the fire, his head tilted toward the sky, a steaming cup of coffee in his hand. For a moment, her heart stopped at the sight of his handsome, rugged profile. She thought about sharing a cup of coffee with him, then thought better about it. Always, at this time of night, the tension simmering between them seemed to reach the boiling point. It would be best if she kept her distance. She turned away and busied herself with her bedroll.

In the distance, thunder rumbled, and she shot a glance toward the sky. Storm clouds scudded, obscuring the moon. The night was plunged into darkness. She shivered and picked up her blanket.

"Think there's room under the wagon for two?"

At the sound of his voice directly behind her, she whirled. "I . . ." She felt her throat go dry. "I'm sure we can manage."

She moved her bedroll over to make room for his. When she got to her feet, he was there beside her. Surely it was her imagination. But somehow, in the darkness, he seemed taller. His shoulders broader. His smile more mysterious. Everything about him seemed more. More dangerous, more menacing. More tempting. Suddenly she couldn't imagine crawling into her bedroll beside him.

"Excuse me." She stepped back. "I'm going to . . . wash up down by the creek."

"Storm's going to break any minute now."

She backed away. "I won't be long."

Lightning streaked across the sky as she lifted the hem of her night shift and began to run. Sweet heaven, what was she going to do? She couldn't go back there. And she couldn't stay out here in the storm. She reached the creek and paused, watching the first gentle raindrops pebble the smooth surface.

"Summer."

She spun around at the sound of Montana's familiar deep voice. Her hand went to her throat.

"How much longer do you intend to deny it?"

Her heart slammed against her chest. "Deny what?"

"What we both want."

"I don't . . ." She shook her head. "I don't want this."

"And me?" He took a step closer. "You don't want me?"

"Oh!" The cry broke from her lips. "Why must you make things so complicated?"

He stepped closer and reached out his hands to her. Seeing her flinch, he moved more slowly, placing one finger beneath her chin and lifting her face for his inspection. "It isn't complicated, Summer. It's simple. I want you."

"Want." Her tone was flat. "That's all that matters to you, isn't it? Whatever you want, you take."

"That's right." He knew that had been true for most of his life. But now, everything was different. Now he wanted more. So much more. He wanted to cherish her. He wanted to take care of her and the children. But how could he tell her? How could he explain? If he tried to put all those feelings into words, they would be flat, meaningless.

And so he merely framed her face with his hands. His gaze burned over her with a fierceness that caused her breath to back up in her throat. "Now I'll make it even simpler. You want me every bit as much as I want you. And if you deny it, you're lying."

Roughly he tangled his fingers through her hair. Slowly, deliberately, he drew her head back, all the while staring deep into her eyes. He brushed her lips with his. At once a spark sizzled between them that rivaled the lightning flashing overhead.

"Your kisses don't lie, Summer," he murmured against her mouth. He drew her a little away from him and stared at the way her breasts seemed to swell at his mere glance. "And your body doesn't lie."

"Oh, Montana. Sweet heaven..." The words seemed torn from her. "Hold me."

For the space of a heartbeat, he paused, as though unable to believe what she'd said. Then he dragged her close and covered her mouth with hot, hungry kisses that left them both shaken.

"I've tried so hard to deny this," she whispered. "But I can't. God help me, I can't."

He kissed her again, more slowly. Suddenly it seemed desperately important that he take great care to show her, with every touch, every kiss, just how he treasured her. He pressed soft nibbling kisses to her eyelids, her cheek, her jaw.

She sighed and moved in his arms, her gaze steady on his, her breathing soft and shallow.

He nuzzled her earlobe, nipping gently before darting his tongue inside to tease and thrust.

Her sighs grew softer, her pleasure more prolonged.

He pressed his lips to the soft, sensitive hollow of her throat, roughly pushing aside the neckline of her gown. As she arched herself to give him easier access, he moved his mouth lower, until he found her breast through the fabric of her gown. She gasped at his boldness. But she didn't want him to stop.

His fingers were strong and sure as they reached for the buttons of her night shift. He slipped it from her shoulders and watched as it slid down her body and pooled at her feet.

"Summer." He whispered her name as if it were a prayer. "You're so beautiful. So perfect." He ran wet, openmouthed kisses down the column of her throat, across her shoulder. Hearing her little moan of pleasure, he brought his mouth lower, to her breast.

Another moan escaped her lips. Her body was a mass of nerve endings. She'd never known such feelings. With a gasp, she clutched at his waist, afraid that at any moment her legs would fail her.

Her fingers were shaking as they reached for the buttons of his shirt. As she slipped it from his shoulders, she encountered a maze of raised scars that crisscrossed his back and chest.

"What—what are these?" she asked in surprise.

"Nothing. Old wounds."

"Oh, Montana..." She ran her fingertips gently along his back. Then, without warning, she pressed her lips to his chest and felt his sudden intake of breath.

His mouth covered hers with kisses that were no longer tender. She returned his kisses with a fervor that matched his own until, trembling, she brought her hands to the fasteners of his pants. When she fumbled, he helped her. As his clothes joined hers in the grass, they dropped to their knees and faced each other.

"Do you know all the things I've dreamed of showing you?" he murmured against her temple.

She shook her head and pressed her lips to his throat, surprised by his sudden intake of breath.

Words failed him. He was overcome with feeling. All he could do was show her. With lips and tongue and fingertips, he moved over her, thinking of all the mysterious, intimate ways to show her, to please her. He laid her down in the grass and moved over her, damp flesh to damp flesh, nibbling, suckling, until she clutched at him and called out his name.

Her breathing grew more shallow. Her body was alive with need. Need she'd never even dreamed of. Never known she possessed.

Montana stared at the woman in his arms. Desire, dark and mysterious, glittered in her eyes. Eyes that seemed to pull him in until he was drowning in them.

She had lost her fear. In its place, he could sense her trust. Trust that he would never take her where she didn't want to go. Trust to lead her on a wondrous new journey to pleasure beyond anything she'd imagined. This wasn't surrender, he knew, but something far better. It was deeply erotic, to know that this woman who valued her independence would honor him with such trust.

Her hair tumbled wildly around her face. She tasted as clean, as fresh, as a mountain stream. She smelled of soap and water and green fields.

For all his life, he knew, he would remember this night of gentle rain and fierce passion. This night when he had first encountered a desire so compelling there was no cure for it. This night when all he could see, all he could taste, all he could feel, was Summer.

"Touch me, Summer," he whispered.

It was the only invitation she needed. Hesitantly she leaned over him, brushing her lips across his shoulder, down his chest. He moaned softly, and she felt a strange new sense of power. Growing bolder, she trailed her lips lower, across the flat planes of his stomach, and felt his muscles contract. But when she moved her mouth lower still, he gave a growl of pleasure before dragging her mouth back to his.

He tasted as dark and mysterious as the passion that held him enthralled. His kiss spoke of hunger, of loneliness, of desperate desire. And all the while, his hands moved over her, exploring, arousing, until she could no longer think, could only feel.

He had wanted to go slowly, to make this first time as pleasurable as possible. But now that she was fully aroused, he could no longer hold his own passion at bay. It clawed at him, desperate for release. He moved his lips down her body and felt the shudders that rocked her as she reached the first peak. He watched as her hands clutched at the ground beneath her and her eyes widened with surprise, then glazed with passion. Giving her no time to recover, he closed his mouth over hers and took her with a fierceness that had her gasping.

She wrapped herself around him and began moving with a strength that surprised him. The rhythm of their movements increased until, dazed and breathless, they began a climb that took them higher and higher until they soared among the stars. And then exploded into millions of tiny, glittering fragments.

They lay, still joined, their breathing ragged, their bodies slick with sheen.

He levered himself above her and pressed his forehead to hers. "Am I too heavy for you?"

She shook her head, too stunned by all she'd experienced to bring herself to speak.

He misunderstood her silence, and felt a sudden slice of fear. He rolled aside and drew her gently into the circle of his arms. "Have I hurt you? Dear God, Summer, have I—?"

"Shh..." She touched a finger to his lips. "It's just... I never dreamed it could be like this."

He felt his heart begin to beat again. He hadn't hurt her. She hadn't turned away from him because of the depth of his passion. "It can always be like this. When a man and a woman love each other."

At his words, she stared at him, thunderstruck.

He realized what he'd just revealed. Taking a deep breath, he said softly, "You wanted it simple. It doesn't get any simpler than this." Or any more complicated, he realized. "I love you, Summer. You're the best thing that's ever happened to me. I want to take care of you. And spend the rest of my life with you."

She couldn't speak. She felt as if all the air had been squeezed from her lungs.

He touched a finger to the corner of her eye. "Are those tears?"

She found her voice. "Of course not. It's raining."

"Is it?" He looked up, blinking against the raindrops.

Suddenly she was laughing. Her heart had never felt so light. Or so free. "What a couple of fools! Don't you realize we could be snug and dry under the wagon?"

She started to get up, but he dragged her back down and kissed her, slowly, thoroughly, until she was gasping.

"We have all night to be snug and dry," he murmured against her lips. "And I promise you this fool will dry you and hold you and keep you warm. But right now, I just have to kiss you again."

She sighed contentedly and wondered how she had lived so long without this. She brought her lips to his. And knew she'd found heaven.

* * *

"That was a fine sermon you gave last night."

They lay beneath the wagon, wrapped in blankets, locked in each other's arms. Rain still spattered on the grass around them, but the worst of the storm had blown over. They knew that sleep was impossible. Neither of them was willing to waste a precious moment of this magical night. There was so much each wanted to know about the other. So much they both needed to learn.

Montana pressed his lips to a tangle of hair at Summer's temple. She sighed at the deep rumble of his voice, and the pleasure of his kiss.

"That part about the Lord being a loving, forgiving father..." He shook his head. "I suppose I heard it before. But it never meant anything to me. Maybe, because I never had a father, I couldn't imagine that kind of love. But now, with the children..."

She moved a little away, so that she could look into his eyes. "You never had a father?"

He shook his head. "Or a mother. I grew up in an orphanage. I was just about Ned's age when my folks were killed, heading west. I don't remember much about them."

An orphanage. Now, suddenly, it all made sense. His dark, simmering anger when the children had told their story. His explosive fury at the Pinkerton agent.

"Didn't anyone offer to adopt you?" Summer asked softly.

"The babies were often adopted first. Or the older ones, who could help out on farms. But no one ever wanted me. There wasn't much call for a boy of six.

And by the time I was old enough to be useful on a farm, I'd become too defiant.''

His words caused such terrible pain around her heart, she had to hold back the tears that threatened. "But if that's the case, how did you learn to be so natural with Hannah? A man doesn't learn that by robbing stages.''

"There were lots of infants in the orphanage,'' he said. "I used to help out. Hell, if I didn't change their drawers, most of them would have had to go around wet all day. You see, nobody really cared about them. I guess I just always had a tender heart where babies were concerned.''

She realized that was another reason why she loved him. Love. It enveloped her like a warm cocoon. She loved this man. Loved him with a fierceness that surprised her. "When did you leave?''

"When I was twelve. I vowed that day that I'd taken my last beating.''

"Beating?'' Her heart stopped, and she thought of the scars that covered his back.

"I guess I just always had an obstinate streak in me. The more I was told I couldn't do something, the more determined I was to do it. You can imagine it caused me a lot of problems in my life. But when I got big enough, I just ran away from the orphanage. And Matt McCoy became just plain Montana. And I've been running ever since.''

"Oh, Montana.'' She wrapped her arms around his waist and pressed her lips to his throat. Despite her best efforts, her eyes filled, and spilled over to dampen his chest.

"Hey. Tears again? That's more than I've seen you shed in all the time I've known you."

She sniffed, and struggled to control herself. "It's just that I can't stand to think about you growing up without anyone to love you."

"I have you, don't I?" he asked easily.

"Yes." She said it fiercely. She understood so much now. Why this outlaw had felt so protective toward three little orphans. Why he used his charm to mask a hidden pain. It made her love him all the more.

He wiped away her tears with his thumbs and smiled down into her face. "I can see that we're going to have to stop talking. Let's see if this will make you smile."

He gave her a slow, lingering kiss that slowly built in intensity until she tangled her fingers in his hair and sighed with pleasure. "Oh, cowboy, you do know how to make a girl forget about crying."

"Not good enough," he murmured, as he began to move his mouth lower. "I don't intend to stop until you've forgotten everything."

He succeeded. Beyond his wildest imagination.

"You still haven't told me." Montana lay with his head pillowed on his saddle.

"Told you what?" Summer curled against his chest. She thought about his boast. If she were a kitten, she'd be purring.

"One single thing about your childhood." He felt her stiffen suddenly.

"There's nothing to tell." She started to push away, until his arms came around her, holding her still. But, though she remained beside him, he could feel her withdrawing.

He caught her by the shoulders and forced her to face him. "As a gambler, I pride myself on being able to read the people around the table. I thought I was reading you. But I was all wrong about you, wasn't I?"

She swallowed. "Why? What did you think about me?"

"Since you'd said you didn't have fields to plow, or crops to harvest, I figured you came from a big, expensive home, with fine, educated people who read the Bible after supper."

She held her silence.

"It wasn't anything like that, was it?" he asked gently.

She shook her head.

"Can you talk about it?"

"I suppose you have a right to know." She sat up, unmindful of her nakedness. Her gaze was fixed on the raindrops spattering into the grass beside them. "I wasn't supposed to be born. My mother..." She shrugged. "Who knows why she allowed it to happen? Maybe she wanted someone to love. Someone who would love her back. Our home was one of the cribs on the back streets of St. Louis."

Montana kept his shock to himself. Everyone knew that the little shacks called cribs were home to the women of the night.

Summer shivered. Montana sat up and draped the blanket around her shoulders, then drew her into the circle of his arms. She clung to him, absorbing his quiet strength.

"Every night, as far back as I can remember, I had to leave home before dark, and stay out all night, until the men were through with...their business. I hated the night, and what it brought."

"What did you do all night?" he asked.

She shrugged. "Huddled in doorways. Counted the stars. Peered in windows and watched families. At dawn I was allowed to return, and my mother and I would sleep. I lived like that until I was ten."

"What happened when you were ten?" he asked gently.

"My grandmother found me. She didn't even know about me. She'd been searching for my mother ever since she ran away from home. My mother refused to go home with her. She was probably too ashamed. But I was taken to my grandmother's home in Kansas. It was the first real bed I slept in. And I was introduced to religion. Gram had a deep and abiding faith. It's what sustained her after her only daughter ran away to a life of—" Summer swallowed. "Religion offered me solace. Gram believed that our Creator wasn't an avenging God, but a gentle, forgiving one. She made wonderful plans for my future. I thought my life was perfect. But..."

Montana waited, knowing how painful this was for her.

"My grandmother died."

"How old were you?" Montana asked.

"Thirteen. Gram's estate went to her son, who never forgave me for the sins of my mother." Her voice lowered. "I'm sure he thought of himself as a fine, upstanding man who was simply sparing his wife and children the shame of being associated with someone like me.''

Montana knew such men. The rector at the orphanage, who had retaliated for the slightest infraction of the rules—with a whip. A lawman in the Arizona Territory who had imprisoned a starving young boy for stealing a loaf of bread. A spoiled young wife who had flirted shamelessly with the new ranch hand, and had him fired from his first honest job when he refused to return her advances. A sheriff named Pain, who directed a gang of outlaws who terrorized helpless ranchers.

''What did you do then?'' he asked.

She smiled. ''Gram taught me that everyone can make choices. So I decided to make my own way in the world. And instead of choosing my mother's way, I chose my grandmother's. I figured the Lord wouldn't mind if I made a living while I preached his word.'' Her lips trembled. ''And now you see why I didn't want to tell you. I didn't want anyone to know about my past.''

Montana wondered if she had any idea how truly unique she was. After such a childhood, it was no wonder she hadn't wanted to allow a man into her heart or her life. What a truly precious gift she had just given him. If it was possible, at this moment he loved her more than ever.

He turned her into his arms and brushed his lips lightly over hers. ''I love you, Summer Chambers. What happened before doesn't matter. And I give you my word. You'll never be alone again. Especially in the night.''

He felt the tremors as she struggled with tears of happiness. He deepened the kiss until, with a sigh, she wrapped her arms around his neck and kissed him back. Together they healed each other's wounds. And wiped away all the pain of their past.

Chapter Seven

"It's about time you woke up, sleepyheads." Montana looked up from the fire as Pansy and Ned emerged from the wagon. Pansy set little Hannah down, and the laughing infant toddled over to Montana and held out her arms. He scooped her up and swung her around before cuddling her close to his chest.

"Where's Summer?" Ned asked.

"She's down at the stream, taking a bath. Come on, partner, you can help me fix breakfast."

"Aw, that's girl stuff." Ned said. "I'd rather gather wood."

"Girl stuff?" Montana uncovered a pan of simmering beef and gravy. "Who do you think made this?"

"You?" Ned's eyes grew wide. He was seeing something new in his hero. "You think you could teach me?"

"I might. But first, the three of you should try some of my biscuits." He handed them cups of milk, and biscuits warm from the fire, smothered in wild strawberry preserves.

"Did you really make these?" Pansy asked as she held the cup of milk to Hannah's lips.

"Cross my heart." He glanced up as Summer approached. Her dark hair still glistened with drops of water. And though she wore a prim pink gown, buttoned to her neck, he could still see, in his mind's eye, the way she'd looked all night in his arms.

"Sit right down," he called. "Breakfast is ready."

"You cook?" She glanced at the blanket spread on the grass, and the assortment of eggs and meats and biscuits, along with a jar of preserves. "Why, Montana, this is a feast."

"That's what I'd planned," he said, brushing a kiss to her cheek. "Just another of my many talents, ma'am."

The children giggled, and she blushed clear to her toes.

He filled their plates, then settled himself cross-legged beside Summer. Without being prodded, he reached out his hands, and the others did the same. "Bless this food," he intoned, "and the family you see before you."

"Amen," the others murmured.

As they began to eat, Montana said with studied nonchalance, "I've got a surprise for everyone."

"A surprise!" Ned clapped his hands. "What is it?"

"Now, if I told you, it wouldn't be a surprise." Montana picked up his fork and calmly tasted his food.

While he ate, the children squirmed. Even Summer, usually so calm and placid, was fairly bursting to hear his plans.

He glanced around and saw that they were all staring at him. He lifted his cup and drained it. He set it down, then chuckled. "All right. I see you can't wait. I'll tell you. We're going into town today."

"What for?" Summer's mouth dropped open.

"Just for fun. We'll shop in the mercantile. And we'll even eat supper at the boardinghouse before we come back here tonight."

"Supper in a boardinghouse?" Pansy and Ned clapped their hands and danced around in excitement. Little Hannah, too young to understand, mimicked their actions, dancing around and around until they were all laughing at her antics.

"Do you think it's safe?" Summer reached a hand to Montana's sleeve.

He patted her hand. "One day won't hurt. By tonight we'll be on our way again. And miles ahead of our Pinkerton agent."

She squeezed his arm and glanced at the happy faces of the children. "Thank you."

He'd have given his life just to see that look in her eyes every day. And to hear her voice, all soft and whispery, thanking him for something so simple. He knew in that minute that he was the luckiest man alive.

"Now everybody eat," he called gruffly. "I slaved over that hot fire, and I expect to see this food gone when I get back from the creek."

As he sauntered away, Pansy smiled at Summer. "I see you found Mama's healing touch."

Summer's cheeks colored as she bent to her breakfast. "I guess I did."

* * *

The little wagon rolled across a meadow bright with wildflowers. Overhead, the sky was a clear, cloudless blue. To pass the time, Summer led the children in a rousing chorus of familiar hymns.

When they ran out of songs, Montana said casually, "Did I tell you about the Gypsy who could read palms?"

Summer and the children turned to stare at him.

A devilish smile touched his lips as he added, "She called herself Amazing Grace."

Ned and Pansy giggled. Summer tried not to laugh. "You're being disrespectful," she muttered. But it was impossible to keep a straight face. Soon she and the children were howling at Montana's string of jokes, each one sillier than the last.

When they reached town, they parked their wagon at the stables, where Montana instructed the blacksmith to check the horses. "We've traveled a good distance," he said, handing the smith a coin. "And we intend to continue the journey. So I'd be obliged if you'd see that they're properly shod."

The little group leaned on the fence and watched for a while as the blacksmith scraped and filed and worked the bellows, creating a hot flame in which to soften the steel and mold it into the shape of the horses' hooves.

Then they made their way up the main street. Pansy and Ned skipped ahead, while Hannah, proud of her newly acquired skill, insisted on toddling between Montana and Summer. With her chubby little hands firmly in theirs, she stumbled only once or twice. When she grew tired of walking, they lifted her by the hands, swinging her between them, which caused her to shriek with delight.

Their first stop was the mercantile, where Montana purchased staples. Sacks of flour and sugar, along with tins of coffee and tobacco, were piled near the door, to be picked up later in the wagon.

Between two aisles stacked high with goods, Montana found Summer and Pansy looking through the bolts of brightly colored fabrics, and admiring a bonnet of wispy pink lace. Summer insisted that Pansy try it on, but it was too big for the little girl's head. It plopped down, covering her eyes.

Pansy thrust it into Summer's hands. "You try it."

"Oh, no. It's too fancy," Summer protested.

"Go on," Montana said, coming up behind her. "I want to see it on you."

Summer pulled it over her dark curls, and they all laughed and agreed it was much too fancy for a preacher.

They paused to examine a shelf of books, and Summer lingered over an ornate Bible with a hand-tooled leather cover and pen-and-ink illustrations. When she saw the price, she quickly set it aside.

They found Ned by the counter, staring at a container of colorful candy sticks.

"How much?" Montana asked.

"Three for a penny," the owner said.

Montana pressed a coin into his hand, and the owner allowed the children to make their choice. For Pansy, it was simple. She chose a pink-and-white-striped candy cane. Ned, studying so many colors, took long minutes before choosing a green-and-white one. Hannah chose a red-and-white peppermint cane and sucked happily, drooling all over the bib Summer quickly tucked around her good dress.

They walked outdoors, enjoying the sights and sounds of the town. Men and women nodded and smiled at them as they passed. Children squealed and chased each other in a game of hide-and-seek. Soon Pansy and Ned had joined in, and Summer and Montana stood to one side, watching and laughing.

They walked along the wooden walkway, peering in shops. In one, a lady was measuring a man's sleeve, while his wife stood nearby, holding up his new jacket. They paused in the doorway of another shop and watched as a rancher was given a haircut.

"Want to go in, Ned?" Montana called.

"No, sir. I'd rather have Summer cut my hair," the little boy said with a shudder. He watched a moment longer, as the barber wielded his scissors dangerously close to the man's ear and strands of long hair drifted to the floor of the shop. "But you go ahead, if you'd like."

"I'd rather have Summer cut my hair, too," Montana said softly.

He turned to her. Hannah had fallen asleep on her shoulder, her pudgy arms wrapped lovingly around Summer's neck. "Want me to take her?"

She shook her head. "She isn't heavy. Besides, she feels good here in my arms."

With his hand gently beneath her elbow, he led her along the street until they came to the boardinghouse.

At Montana's knock, a smiling, apron-clad woman opened the door. "I'm Charity Danville. What can I do for you folks?"

"Are we too early for supper?" Montana asked.

"You're just in time. Please come in."

The woman led them past a formal parlor to a large, comfortably appointed dining room, with a table that ran the length of the room and enough chairs to seat at least a dozen people. The table was covered with lace, and silver and crystal gleamed in the light of dozens of candles set about the room. The wonderful fragrance that wafted in from the kitchen had their mouths watering.

Several men stood around talking and laughing, and they looked up at the arrival of the strangers.

"These are my regulars," Charity said, introducing several shopkeepers, as well as the mayor and Sheriff William Sharp, who she said had recently lost his wife.

Montana and Summer introduced themselves and the children.

"These are the folks I was talking about," the sheriff said. He turned to Summer. "I was just telling my friends that I attended your revival last night, Sister Goodness. I was moved to tears by your sermon."

"Why, thank you, Sheriff Sharp," she murmured. "I hope I strengthened your faith."

"That you did."

"And I hope," she said, taking the seat that Montana held for her, "you'll continue to trust in the Lord."

"I'll try. I only wish I had your faith," he said as he sat across from her.

There had been a time, Summer realized, when such words were nothing more than a game to her. Now, she meant them. It still shocked her to realize how much she had changed. And yet, oddly, it pleased her.

Charity Danville provided a small wooden high chair for Hannah, which she positioned between Summer and Montana. Then, when the others were seated, she and her young daughter began to carry in tray after tray of food. As they took their seats, Charity said, "Perhaps you will honor us with a prayer, Sister Goodness."

Summer and Montana held hands, and the others followed suit. "We thank thee for this food," Summer murmured. "And these fine people who have offered us the food of friendship."

"Amen," the others said.

With a light heart, they began to eat. There was succulent roast beef and mashed potatoes, gravy and biscuits, and greens from the garden. And for dessert Charity offered freshly baked apple pies, still warm from the oven.

Seeing Ned's plate empty, the woman said, "There's another piece of pie, son. Would you like it?"

"No, ma'am," he said, touching a hand to his stomach. "I think if I ate another thing, my stomach might come apart at the seams."

Everyone laughed.

"Then how about you?" she asked Montana.

He lifted his plate. "I guess I can force myself."

She moved around the table, topping off cups with fresh coffee.

"That was a fine meal," Montana said with a sigh.

"Thank you." As she and her daughter began to clear away the dishes, she said, "I hope you good folks will come again."

"Thank you, ma'am." Montana lifted Hannah from her chair and trailed Summer and the other children to the door. There he paid the woman for their meal, and they took their leave.

As they walked through the town toward their wagon, they could see, in the glow of candlelight, families gathered around supper tables. For the first time in their lives, Summer and Montana felt they shared a common bond with such people. They, too, were part of a family. A family united not by blood but by something far greater—love.

Montana glanced at Summer, seated beside him. "You're awfully quiet."

The three children, worn out from all the excitement, were asleep in the wagon.

"I was just thinking how wonderful this day has been. Wasn't it nice to see the children playing hide-and-seek?"

He nodded.

"The other children didn't seem to mind that Pansy and Ned were strangers. They just accepted them without question"

"The folks at the boardinghouse didn't seem to mind that we were strangers, either," he reminded her.

She turned to him. "Why, you're right." A smile came into her eyes and warmed her words. "Could it be that we're becoming respectable?"

"Would you like that?"

She nodded. "Very much. For the sake of the children, of course. I owe them that much, if I'm going to try and make a home for them." Her voice lowered with emotion. "If it takes me forever, I'm determined to live down my past."

"It wasn't your past," he said firmly. "It was your mother's. Trust me, Summer. You don't have anything to prove to anybody. You're good and fine and decent."

Moved by his words, she linked her arm through his, and pressed her cheek to his shoulder. "Careful, cowboy. You're beginning to sound like a man in love."

He pulled back on the reins, bringing the horse and wagon to a halt. Then he drew her close and tipped up her face for a slow, lingering kiss. "I do love you, preacher. And don't you forget it."

She touched a hand to his cheek, marveling at the wild rush of joy she felt at his words. "And I love you, Montana. With all my heart."

He flicked the reins, and the horse and wagon rolled toward their campsite. "I wish we could stay the night," he muttered. "I surely would enjoy showing you some more of my many talents."

"Hush. The Lord loves a humble man," she said with a laugh. She climbed down from the wagon when it came to a halt. "I'll just fetch the clothes I washed this morning, and you can make certain we haven't left anything else behind."

Before they had taken two steps, they heard the sound of Pansy's frantic call, and the words that had struck fear into the hearts of parents from the beginning of time.

"Come quick! Hannah's burning with fever!"

Summer studied the whimpering infant in her arms. For the past two hours, she had bathed her with cool water from the creek, but the fever had only grown worse. This little cherub, who was always so full of smiles, was now struggling for every breath.

"Has this ever happened before?" she asked Pansy.

The little girl nodded. "Yes, ma'am. We almost lost her once before."

Summer's heart missed a beat. "How did you save her?"

Pansy shrugged. Her eyes were wide with fear. "I don't know. Mama and Papa took her into town, and the doctor fixed her just fine."

"Doctor." Summer looked up at Montana, who had been pacing helplessly. "Did you notice if there was a doctor back in town?"

He shook his head. "I didn't pay any attention. But there has to be one." He took her arm and helped her up to the seat. The children scampered up beside her. Within minutes the horse and wagon were rolling through the darkness, toward the lights of town.

At this time of night, there was little sign of life in the town. Ranchers and shopkeepers were up by dawn, and they retired by dark. But after several knocks on the door of the boardinghouse, a lantern was lit and Charity Danville, wearing a modest wrap, threw open the door.

She glanced at Montana, then beyond him, to the figures on the wagon seat.

"I'm sorry to wake you, ma'am," he explained. "Is there a doctor in the town?"

"A doctor." The woman struggled to clear the cobwebs of sleep from her mind. "I'm sorry. The only doctor in town is old Dr. Cooper Ethridge, and he's—"

"Where can I find him?" Montana demanded.

"Why he's at the end of the street, in that big old house. But he's—"

Montana had already swung away and was climbing up to the wagon seat. He flicked the reins, and the wagon rolled away before Charity Danville had a chance to finish her sentence.

She lifted her lantern and watched as the wagon disappeared along the street. With a shrug, she closed the door.

The big old house lay before them, shrouded in darkness. Montana helped Summer and the children from the wagon, then hurried ahead to pound on the door. He waited, but heard no answering response from within. He brought his fist against the door so hard it rattled the windows. And still there was no response.

"Maybe the doctor is out somewhere," Summer said nervously.

"Then we'll just break in and wait until he returns." Montana's jaw was set, and his eyes were as hard as granite.

"We can't break into the doctor's house."

"The hell we can't," he said, twisting the knob.

At that moment, the door opened, and he nearly fell inside. Startled, he looked up to see a stooped, elderly man in a flowing nightshirt, holding a flickering candle. A mane of white hair and a neatly trimmed white beard were in shocking contrast to piercing blackbird eyes. Eyes that took in each member of the little group clustered on his porch.

"Thought I heard a knock," he said, in a strange, whispery voice.

"You thought?" Montana didn't bother to mask his impatience. "I nearly broke my hand on your door."

"My wife, God rest her soul, used to call it the sleep of the innocent," the old man whispered. "A storm could blow the house away, and I'd sleep through it. How can I be of help to you?"

"It's our baby," Montana said, indicating the still, pale figure in Summer's arms.

"Ah." The old man was clearly moved. He stood aside and indicated that they should enter.

Frightened, the children clutched at Summer's skirts as the old man hobbled slowly around the room, holding his candle to the wick of several lanterns until the gloom had been chased away.

The sofas and chairs in the parlor were draped with ghostly white dustcovers. The house had a musty, unused odor that reminded Summer of a tomb. A chill raced along her spine as the old man searched for his spectacles, then opened a Bible and turned to them.

"What are you doing?" Montana demanded.

"Why, preparing to say some prayers for your dead child," he said matter-of-factly.

Seeing the spark of fury in Montana's eyes, Summer quickly stepped forward. "Hannah isn't dead, Dr. Ethridge."

"Oh, my dear, forgive me," the old man said. "But then, why did you come to see me?"

Summer struggled to keep the panic from her voice. "We came here because we thought you could save her life."

"Ah. I see." The old man stepped closer and placed his hand on the baby's fevered brow. "I wish I could help you. But, you see, I am not a doctor of medicine.''

''But what—?'' Montana began, but the old man stopped him with a wave of his hand.

''I am a doctor of divinity. A minister of the Lord. And the only help I can give your child is my prayers.''

Chapter Eight

Seeing the fear in Summer's eyes, Montana draped his arm around her shoulder protectively. "Is there another doctor in town?"

"I'm afraid not," the old man said in his whispery voice. "Though it has been our fondest wish for many years."

"Oh, Montana. What will we do?" Summer cried. Her words betrayed her anguish.

Pansy tugged on her skirt. "We can pray. Remember what you said in your sermon last night? The Lord hears even the lowliest of his creatures."

Dr. Ethridge leaned toward the little girl with an air of barely controlled excitement. "What did you say, child?"

"I said the Lord hears—"

"Before that. Did you say 'sermon'?"

Under the old man's intense scrutiny, Pansy backed away from him and reached up to curl her hand inside Montana's big palm, seeking his reassuring touch. "Yes, sir."

The old man's gaze swung to Summer. "You are a minister?"

At his piercing gaze, she swallowed. "I...I am a preacher. But I'm not an ordained minister." She couldn't imagine why she was telling this stranger the truth. But there was something so compelling about him, she could no more lie to him than she could to herself. Or to God, she realized. That was it. This old man looked exactly the way she pictured God.

"And a child shall lead them," he muttered aloud. "Come," he said suddenly. "This little one is right. First we must join hands and pray."

"Pray?" Montana hung back as the old man reached out a hand to him. "What Hannah needs is healing, not praying."

"First we must ask the Lord for wisdom," the old man said gently. "Then he will show us how to set about making the child well."

Reluctantly Montana grasped Dr. Ethridge's withered palm, and the others followed suit.

"Lead us in prayer," the old man said to Summer.

She squeezed her eyes tightly shut. The words were wrenched from her heart. "Father," she intoned, "look upon this child, who is so dear to us. Help us to find a way to help her. Send your healing powers upon her. And upon all of us. Amen."

In the silence that followed, they could hear the disturbing sound of Hannah's labored breathing. It struck terror into all their hearts.

The old man suddenly caught up a lantern and turned away. "Follow me," he commanded. He led them toward the rear of the house, to a large, airy kitchen. "I do not know if the illness is the same," he whispered as he began to fill a large kettle with water, "but many years ago, my wife saved our son when he could barely breathe." He turned to Summer. "Are you willing to risk it, my dear?"

"I'd try anything to save Hannah," she said. "What do you want us to do?"

"We will need plenty of wood for the fire. And water from the stream that flows out back."

Montana was already headed toward the woodpile. "Pansy! Ned!" he called, "Take all the containers you can carry, and hurry to the stream!"

Dr. Ethridge lowered himself slowly into a chair and held out his hands, which shook with palsy. "If you'll trust me to hold the babe, my dear, there are blankets upstairs in the linen chest."

There was no question in Summer's mind. Though she didn't know why, she knew instinctively that he was a man worthy of her trust.

She placed the feverish little Hannah in his arms, then hurried up the stairs, returning minutes later with an armload of linens.

Soon the steam in the kitchen was so thick, they felt as though they were peering through a fog. The air was ripe with the bite of camphor.

Montana tossed another log on the fire, then stood back, watching as the flames grew. He wiped his palms on his pants and crossed to where Summer sat at the kitchen table, holding Hannah under a tent of linens, positioned over a basin of hot water. Each time the baby breathed, she inhaled the steamy vapors.

"Any improvement?" Montana asked.

Summer shook her head. Though her arms ached from the effort, she refused to relinquish her. She was prepared to do whatever was necessary to save the little one in her care.

Montana squeezed her shoulder and pressed a kiss to her cheek. "This will work," he murmured. "I know it will. You'll see. She'll be fine."

A tear glistened in Summer's eye, but she quickly blinked it away. This wasn't a time for weakness. She had to be strong. Not only for Hannah, but also for Pansy and Ned, who were huddled nearby, watching with haunted eyes.

"Perhaps the children would like to sleep awhile?" Dr. Ethridge whispered.

Summer shook her head. "I can't ask them to leave. They're devoted to their baby sister."

"I understand, my dear. Come, children," he called. "Sit with me awhile."

Pansy and Ned crossed the room and settled themselves on a rug in front of the fire. To ease their minds, the old man coaxed them into conversation. Soon they were laughing and talking. But gradually, as the hours passed, their voices began to fade. They lost the battle to remain awake. The old man's head bobbed, and he, too, joined them in sleep.

Please, Lord, Summer thought, pressing her lips to the baby's cheek. These little children had already lost so much. She couldn't bear to think of the heartache if they were forced to lose Hannah, as well.

Outside, Montana swung the ax, splitting the log, his muscles protesting every movement. Though he'd chopped enough wood to see Dr. Ethridge through next winter, he had a need to stay busy. That way, he wouldn't have time to think about what would happen if Hannah didn't make it.

How could it be, he wondered, that one insignificant creature could make such a difference? Just weeks ago he'd been a carefree gambler whose only concern was a good cigar and a winning hand. A two-bit outlaw, always just one step ahead of the law. Now, he would face the gallows, if it would give Hannah life.

Straining under the load of logs, he deposited them next to the fireplace, then draped the sleeping children and old man with blankets, before crossing the room to where Summer sat. Her head was thrown back. Her eyes were closed.

Hannah was asleep in her arms. Her breathing was soft and easy.

He dropped to his knees beside them. And wept tears of gratitude.

Sometime during the early hours of the morning, Summer awakened to find Montana asleep, still kneeling on the hard floor, his arms around her knees, his head pillowed in her lap. Hannah was sleeping peacefully in her arms.

Hearing a sound across the room, she glanced up to see Dr. Ethridge watching her.

Gingerly she extricated herself from Montana's grasp. He was so exhausted, he continued to sleep. She crossed to the fireplace and laid the baby between Pansy and Ned so that Hannah would be the first thing they saw when they awoke.

The old man eased himself from his chair and motioned for her to follow him to the parlor. Filling two cups with hot tea, she entered.

"I'll never be able to repay you for what you've done." She placed the cup of tea on the small table beside him.

"It was not my doing," he said in that strange, raspy voice. "It was the Lord's. And it was he who helped me remember my wife's treatment of that illness, for that was more than fifty years ago. There are times now when I can't even recall yesterday."

Summer shook her head in wonder. "We never could have properly cared for Hannah in our wagon. If you hadn't been kind enough to open your home to perfect strangers—"

He held up a hand to stop her. "There are no strangers in this world. We are all brothers and sisters." He sipped his tea a moment, then fixed her with a piercing look. "Pansy and Ned told me how their parents were killed. And they spoke glowingly of you, my dear. They said that you are a woman of deep and abiding faith, and that you and your husband offered them shelter. And when a Pinkerton agent came for them, you fought and ran, rather than allow them to be separated. Is that so?"

She wanted to lie. It was on the tip of her tongue. But she couldn't. Not in the presence of this man. She took a deep breath. "Some of what they said is true. I did offer them shelter, but I didn't do it for any noble reason. I...simply couldn't turn away from them. As for my faith . . . it is a sham."

She expected censure in his eyes. Instead, she saw only a strange, haunted smile.

"Perhaps you don't understand, Dr. Ethridge. I am a charlatan. I preach, not out of any sense of faith, but because it is the only thing I can do, and it pays well."

"You do not believe what you are preaching?" he asked.

''Well,'' she grudgingly admitted, ''at the time I'm speaking, I believe every word. But that doesn't mean that I am good or noble. Far from it. I didn't always believe. In the beginning, I saw it as simply a form of entertainment. You see, I am really an actress, not a preacher.''

He made a steeple of his fingers and regarded her. ''I see.''

''And as for Montana,'' she continued, ''he isn't my husband.''

''What is he?'' the old man asked kindly.

''I'm a gambler, a thief and an outlaw.''

They turned to see Montana standing in the doorway. He walked closer, to stand beside Summer's chair. Instinctively he rubbed the back of his hand across her cheek in a gesture of affection.

''He isn't telling the whole truth. He's also good and noble—'' Summer began.

''There's nothing noble about what I did, Dr. Ethridge,'' Montana cut in. ''I saw Summer and the children as a way to evade the long arm of the law. I figured most local sheriffs wouldn't bother with a man who had a wife and children.''

The old man regarded the two of them. ''So, what you are telling me is that your past has been...less than heroic.''

They both nodded.

Montana sat on the arm of Summer's chair and dropped a protective arm around her shoulders.

Dr. Ethridge posed an unexpected and shocking question. ''Would you like to leave the children here with me?''

"Leave them?" Montana's eyes narrowed with sudden anger. "Why would we do a thing like that?"

"So that you can go back to your former lives," the old man whispered.

Montana's voice deepened with feeling. He caught Summer's hand and laced his fingers with hers. "I guess we didn't make ourselves clear. Those three children have come to mean everything to us. We don't intend to ever give them up."

"But you said you weren't married…" the old man began.

"We intend to change that as soon as we can."

"Ah. And the law?" Dr. Ethridge asked. "Will you continue running, hoping to evade the law at every turn?"

Montana shrugged. "I don't see any other choice. There's a lawman trailing us right now who intends to separate those children, not only from us, but from each other. We can't let that happen."

They looked up at the sound of the children's voices. At once Summer and Montana flew to the other room, leaving Dr. Ethridge staring after them with a look of solemn concentration.

"Why do you whisper, Dr. Ethridge?" Ned asked around a mouthful of hot porridge sprinkled with cinnamon and sugar.

"Ned, it isn't polite to ask personal questions," Summer admonished.

"That's quite all right," the old man said. He turned to Ned. "I believe the Lord is punishing me for the sin of pride. You see," he said to the others, "I was once a famous preacher, known throughout the West as the Oracle. My fame was so great, President Ulysses S. Grant asked me to speak at his inauguration.''

Summer's mouth opened, but no words came out. She felt a wave of shame at the realization that the children had boasted about her preaching prowess to a man of his stature.

''As my fame grew, I began to believe that the people came to hear me, instead of my message. But at the height of my success I lost everything that mattered to me in life. My wife. My only son. Both died of smallpox. It was then that I lost my voice, and my body was racked with palsy.''

''How terrible,'' Summer murmured.

''No, my dear,'' he responded with a gentle smile. ''It was a blessing in disguise. For, you see, with my voice silenced, I was forced to look inward. I regained my faith. Now, because my health is so poor, I live quietly, ministering only to those most in need. My only regret is that I can no longer preach the word. It would bring great comfort to the good people of this town.'' He fixed her with a piercing look. ''Perhaps the Lord brought you here to fill that need.''

Summer saw the way the children turned toward her with eager, expectant looks. She recalled the joy on their faces as they'd joined in a game of tag with other children. Then she glanced at Montana, and quickly looked away.

''We couldn't possibly stay. We have to move on as soon as Hannah is strong enough to travel.''

The old man nodded. ''I understand.'' He took another bite of his porridge. ''This is the tastiest meal I've had since my wife passed on. I will be sorry to see such a fine cook get away.'' He glanced around with a bright smile. "I'm afraid I can't accompany you upstairs. I haven't been able to take the stairs for some years now. But I want you to make yourselves comfortable up there. The rooms are yours for as long as you stay. In fact, consider my home yours."

"You're too generous, Dr. Ethridge," Summer said.

"Oh, my dear. This is purely selfish on my part. It is a joy to see life again in these old rooms."

Upstairs, Summer removed the dustcovers from the beds and opened the windows wide to let in the fresh air. She looked around the big, cheerful rooms and was reminded of her grandmother's house. There had been much warmth here. And love.

The feather beds were large and sturdy. In one corner of the room was a child's cradle, and in a closet were toys. A brightly painted top. A lovingly crafted wagon.

The children were delighted, and they played quietly until, worn out from their emotional night, they tumbled into bed, while the sun climbed higher in the sky.

Summer sat in the comfortable old rocker and held Hannah to her heart until she, too, fell asleep. Summer laid her in the cradle and crawled gratefully into bed.

Only Montana remained awake and alert. He wished with all his heart that he could join Summer in bed and hold her. But he dared not relax his guard. Instead of resting, he pulled a chair beside the window, keeping an eye on the road below. And praying they could leave this town before the law caught up with them.

* * *

Refreshed and renewed, Summer awoke from her nap to the sound of Hannah's cooing. Sitting up, she saw that Montana had fallen asleep in the rocker, one hand resting protectively on the cradle. She crossed the room and scooped the baby into her arms, hugging her fiercely, then tiptoed from the room, leaving Montana to rest.

She found Pansy and Ned in the next room, playing quietly with toys they'd found in the closet. With a finger to her lips, she beckoned them to follow her downstairs.

In the parlor, Dr. Ethridge was seated in a chair by the window. He looked up as they entered. "Well, you are all looking much better than the last time I saw you."

"Thanks to you," Summer said. "Would you like me to fix you some dinner?"

"It isn't necessary, my dear. I told Charity Danville that I had company, and she and her daughter brought us a feast. All you need do is set the table."

"You're too kind," Summer said.

"I have ulterior motives," the old man said, with a twinkle in his eye. "I'm hoping to persuade you and Montana to stay here, so that my home can once more be filled with the sound of children."

"Oh, Dr. Ethridge. If only we could." With a shake of her head, Summer made her way to the big kitchen, leaving the children under the watchful eye of the smiling old man.

Moments later, she heard the sound of hurried footsteps and turned as Montana burst through the door. "I can't believe I fell asleep," he called gruffly.

"I just caught sight of them going into the sheriff's office. There's no telling how long they've been in town."

"Who?" Summer whirled, her hand at her throat. But she already knew the answer.

"Wade Farmer, our Pinkerton agent, and none other than Sheriff Otis Pain."

It took only moments for Summer to recover from the shock. "Hitch the horse," she said resolutely. "I'll fetch the children."

She would not think about what they were leaving. She would not allow herself to dwell on the sort of home they could have made here, among these good people. There was time, just barely, if they moved out at once, to escape.

Summer raced to the parlor and struggled to keep the panic from her voice. "Come, children. Say your goodbyes to Dr. Ethridge."

The old man blinked in surprise. The children, who were clustered around him, fell silent.

"Montana just spotted the Pinkerton man in town, along with the crooked sheriff who has vowed to see Montana hang."

Pansy and Ned began to cry. Then little Hannah's lips began to quiver and soon she, too, was crying.

"Hush now," Summer whispered. "There's no time to waste."

Dr. Ethridge hugged each of the children, then got slowly to his feet and made his way to her. Placing his hands on either side of her face, he stared deeply into her eyes. "This is no way to live. Always running. Always looking over your shoulder."

"You don't understand," she said, fighting the tears that threatened. "I love Montana and the children. I couldn't bear to lose them."

"Then, if you would keep them, stop running and place your trust in the Lord."

Tears blurred her vision as she gathered the children around her. "Pansy," she said softly, "take your brother and sister to the wagon."

"Yes, ma'am."

She turned back, hoping to put into words the gratitude she felt toward this kind, gentle man. Her eyes widened as she saw him drop to his knees and collapse onto the floor. She let out a cry, and raced to his side.

Moments later, Montana hurried inside, summoned by the children. "What is it?"

"I don't know." Summer had managed to cover the old man with a blanket and cushion his head with a pillow from the sofa. "I can't rouse him." She lifted her gaze to Montana. The tears were gone. Her vision was clear. As was her course of action. "Whatever has happened to him, I can't leave him."

"But what about—?"

She crossed to him and touched a finger to his lips, closing her eyes against the pain. "You'll have to take the children and go without me."

He lifted his hand to cover hers. "We're partners, remember? If you stay, so do I." He checked his pistol. "I guess this town is as good as any for a gunfight."

She shook her head. "Dr. Ethridge is a man of God. We can't resort to guns in his house."

His voice was low, angry. "So. You want us to give up, is that it?"

She glanced at the still, silent man beneath the blanket, and thought of his last words to her. "We won't give up. We'll put our trust in a power even stronger than guns."

Wade Farmer and Sheriff Otis Pain were taking no chances. They had rounded up the mayor and sheriff and most of the shopkeepers, and warned them about the outlaws posing as a preacher and her husband. They had recited a litany of crimes committed by the man known as Montana. Then, to add weight to their charges, they had told how these two had eluded capture by pretending to be a family, when in truth the children were runaway orphans.

The angry mob that made its way to Dr. Ethridge's home was hungry for blood, fearing for the fate of that kindly old man at the hands of these criminals. They surrounded the house and burst in with guns drawn, only to find Summer, Montana and the children kneeling around a figure on the floor.

"What have you done to him? Step away from Dr. Ethridge," the sheriff commanded, gun drawn.

They got to their feet. Summer held Hannah to her heart and clutched Pansy's hand in hers. Montana lifted Ned in his arms and took a step back.

"Dr. Ethridge has taken some kind of spell," Montana said.

"Careful," the Pinkerton agent called. "He's a gunfighter. Better search him."

At once several of the men checked Montana's holsters. Then they shook their heads. "No weapons," one of them called.

"So, you ran out of places to hide. You're finally ready to turn yourself in," Sheriff Pain called mockingly. "Set the kid down, and we'll tie your hands so you don't get any ideas about running."

Hearing his voice, Ned stared at the sheriff, then turned away and buried his face in Montana's neck, whimpering in fear.

"Hey now, partner," Montana crooned, stroking the boy's head. "You've got to be brave about this. I told you, I'll come back when I've done my time."

But the boy continued to cry, and Montana was forced to set him down while he held out his hands to the sheriff.

"This was a lot easier than I thought," Wade Farmer said. "In the name of the Pinkerton Agency, I claim full authority over these children."

"He's going to send us to an orphanage!" Pansy shouted. "And give our baby sister away to a mean woman who won't love her like we do!"

"Now, now..." Farmer began, but the mayor stopped him.

"Is that true?" he asked. "Are you chasing these children just so you can separate them?"

Wade Farmer shrugged. "That's none of my business. Or yours. The banker who's paying me just said to see they're brought back."

As he started to take Hannah from Summer's arms, Ned managed to find his voice through the tears that choked him. "That man," he said, pointing to Sheriff Otis Pain, "is the man who shot my mama and papa."

Everyone turned to stare at the sheriff, who was busy tying Montana's hands.

Summer gasped and turned to Pansy. "But I thought you said you didn't see who shot them."

"I didn't," the little girl said. "I was in the cabin with Hannah. But Ned was playing out in the fields." She turned to her trembling little brother, who couldn't seem to tear his gaze from the man wearing the sheriff's badge. "Tell the truth, Ned. Is that the man?"

The little boy whimpered and hid behind Summer's skirts. Then, seeing the piercing blackbird eyes of Dr. Ethridge fixed on him, he seemed to gather his courage, and he stepped forward. "He's the one. I was lying in a furrow behind the plow. He had some other men with him. He wanted money, and Papa said there was none. And then he shot Papa and Mama." The boy's lips quivered as he added, "And he was laughing as he rode away."

Sheriff Pain's eyes narrowed in fury as he jammed his pistol into Montana's chest. "It's the kid's word against mine. And I'm the one with the badge here."

"Hold on." Sheriff William Sharp stepped forward. He motioned for the other men to train their weapons on Sheriff Pain. "This is my town. And I'm the law here. Otis Pain, you're under arrest on suspicion of murder. I'll take that gun."

Wade Farmer, eager to disassociate himself from the crooked sheriff, strode across the room and started to wrench Hannah from Summer's arms, saying, "None of this has any bearing on the children. I'm still taking them back to Hollow Junction.''

The children began to weep, and even Summer had to bite down hard to keep from crying out. But she had vowed that she would offer no resistance.

Sheriff Sharp hesitated, clearly uncertain whether or not to intervene in official business.

Seeing his indecision, Dr. Ethridge sat up, looking like a ghostly figure with the blanket wrapped around his stooped shoulders. Though his voice was barely audible, he managed to whisper, ''Suffer the little children to come unto me.'' He pointed a bony finger at Montana. ''This man was willing to give up his freedom in order to keep the children together. I think that says much about his character.''

That was all Sheriff Sharp needed. He trained his gun on Wade Farmer and said, ''These children are under my jurisdiction. I'll not have them separated, as long as they remain in my town.''

Dr. Ethridge smiled. ''Our town would be well served by these good people. I would be willing to share my home, in exchange for the kind of care they have shown me this day. And I would tutor them in the ministry, should they be so inclined.''

''You would open your home to an outlaw and his woman?'' the mayor asked in surprise.

Sheriff Sharp pulled a Wanted poster from his pocket and handed it to the mayor. ''This poster calls Montana 'the gentleman bandit,' and points out that he never caused physical harm to any of his victims.'' He reached out a knife to Montana, whose hands were still bound, slicing the ropes. ''Most of the people you robbed refused to file complaints. My guess is, they were ill-gotten goods to begin with. Still, you have stolen. And you'll have to make restitution to any who press charges."

"If he has a home here, and a means of . . . respectable employment, he can easily make restitution," Dr. Ethridge pointed out logically.

Montana turned to where Summer stood quietly with the children. Though they spoke not a word, their gazes met and held. And they both knew. The wily old man had just spoken the one word neither of them could refuse. *Respectable.*

"Of course," the old man went on, eyes twinkling, "there would have to be a wedding right away. I can't have a man and woman living under my roof without benefit of marriage."

At the word *wedding,* the children began dancing up and down, and Hannah, imitating them, joined in.

"I think," Charity Danville said, "that my daughter and I could prepare a wedding supper by tonight. That is, Dr. Ethridge, if you're feeling up to it?"

"Never felt better." The old man threw off the blanket and crossed the room in search of his spectacles. Summer and Montana both noticed at the same moment that his step was as spry as a young man's.

He turned to the assembly. "I'll look forward to seeing you back here this evening." He glanced at Summer. "Six o'clock, my dear?"

Before she could respond, he said to the mayor, "Better make it five o'clock. Wouldn't want to give them time to change their minds, now, would we? Invite the whole town. They can come and meet our new preacher and her family."

Amid much laughter, the crowd began filing from the house, with Sheriff Pain and Wade Farmer in tow.

When the last of them was gone, the children gathered around Summer and Montana and were swept up into their arms, where they clung, laughing and weeping.

"Is this going to be our home?" Pansy asked.

"I guess so," Montana muttered.

"Forever and ever?" Ned asked.

"For as long as Dr. Ethridge wants us to stay," Summer admitted.

When the children's tears were dried, and their fears swept away with kisses, they raced upstairs to retrieve the toys they'd abandoned earlier.

Summer and Montana turned to face Dr. Ethridge.

"Why, you old con," Montana muttered, fixing him with a knowing look.

Dr. Ethridge merely regarded him with a charming smile. "It takes one to know one, young man. In my youth, I was the best there was. Even better than you, if truth be told...until I saw the light." His eyes twinkled with a mischievous look. "Resurrecting that old talent has been quite exhilarating." He started across the room. "I believe I'll fix a cup of tea. And leave you two alone. I'm sure," he added with that same playful smile, "there are things you'll want to discuss."

As he took his leave, Summer and Montana fell into each other's arms and roared with laughter.

"Can you believe that old codger?" Montana said with a shake of his head. "We just fell for the biggest con of all. He tricked us into spending the rest of our lives in his town, ministering to his flock."

"But don't you see?" Summer brushed her lips over Montana's and felt a swift rush of heat. "By forcing us to admit our faults in front of the entire town, he's given us a chance to build a life together, where we'll never again have to look over our shoulder and wonder when our past will catch up with us. That sly old fox just gave us everything we've ever wanted."

Montana drew her into the circle of his arms and looked into her glowing eyes. "I'm about to take on a lifetime of responsibility for a woman and three children. I'm forced to forsake the only way of life I've ever known. And instead of feeling panic, I feel free. For the first time in my life."

Freedom, he thought as his mouth covered hers in a searing kiss. This was Summer's gift to him. And he intended to repay her with loyalty and devotion. And laughter. A great deal of it. And love. Oh, yes. Enough love to last a lifetime and beyond.

*　*　*　*　*

The Ballad of Josie Dove
Mary McBride

Chapter One

New Mexico Territory, 1878

Winning four hundred dollars at poker was one thing, but winning a woman was something else entirely. If he had known this was going to happen, Will Curry would have burned those four kings before he ever laid them faceup on the table. Hell, he never would have come to Las Vegas in the first place. His deputy could have had the sole glory and the dubious pleasure of escorting their prisoner to the authorities in San Miguel County. But no. Will had made the trip himself because he had a yearning for some high-stakes poker. Then he'd gone and won. Damn it.

"Quit following me, will you?" Will lengthened his already considerable stride on the dark, dusty street. Behind him, the whisk of petticoats quickened.

He went faster, hunching his shoulders and jamming his thumbs through his gunbelt to stifle his natural inclination to draw on the menace at his back. "Go away, lady. Scat."

"Can't." The word came out in a chuff of breath as she ran to keep up. "Got no place to go."

Lord have mercy. Will gritted his teeth and dug his bootheels into the dirt, and the woman ran smack into him. Because he was six foot three and a solid two hundred pounds, it barely fazed him, but it took an instant toll on the tiny female. It knocked what little wind she had left clear out of her, and judging from her expression, the collision set her to seeing a whole firmament of stars.

He should have just taken the opportunity to ditch her for good then, but instead, he reached out and took hold of her shoulders to steady her. A big mistake, he realized, feeling the satin warmth of her skin and the delicacy of the bones beneath it. In that instant, Will had to remind himself she was a whore, a hard woman, and not the fragile creature his fingertips were telling him she was. The dark, rich tumble of her hair was meant to beguile every bit as much as the skimpy cut of her red dress. And the innocence swimming in her wide eyes was only because she'd just had the very daylights knocked out of her. Not to mention the very devil.

"Go on back to Sharkey's now," he said sternly, releasing his grip on her shoulders and taking a step backward. "This has all been a mistake. A terrible, confounded mistake."

"You won me." She crossed her arms, bit her lip, then took a few deep breaths that threatened to lift all that shimmering flesh right out of her corset. "That's my contract in your pocket."

Will jerked his gaze from her breasts to the breast pocket of his coat. "This?" He yanked out the folded paper and glared at it. "I thought your boss was betting his stake in a silver mine. Not his claim on some whore."

She threw those bare white shoulders back and stood taller, which must have made her all of five foot four. "Well, you won me just the same, mister. You're holding my contract. It's probably worth two hundred dollars. Three, maybe."

"Oh, yeah?" Will ripped it down the middle and waved both halves in her face. "What's it worth now?"

Her big eyes got bigger. "What in blazes do you think you're doing?"

Losing his temper, Will thought, something he'd only done two or three times in his thirty-six years. He'd always prided himself on his cool control, but this ornery little bit, with all that skin and her chin sticking in his face, had him boiling.

"What am I doing? Just watch," he said through clenched teeth, as he proceeded to tear the halves into quarters, and then tore those, and kept on tearing until he tossed the mutilated contract into the air, then stood grinning maliciously and rubbing his hands together while the shreds came down on them both like their own private snowfall.

"There you go, lady." Will whacked a bit of paper off his sleeve. "Now leave me alone. Go on back to Sharkey's where you belong."

She shook her head, gazing mournfully at the confetti in the street.

"Well, then, go someplace else." He gestured toward the score of buildings that had sprung up almost overnight in anticipation of the arrival of the Atchison, Topeka and Santa Fe next summer. Every second one of them was a saloon or gambling hall with sporting rooms attached. "Take your pick, lady. This is a paradise for whores. Just leave me be."

Will spun on his heel and covered the distance to his hotel in less than a minute, took the inside stairs two at a time and, once in his room, slammed the door and threw the bolt. He stood there for a minute, sweating, swearing, more like a man under siege than one who had just been dealt the best damn poker hand of his whole life. Then he went to the window, muttering, and edged back the curtain and peered down into the street.

All he could see were bits of paper blowing in the breeze. The woman was gone. He didn't even want to wonder where. Good riddance.

"Whoa! Where are you going, Josie?"

Josie Dove halted in the middle of the lobby. "Upstairs. And don't you dare try to stop me, Tick Farley. I've got business." She planted her hands on her hips and aimed a hot hundred-degree glare at the young desk clerk.

He didn't melt the way she had hoped. The kid smirked instead. "Business? Who with?"

"None of yours. And I don't know his name." She pointed her chin toward the stairs. "The tall man who just came in here a minute ago."

"You mean Will Curry?"

Will Curry. Oh, it suited him, Josie thought. Strong and determined and, well...clean. She could still picture the man's finely shaped hands as they held his cards just so. Not too tight, but tenderly. Caressingly. The same way he'd held his glass of whiskey. Like a patient lover. She could still see his clean, clipped nails.

"That's right. Will Curry. What room is he in?"

Tick's mouth slid to the side. "Didn't he tell you?"

"He forgot."

"Yeah. Right."

Josie sighed. She was going to find that fine-handed man, one way or another. One way would have been to rip the registration book right out of Tick's grimy grasp and read it herself. The other way, which she had learned from studying the girls at Sharkey's, would be to saunter across the lobby, lean across the desk, and whisper promises that she had no intention of keeping.

The boy had trouble talking and staring down her dress at the same time. "Tomorrow night?"

"Uh-huh," she crooned.

"All night?"

"Uh-huh."

"Free?"

Josie blinked "Yes" and smiled "Yes" and shifted her cleavage invitingly and affirmatively.

"Room 208."

"Thanks, Tick. You won't regret it."

Before the boy could reply, Josie was up the stairs, her hand already fisted to knock on Will Curry's door. But by the time she reached room 208, she'd decided on something better. She scratched on the painted wood and whimpered like a lost dog. Pretty convincingly, too, she thought. And why not? It wasn't so far from the truth.

She heard a considerable amount of grumbling on the opposite side of the door. She smiled and scratched some more. Then, after a boot thunked against the wood, she whimpered louder, loster. Finally, when the door jerked open, Josie scurried inside and grabbed for the bedpost. If he threw her out, he'd have to throw the bed, as well. Which the man could probably do, considering his size. Still, Josie held on tight.

Only Will Curry didn't make a move in her direction. He stood in the doorway, his arms braced against the frame, staring out into the dark hallway. "God Almighty. I should have known." He shook his head. "You're worse than flypaper, lady."

"You won me."

"I don't want you. How many times do I have to tell you?" His deep voice deepened even more. "I do not want you. Can't you get that through your head?"

"I guess not."

He turned now and faced her. "Well, try. All right? It's nothing personal. You can follow me for the next five years. Hell, you can follow me for the next fifty or five hundred years. But I still won't want you. Do you understand?"

Yes. She thought she did. "Oh, my God!" Josie wailed.

She let go of the bedpost and plopped onto the mattress. "Of all the damn bad luck. I finally find the perfect man, and he turns out to be—" Her words broke on an agonized moan, and then she flopped back, grabbed a pillow and put it over her face. She moaned again, but the feathers soaked up most of the noise. Then she just lay there. Silent.

Smothered?

Lord help him. Will took a step toward her. "Lady, are you all right?"

She mumbled something he couldn't understand, and she kept mumbling while he lit the lamp on the nightstand, then turned up the wick to get a better look at her. Other than red satin and a lot of bare limbs, he couldn't see much.

He cleared his throat. "Did you hear me? I asked if you're all right."

"I heard you. No. I'm not all right." She lifted a corner of the pillow then, and one big green eye glared at him while taking him in from head to toe. Once. Twice. "Oh, God," she wailed again. "Look at you. Just look at you."

"What?" Will looked down. He was wearing his union suit. It had been washed so many times it was a pale pink now. A couple of holes here and there, but none that showed anything important. It had shrunk some and the buttons strained across his chest, but... "I'm decent," he said.

"Decent! You're gorgeous. And your hands are so refined. So clean." She slammed the pillow over her stomach and gave it a punch. "Just my luck to finally find a man like you, and you turn out to be..."

"To be what?"

"You know."

"No, damn it, I don't know." Will could feel his temper on a downhill slide. "What?"

"A man who likes men," she said at the same time she held up one very limp-wristed hand. "Better than women."

"Oh, for Christ's sake. You think I'm..." Will's mouth snapped shut. It wasn't such a bad idea at that, letting her think he was that way. In fact, he wished he'd thought of it himself. Damned if it wasn't one surefire way of getting shed of her.

He hung his head, as much to look ashamed and perverse as to hide the grin creeping across his lips. Then he sighed. Mightily. And shrugged as if his shoulders bore intolerable burdens. "Well. What can I say? You found me out. Don't tell anybody, though.

Okay?'' *Please. I'd sooner be taken for a rustler or a cheat.* Lord, he was sweating already just thinking about living it down.

She was back under the pillow again, muttering.

"I said don't feel obliged to pass that information along, lady."

"Oh, who cares?" She lurched upright, hugging the pillow to her bosom, her face all scrunched and her eyes shimmering with tears like liquid emeralds. Taking a swipe at the one that trickled down her face, she said, "I'll go. Just give me a minute to get myself together."

A minute passed—long enough for more tears to drip onto the pillowcase. Her hands were wet from wiping them away. Hardworking hands, Will noticed. They didn't match the rest of her.

"Quit crying now." He lowered himself beside her, his arm just brushing hers. "It can't be as bad as all that."

"It's worse. I was watching you all night while you played cards. Studying you. 'If ever a man could help you, Josie,' I said to myself, 'he's the one.' Then, when Sharkey threw my contract into the pot and you won, I thought for sure it was a sign from heaven above. 'Everything's going to be fine now, Josie. He's the one.'"

She gazed at him now, her lips trembling, her wet eyes roving over his face. "I thought you were the one. Only you're not."

"What one?"

After a sniff, she said, "The one to teach me everything I need to know about loving. To help me be the best whore in the territory. The best one in the whole West. But now I know you can't, of course."

She slapped the heel of one hand to her forehead. "How could I have been so dad-blasted wrong?"

Will shrugged. "Maybe you're in the wrong line of work," he suggested lamely.

His comment earned him a damp snort, a roll of her green eyes and a curt "No kidding."

"Well, quit, then," he said.

"And do what? I haven't any skills. None I know of, anyway. Hell, I don't even know who I am."

He glanced at the watch he'd left open on the nightstand. "Two o'clock in the morning. Little wonder you're confused, lady. I hardly know who I am either till I've had a good night's sleep."

"You don't understand," she said with a sigh. "I really don't know who I am."

Will shook his head, wondering vaguely if he'd fallen asleep and tumbled into one of those strange dreams where conversations seemed to make sense but really didn't, where dogs scratched at doors, then busted in as women and proceeded to bawl and pace around the room the way this one was doing now. The way she was punching that pillow, Will was willing to bet there'd be feathers all over the room pretty soon. Feathers and tears. God Almighty. This was a nightmare.

"Sure you know who you are," he told her. "Why, only a minute ago you said your name was . . ." Well, hell. He'd clean forgotten. No, wait. "Rosie. That was it. You said your name was Rosie." He grinned, pleased with his powers of recollection, once again secure in his natural ability to solve problems. "So there you go, Rosie."

She stopped in the center of the room and glared at him. There was wet murder in her eyes. "Josie."

Aw, hell.

"Josie Dove. Only that's not my real name." She started pacing again, pummeling and puffing at the strands of hair that kept falling in her face.

"Well, what is your real name, then?" he asked. But instead of an answer, Will got a pillow right in his face.

"That's what I've been trying to tell you!" she shrieked. "I don't know my real name! I don't know who I am!"

Chapter Two

A sane man would've just smiled affably and told Josie Dove that was a pity. A real shame. See you around, sugar.

A man with any sense at all would've nudged her out the door—red dress, bare skin, tear-streaked face and all—bidden her a fond good-night and an even fonder farewell, then ridden out of town the next morning. Alone.

Will eased back in the saddle. He swiped his hat off and ran his shirtsleeve across his forehead. He'd always been sane. Always had more than his share of good sense. Until last night. He wondered...

"They don't put anything in the drinks at Sharkey's, do they?" he called over his shoulder.

"Like what?" Josie called back.

"I don't know. I've heard stories about saloons back east and out in San Francisco where they dope a fella's drink and the poor fool's liable to wake up on his way to China or Brazil. I was just wondering."

"All Sharkey puts in his drinks is a little whiskey and a lot of water." Her laughter carried the distance between their mounts. "Why? You feel like you've been shanghaied?"

"A little." *A lot.* He jammed his hat back on, gave the brim a tug for good measure.

"You didn't have to do this, Will. I told you that. Remember?"

"Yeah." He remembered how lost she'd looked once she stopped crying. How she'd curled up on his bed, "just to rest my eyes a minute," and then fallen asleep immediately, leaving him standing there in his long johns, looking at his own bed, at the half foot on either side of her left over for him. He remembered, though she vehemently denied it, how she'd cried and shivered in her sleep and clung to him while he tried to cling to his scant six inches of mattress.

Most of all, he remembered the way the scrawny desk clerk had ogled and leered at her in the morning, and how it had scared her, even though she'd sworn up and down it didn't.

"You could have just lent me some money to get out of town," she called to him now. "I'd have paid you back. I may be a whore, but I'm an honest person. Truly I am."

He heard her heels thunk into the side of the little chestnut mare he'd acquired for her, and the next minute she was right alongside him. Her red dress was hiked up and her bare knee—pretty as a peach—clacked against his.

"I said I'm an honest person, Will Curry."

"I heard you."

"Well?"

"If you don't have the merest inkling who you are, Josie, then how do you know you're honest?"

Her forehead wrinkled briefly, then smoothed. "I just know it, is all." Her mouth set tight, like stretched wire.

"Well, you're stubborn, anyway," he said with a sigh.

And one hell of a horsewoman, too, he thought, noting once more the ease with which she sat her mount. Astride, yet. When the old codger at the livery stable in Las Vegas tried to sell them a side saddle, Josie had been fit to be tied. "I'd rather walk," she'd said, sniffing in an indignant whiff of air.

Then, out in the corral, she'd gone straight for the best horse. Not the handsomest. The little chestnut mare had scarred flanks, a raggedy tail and a mane full of nettles, but her chest was deep and her eyes were as clear as a summer day. She was the same horse Will would've chosen himself if he had the time, which he didn't, since Josie had announced, "I'll take this one," before he could even open his mouth.

His curiosity started itching again. A person didn't acquire those skills overnight, especially when those nights were spent in a sporting house. "Where was it you said that woman found you?"

She sighed, leaning forward to pick another burr from the mane she'd been working on all day. "You already asked me that."

"I'm asking again."

"She said I was wandering along the North Canadian in Union County when the soldiers found me. Sick and talking out of my head, I guess. They brought me to her place, just outside of Clayton. I don't remember any of that, of course. All I know is I opened my eyes one day and there was Mrs. Schumacher smiling at me.''

"And you didn't know your name?''

"Nope. I didn't know anything." She tossed another burr over her shoulder, then said, almost gaily, "My head was as empty as a poor man's pocket.''

Will shook his own head now. It galled him, as it had earlier, that she wasn't more concerned by her condition. Whatever it was. A person didn't just wake up empty-headed and not worry about it. Not a normal person, anyway.

"And when'd you say that was?" he asked her. "The winter of '76?"

"Around then. I came to my senses at Mrs. Schumacher's in April of '77." She combed her fingers through the mare's mane and snagged another nettle. "She was the one who gave me my name. Josie was all, at first. Just because she liked it. And then, after a couple weeks, she came up with Dove.''

Will frowned, thinking of the mournful, nearly heartsick call of those birds. "Because you were sad?"

"Sad?" Josie clucked her tongue. "No, silly. Because of my occupation. See, Mrs. Schumacher was figuring on training me to be one of her fancy girls. She said last names, more often than not, reflected an occupation. Schumacher, if you don't know, is German for *shoemaker*. One of the girls was named Baker. And one of them was a Smith." Tipping her chin up, she squinted under the brim of his hat. "What do you suppose Curry means?"

"I never gave it much thought."

Josie shrugged. "Well, anyway, Mrs. Schumacher said, since I needed a name that said what I or my ancestors did, and since I was training to be a soiled dove—she never said 'whore,' because she thought it was undignified—then that was probably the perfect name for me. So that's who I am. Josie Dove."

Will simply stared at her.

She smiled. "Close your mouth, Will."

He snapped his slack jaws shut, shook his head again. "Aren't you the least bit curious about your real name? About who you really are?"

Her smile tightened before it disappeared altogether. "No," she said. "Not the least little bit." Then she slammed her heels into the mare and left Will eating dust.

Josie sat hugging her knees, staring into the heart of the campfire where the red coals pulsed with heat. This wasn't going at all the way she had planned. Despite his fine hands, Will Curry wasn't the man she'd been seeking. But here she was with him anyway, out under an open sky somewhere west of Las Vegas, somewhere east of a town called Agate where he claimed to live.

She hadn't had much choice, she thought dismally, after making those outrageous promises to Tick Farley the night before. She'd meant it, though, when she told Will she was an honest woman, one who didn't break promises. To Josie's way of thinking, her promise to Tick hadn't been broken so much as, well...stretched. About twenty-five miles.

She sighed and lifted her eyes to the man who sat on the opposite side of the campfire, his boots to the fire and a tin plate of beans and bacon balanced on his leg. His dark brown hair was slicked back with creek water and glistened in the firelight that sculpted the planes of his face and flickered along his jaw. He had fine eyebrows, Josie observed, and probably the truest blue eyes she'd ever seen. Deep sapphire eyes that crinkled at the corners when he smiled. Which wasn't often. Eyes that had a way of homing in on her, curiously and relentlessly.

Will Curry was a fine-handed, handsome man. But he was the wrong man, and he asked too many questions. Like wasn't she the least bit curious about who she really was. The truth was that she had been at first. Intensely, nearly insanely curious. But now she didn't want to know.

"You don't want to know, *liebchen,*" Mrs. Schumacher had cautioned her.

With her eyes closed, Josie could clearly picture Lottie Schumacher's wealth of hair, dyed a sultrier shade of red than nature ever dreamed of, her carefully painted mouth, and her fingers, nearly hobbled by rings. The madam had struck Josie as not only a vision of sophistication, but a fount of wisdom, as well. How she ever wound up in a poor corner of the territory was a mystery to Josie, but then, Mrs. Schumacher had seemed fond of mystery.

The elegant redhead with the deep-throated German accent was probably the closest thing to a mother that Josie would ever know. The woman had named her, after all, the way a mother would. And she had taught Josie three important things, the first of which was that she was better off not knowing anything about her past.

"I knew a young woman in Dresden many years ago who had lost her memory. Just like you. It bothered her. That loss. It worried her every minute. And when she finally found out the truth about who she was, she was oh-so-sorry. You see, *liebchen,* the young woman had committed a terrible, a truly unspeakable crime and that was why her mind had gone blank. To protect her from that knowledge. So you don't want to know, Josie. Ever. You've forgotten your past for a good reason, *liebchen.* This way, you are sweet and fresh and new. This way is best. You see?"

It still made sense to Josie. She didn't know about being sweet, but she liked the notion of being fresh and new. She felt like a good person, not one who would commit an evil crime, but still there was a dark spot inside her, a little like a bruise under the skin of an apple—a constant shadow that she was more than willing to ignore. If she had indeed done something terrible, she didn't want to know about it.

The second thing Mrs. Schumacher had told her, which also made perfect sense, was that, because Josie had no skills or education that she was aware of, and unless she married—"I don't even know any men!" Josie had exclaimed—then she would probably have to earn her livelihood as a soiled dove.

"Believe me, *liebchen,*" the madam had said, "it is better than being a wife. You will be able to earn not only money, but your independence, as well."

That had sounded fine to Josie. In fact, everything that Lottie Schumacher had said struck her as sound and altogether sensible. Solid advice. Even the third thing.

"When you have regained your health, Josie, you will watch the other young women and you will listen to them and you will learn. To be a success in this business, a woman must do more than simply lie on her back. Loving is one thing, but loving *well* is an art."

Mrs. Schumacher had smiled then—a very mysterious smile that curled her perfectly painted lips like red ribbons. "So, after you have seen everything and heard everything, then you will choose a single man with whom to practice until you are perfect. That is best, you see. One man with patience and fine hands and much experience, who will teach you all the wonderful things a woman is supposed to feel. That way, you see, you will know how to act with the others, with the ones who fail to make you feel so good. Believe me. I know. That is the only way to be successful and happy in this business."

"How will I know who to choose?" Josie had asked.

In reply, Mrs. Schumacher had touched a red-tipped nail to her own powdered bosom. "You will know. Right here. There will be a spark. In your heart it will feel as if someone had just struck a match."

And it had, too, damn it, Josie thought. When she first saw Will Curry last night, there had been that little flare in her heart. As if a match had been scratched across it. As if a shooting star had gone streaking across a midnight sky.

She glanced across the campfire now at the fine hands of the man she had finally chosen. Hands so sure and graceful as they lifted a forkful of beans from the plate on his knee to a mouth that was also graceful and beautifully carved. Her stomach fluttered at the sight. Her heart flickered, and she sighed. Woefully.

"What a waste."

"Pardon?" Will put down his fork. Over the flames, his deep blue eyes latched on to hers.

She tightened her arms and planted her chin on her knee. "Nothing. I was just thinking out loud."

"What about?"

"Oh, I don't know. About kissing, I guess."

He shook his head while his wonderful mouth thinned in disapproval. "You're a mite too candid, lady. Or maybe *brazen*'s a better word. Talking like that could get you in a whole lot of trouble."

"It's supposed to, isn't it?" Josie grinned. "I mean, the kind of trouble you're talking about is my occupation, after all." She lifted her chin a notch. "For your information, Mr. Curry, prostitution is the world's oldest occupation."

Will slapped his plate down on the ground. Then those blue eyes narrowed, skewering her. "I doubt that, Miss Dove. I doubt that most sincerely."

"Oh, yeah? Why?"

"Because," he growled, "the first poor fella who went looking for the first damn prostitute had to have some change in his pocket. That's why."

Josie felt her confident grin go flat all of a sudden. "What have you got against women who work for a living?" she asked. Then, hearing her own question, she answered it before Will could. "Oh, that's right. Never mind. I keep forgetting."

"What?"

"That you don't like women."

"I like women all right," he snarled.

"You know what I mean." She sighed and reached toward the fire, extracting a stick that was still glowing on one end and poking it sullenly at the coals. "It's such a waste."

Will muttered a succession of curses, regretting ever letting her believe he was so inclined. He told himself he ought to set the record straight right now. But then he'd have to deal with her as a woman, rather than a puzzle, and he wasn't certain he was ready for that.

"What have you got against working girls?" she asked him again. Her green eyes shot sparks, challenging him, and her pretty mouth froze in a stubborn line while she waited for his answer.

"Nothing." Will shrugged. "Live and let live, I always say. I just personally don't believe in paying for sex." And the few times he had, Will thought, hadn't been worth what he paid. The women had been drunk, indifferent to the point of boredom when they weren't in a rush to get it over with. Those acts not only had shamed him, but had dashed his hopes of discovering the magic he'd foolishly believed was associated with a man and a woman lying down together. The magic he used to long for, but had come to accept as nonexistent, or a will-o'-the-wisp that was always just beyond reach. His reach, anyway.

Across the fire, Josie was frowning again, poking a stick at the coals. Her lithe, slim legs were tucked under her red satin skirt, which was a relief since Will was tired of trying not to look at them. Still, there were her sleek arms, not to mention the significant swell of her breasts above the top of her dress.

"Live and let live," he muttered again, dragging his gaze away from the fire to the cool darkness beyond.

"I agree completely," she said. "Even for folks with inclinations like yours." Her voice was as casual as if she were talking about the weather. Then she sighed again. "I suppose you have a special gentleman friend."

"God Almighty, lady. Give it a rest, will you?" Will lurched to his feet so fast anyone would have thought his pants were on fire.

His movement startled Josie, who gave a little gasp and drew back. The stick was still in her hand, and its glowing tip broke off and fell into the folds of her skirt. Will saw it drop, and no sooner had it fallen than the red skirt started smoking and going up in flames.

It was Josie who lurched to her feet now, slapping at the fiery fabric and screaming to beat the band.

Will reached out to grab her before she took off running and burned herself to a crisp. In her panic, she started slapping him.

"Get down!" he shouted. Then, when she didn't, he knocked her legs out from under her. Josie hit the ground hard, and Will promptly fell on top of her, smothering the flames.

They lay there a long moment—Will on top, Josie flattened beneath him, burned satin and nothing else between them. He could feel her heart pounding nearly as hard as his own. Right against his own. He levered up on his elbows, looked down to find her pretty face just inches from his own and a peculiar grin on her lips.

"Holy hellfire," she breathed softly.

"It's out now. You're all right."

"Oh, I know that." She blinked. "That isn't what I meant. I meant you, Will. Your face right now. Your eyes. You look..."

"Like somebody who's just had the daylights scared out of him," he finished for her.

"No," she whispered. "Like somebody who's contemplating a kiss."

She could see that? It was true. Not that he wanted to *do* it so much as just sort of savor the thought of it. A kiss. Feeling those soft lips against his. What kind of idiot, Will wondered, put out one fire and then was instantly lit up by another? He ought to deny it, but the words wouldn't come.

Josie whispered again, her warm breath riffling against his mouth. "Go ahead, Will."

He did. He lowered his head and pressed his lips against hers—lips that were even softer than he'd imagined. Gently at first. But then, when her arms slinked up around his neck and her fingers threaded through his hair, the kiss got clean away from Will. He was barely aware of anything except Josie's mouth—sweet and wet as molasses—until somebody groaned and, to his dismay and utter embarrassment, he realized it was him.

Will levered up and off Josie as if she were still on fire. As if he were. And, damn it, he *was*. He thought right then he'd rather feel his shirt and pants go up in flames than the way his body felt at that moment. At least he'd know how to put out a clothes fire. He slapped at his pant leg anyway, and the dust lifted like thin smoke.

"That was some kiss, Will." Josie was leaning back on her elbows, gazing up at him.

"Well, it's over," he muttered.

"I knew you'd be a good kisser," she said, "the minute I laid eyes on you."

Will ground out an oath and walked to his bedroll, while Josie kept babbling about kissing and her amazing powers of observation and matches in her heart. He shook out his blanket with a vengeance, slung himself down on it, crossed his arms and closed his eyes. Unfortunately, he couldn't close his ears.

"Of course—" Josie was still going on "—there's nothing that says a man of your persuasion wouldn't be a good kisser, is there? I mean, it's still just two pairs of lips, right? No matter whose they are."

"Go to sleep, Josie," he ordered.

He heard her sigh as she got to her feet, then mutter and whine about her burned dress awhile before she settled into her bedroll. He heard her rooting and thumping around like a dog trying to carve out a place to sleep. The last thing Will heard her say before she fell asleep was "Such a confounded waste."

*   *   *

The next day, Will pretty much confined his conversation to "Yep" and "Nope" as they rode through the sage-dotted hills south of Santa Fe. In fact, it was late afternoon before he spoke his first whole sentence.

"Agate's another two or three hours west, but we can camp here if you're too tired to go on."

Josie rode up beside him. "I'm not tired," she said. "I slept fine last night."

Will slanted her a challenging look from under his hat brim. "When you weren't crying and shivering, you mean?"

"I did not."

"You did, too," he shot back, churlish as a kid. He knew, for God's sake, because he'd been awake half the night, holding her, trying to comfort her. Not that she'd been the least bit grateful, then or now.

She planted her hands on her red satin hips. "Don't you think I'd remember it if I had?"

Will shook his head, half in bafflement, half in disgust. "Lady, I've about concluded that you only remember what you want to, while conveniently forgetting the rest." Then he dug his heels into his horse and pulled ahead.

Two hours later, at sunset, they crested San Angelo Hill. Just below, the little town of Agate sat, kind of squat and comfortable, among the cottonwoods along San Angelo Creek. Lord, he was glad to be home, Will thought.

For a minute, he even forgot to worry about what he was going to do with Josie Dove once he got there.

But there was one worry that he knew for certain he needed to attend to before they rode into town.

"Look," he said, "about my leanings..." He swiped off his hat and ran the brim through his fingers. Lord, he hated talking about sex. He hoped she'd think the pink in his cheeks was just a reflection of the setting sun.

Josie grinned. "I won't say anything. I can understand your wanting to keep a lid on it. Guess you do your business out of town, huh?"

"No, God damn it," he growled. "You don't understand. I lied. I'm, well... I'm not that way."

She didn't say a word at first. Just stared at him, her mouth hanging open slightly, her eyes big and wide, looking more stunned than aggrieved. "You're not?" she said finally, her question coming out on a gust of breath.

"No, I'm not. And I'd appreciate it if you'd just add that to your list of things to forget. All right?"

She nodded enthusiastically. "All right. It's already erased from my brain."

"Good. Let's go then. Time for me to be getting back to work." He started to nudge his horse forward, down the hill, but Josie stopped him.

"Wait a minute, Will. You never did tell me just what it is you do for a living."

"I don't remember your asking." He gave her a little sideways grin as he unlatched his saddlebag and reached in for the badge he kept stowed there, then dipped his chin in order to pin it on his shirt. "There you go, Josie. That's what I do. Now let's get going."

She just sat there a minute, smiling, watching him move down the hill. Watching his fine hands and their firm grip on the reins. His broad shoulders narrowing to his gunbelt. The way his backside met the saddle. Lord, he was such a beautiful man. And a *real* man, too, it turned out.

But then Josie stopped smiling. That bruise, that little shadow deep inside her, twitched hurtfully. If Mrs. Schumacher was right and Josie had indeed done something terribly wrong in her past, she sure didn't need to be taking up with a lawman. Fine-handed or not.

Chapter Three

And the last place Josie wanted to visit was the jailhouse, but that was where Will took her upon their arrival in town. She stood just inside the door as Will strode to a desk where a potbellied man was slumped and snoring in a swivel chair.

"I'm back, Burley," Will said, picking up a stack of mail, riffling through it, then whacking the man's boots where they were propped on a corner of the desk top. "Wake up, Burley."

The deputy lurched up with a snort. He scrubbed his face with the palms of his hands, then twitched his salt-and-pepper mustache and smiled groggily. "Hey, Will. I must've dozed off there for a minute."

"I can see that." Will's gaze canted toward the two cells at the rear of the office, where two lumpy blankets covered two rickety cots. "Who's that you've got locked up?"

"Hiram Freeze and Joe Broder. Who else? They each had a snootful and got into it again. Broke a mirror over at the Green Parrot, so I'm letting them sleep it off here, where they won't do any more damage." The deputy shrugged. "Otherwise, it's been real quiet. How was your trip, Will? I see you brought a little something back." Burley angled his head toward the door.

Will sighed. "Burley Watson, meet Josie Dove."

"How do, missy?" Below his shaggy mustache, the deputy's mouth split in a grin. "You sure are a pretty one. Isn't she pretty, Will? Why, I don't think I've ever seen—"

Will cut him off with a curt "Yep." Then he said, "You can go on back to sleep now, Burley. I'll see you in the morning." He strode to the door, took Josie by the elbow and muttered, "Come on," as he propelled her outside.

"I thought I could put you up in a cell for a night or two," he said, "but I guess that wasn't such a good idea."

It was a terrible idea, Josie thought. Those iron bars had given her the willies. "Couldn't I just stay with you?" She gazed up hopefully at him, a little smile perched on her lips.

"Nope."

But neither, as it turned out, could she stay at the town's only hotel—"Sorry, Will, there's people doubled up in all my rooms right now"—or its sole boardinghouse, where the female proprietor took one look at Josie in her scorched red satin and slammed the door in her face.

"Well, I guess I'll have to stay with you," she said, trying not to sound too happy.

"I guess not." Will grasped her by the elbow and started down the street.

"Where are we going now?"

"The Green Parrot. That's one place you won't be turned away."

Just from his tone of voice, Josie knew the Green Parrot was going to be like Sharkey's, a smoky place that smelled like beer, where people kept disappearing up the stairs and into the back rooms. She balked. "I'm not in that much of a rush to ply my trade," she said. But Will kept dragging her along until he pulled her through a pair of batwing doors into the dim, foul-smelling saloon.

If ever he'd seen a den of iniquity, Will thought, this was it. He stood in the doorway with Josie in the curl of his arm, wondering why the place looked worse, darker and tawdrier, than it ever had, and then it dawned on him that it was because the mirror over the long oak bar was broken. The unreflected light from the brass chandeliers seemed as yellow as old newspapers now. All the eyes that stared his way—his and Josie's—seemed dull and lusterless.

"Well, who's this, Sheriff?"

Will looked down into the thin, eager face of Jake Vestal, the saloon's proprietor. The man reminded him of a weasel who'd just glimpsed a plump little hen. Or a pretty little dove.

"Heard your mirror got busted," Will said. "Anybody hurt?"

Jake shook his head, much more interested in Josie than in his broken mirror. "What's your name, honey? Are you looking for work?"

Before Josie could reply, Will did—gruffly. "No, she's not. Not now, anyway." He clamped his arm around her waist. "Come on."

"You don't belong in a place like that," he muttered, once they were out in the street again.

Josie grinned. "That's what I've been trying to tell you. Where are you taking me now?"

"My place." He set his jaw and lengthened his stride. "Temporarily. Just till I can figure out what to do with you."

"This is nice, Will," Josie said. "Sort of."

The small adobe structure on the west side of town was closer to a shack than a home, she thought, but, seeing as she had no home herself, who was she to criticize? Will struck a match and lit a lamp. Josie stopped peering at her surroundings and instead watched the way the lamplight warmed his face and carved out hollows beneath his strong cheekbones.

She was determined to ignore the way his forehead was rutted with irritation at the moment, and the grim slant of his wonderful mouth. Her gaze strayed to his hand as he put the lamp down on a table. Her heart flickered again.

"Where's your bed?" she asked. "I mean, where do you sleep?"

Will walked to a doorway and drew aside the blanket that served as a door. "You can take the bed in here. I'll make do with the sofa."

"Oh, you don't have to—"

"Stop it." His voice was a barely controlled bellow. "I'm tired. I don't even want to talk about this tonight. All right?"

He stalked into the bedroom and lit another lamp, whose light revealed rumpled sheets and a tattered quilt on a narrow iron bed. There was a book on the nightstand, topped by a pair of steel-rimmed spectacles.

Josie picked up the glasses. "Yours?" she asked, squinting through them.

Will snatched them out of her hand. "Sure they're mine. Who else would they belong to?"

While he proceeded with a valiant attempt to straighten out the bedcovers, Josie picked up the leather-bound volume and read the gilt title on its spine. *"Great Expectations!"* she exclaimed. "Oh, this is a wonderful book, Will. I read it twice. No sooner finished it than I started again right back on page one."

Will tucked the quilt under the mattress, then straightened up. "When did you read it?" he asked.

"What?" Josie's eyes jerked from the volume to his face. His blue eyes were dark and narrow with suspicion.

"When did you read that book, Josie?"

"I...I don't know." Her heart was pounding, all of a sudden. A lump lodged in her throat, and her fingers tightened on the book till her knuckles turned white. Something. What? Who? She shook her head. She didn't want to know.

"Josie?" Will was beside her now, but she didn't even remember his coming around the bed. "Josie?"

"Here." She jammed the volume into his hands. "You'll be wanting this."

"You remembered something, didn't you? This book brought it back."

"No," she said, then tried to coax her tense mouth into a yawn. "I'm just tired, Will. More than I thought. Would you mind pulling that curtain closed on your way out?"

He minded, but he did it anyway, despite his urge to ask her more questions. She'd remembered something just then, and Will wanted to know what. The sooner he found out who she was, the sooner he could send her packing, off where she belonged. Because she didn't belong here.

Will tossed the book onto a pile of papers, then glared around the cramped, half-furnished room that served him as parlor and kitchen and dining room. Now it was his bedroom, too, he thought glumly, settling his large frame on the too-small sofa. The sooner he solved the mystery of Josie Dove, by God, the sooner he could have his confounded bed back.

He was a lawman, damn it. Solving mysteries was his job. He was good at it. He just wasn't any good with women.

"For pity's sake, Will. Stop and let me catch my breath."

Will halted halfway up the outside stairs, turned and looked down at Josie in her new white shirtwaist and long blue skirt. The scorched red satin dress was in a trash barrel in back of the dry-goods store now, but— even primly covered—Josie's curves were still in evidence. More so because she was breathing hard.

"Where in the world are you taking me *now?*" Panting, she lifted a hand to shade her eyes as she read the sign overhead: Curtis Malone, Photographer.

Fetching Portraits. Studio or in the Great Outdoors.
"A photographer? What in blue blazes are you doing, Will?"

What he was doing was following the plan he'd figured out the night before. What he was doing was cleaning her up and then having her picture taken to send to newspapers all over the territory, in the hope that someone would recognize her and take her off his hands. What he was doing was trying not to look too long at her pretty face and soft curves.

Then he was trying not to notice the overly fond way Curtis looked at her while he was setting up his camera, or to mind the way the man's hands lingered just a tad too long when he was posing her.

Then, walking her home, Will was trying to remind himself that, under the swell of her starched, high-necked bodice and the sway of her fine new skirt, Josie was still a working girl.

He was thinking so hard he nearly tripped when Josie drew up short by the vacant lot next to the livery, where the Carson boys—all four of them—were playing a lively game of catch.

"What's wrong?" he asked, noticing that her face had gone as white as her shirt. She had turned her back to the Carson kids and closed her eyes. "Josie? What's the matter?"

She bit down on her lip a moment before she answered. "Nothing. I don't know. One of those boys just reminded me of somebody, that's all. Let's go."

Then she took his arm and tugged him along without ever looking back at the vacant lot. Once they were at his place, she paced around the room, wringing her hands and chewing her lip.

"I gotta get back to work," Will said, pulling his hat brim through his fingertips. Much as he'd wanted to get away from her earlier, he hated leaving her now, when she seemed so distressed. "Are you gonna be all right?"

"Oh, sure." She let her hands fall to her sides and gave him a faint smile. "I'll be fine. You go on."

He was halfway across his weedy little yard when she called out to him. There was a funny note of urgency, almost fear, in her voice.

"Will?"

"Yeah?"

"Could you ask those boys to play someplace else? You're the sheriff. Could you do that?"

"Well, sure I could, Josie, but they're not causing any trouble, and I..."

"I know, but..." Her deep frown smoothed out suddenly and she smiled. "No. Of course they're not causing any trouble. I was just being silly." She waved him on, shooing him toward the street. "It's all right. Really. You go on to work and I'll see you later."

Then she stepped back inside and closed the door, leaving Will scratching his head and wondering what all that had been about.

At five-thirty, when Josie heard Will's footsteps in the yard, she felt that little spark in her heart again as she whisked off her apron and gave her hair a pat. A quick glance around the room was enough to convince her that her hard work was evident. The place was straightened and dusted. The lamps had clean chimneys. There was a new calico curtain on one of the windows and stew bubbling on the stove.

She looked out the window to see Will's head angled under the pump and her heart fluttered again. How anybody could look so good just cleaning up for supper was an amazement to her.

She was peppering the stew when Will finally came through the door. "Supper's almost ready," she called over her shoulder. When there was no reply, Josie turned to find him staring—gawking really—at the clean room.

"What's all this?" He gestured from the stove over the dusted tabletops and wound up pointing at the window.

"Nothing," she said. "I just tidied up some. Sit down now. Your supper will be on the table in two shakes."

Will's gaze came back to Josie. She couldn't quite decide whether he was surprised or confused, especially when his sole remark was "It's Monday," as he moved past her into the bedroom.

It wasn't quite the reaction Josie had been anticipating, but then, she already knew Will Curry wasn't a man who made bouquets with words. And flowery speeches weren't what she wanted from him, anyway, she reminded herself. She wanted to learn everything his fine hands could teach her. Soon. Maybe tonight.

She had just ladled his stew into a bowl when Will reappeared, buttoning a boiled shirt and looking handsome and mad all at once.

"You should have asked," he said irritably, while he stabbed in his shirttails and glowered at the table with its folded napkins and carefully laid out utensils. "It's Monday."

"You said that, Will."

He ran his fingers through his wet hair. "I have supper out. Every Monday. With Helen Hogan. A widow I've been keeping company with for some time."

"Oh."

She'd been smiling up until then, but Will watched her smile dry up like a creek in summertime. Well, hell. If she'd asked him first, he might have prevented her disappointment. She should've asked. Or maybe he should've said something, but then, he hadn't guessed a prostitute would start behaving so domestically. He didn't even know they could clean, for God's sake, or sew, or—he caught a good whiff of the hearty stew—or cook. And Josie's stew smelled better than any of the fancy dried-out concoctions Helen had put on her table over the years.

"I'm sorry," he said, more gruffly than he meant to. "You go ahead and eat, Josie."

Her wounded eyes lifted to his. A hopeful little smile flickered across her lips. "What time will you be back?"

"Late," he said. "Real late."

"Midnight?"

Will shook his head.

"One o'clock? Two?"

He could feel his cheeks heat up now. He stared down at his boot tips a minute before muttering,

"Later. More like morning," and heading for the door.

Helen Hogan's two-story frame house was on the east side of town, as far from the honky-tonks and the hotels that catered to prospectors as the dusty streets of Agate would allow. Will walked there slowly. Twice, he almost turned back, but he told himself Helen was expecting him, and seeing her as he always did on a Monday was the right thing to do.

The smart thing to do, too, under the circumstances, he decided. Josie, with her pretty face and undisguisable curves, had his blood simmering. He'd been walking around town all day, his mind only partly on his job, his brain insisting on locating itself—like a rock—between his legs. Spending the night with Helen ought to take care of that problem, even if only temporarily.

Women! They'd never been much more than an itch he had to scratch from time to time. A thorn in his hide. A necessary evil. Worse, they made him feel uncomfortable and foolish for wishing for more. They made him feel guilty and a failure.

He'd been a failure thirteen years ago with his bride. Evie had cried so hard on their wedding night even though he'd tried to be gentle and slow. After that, there had always been an excuse for not joining him in their bed, the biggest one being that their first time had taken and Evie was carrying his child. Then his baby had been born dead and his wife had died cursing him for ever touching her.

"You killed me, Will," she had whispered.

He'd only meant to love her.

Now there was Helen, who had her eye on a wedding ring, who let him but took no pleasure in his touch. He'd read a book once—one he'd picked up in Albuquerque—with suggestions, but Helen had slapped his hand when he touched her where the book had directed. Every Monday—afterward, when she thought he'd fallen asleep—she'd get out of bed and wash. Scrub and rinse, then scrub and rinse again, as if she meant to remove any trace of him. Then, every Tuesday morning, she'd pretend it had never happened, that they had just had supper and nothing else.

Will opened her gate now and walked to her door like a condemned man. When Helen answered his knock, she looked as sour as a prison warden, and severe, with her yellow hair pulled back in a tight knot.

She crossed her arms and jutted her chin up into his face. "You've got your nerve coming here, Will Curry."

"It's Monday," he said lamely.

"Surely you don't expect to see me while you've got that . . . that woman in your house."

Will soundlessly cursed Burley for his big mouth and *that woman* for her very existence. "It isn't what you're thinking, Helen."

"I'm thinking I don't want to see you, Will, until she's gone. How dare you come *here*—" Her hazel eyes scorched a path down the street "—when she's *there?*"

Well, she wouldn't be for long, Will thought morosely as he sat at his desk five minutes later. All in all,

Helen had a legitimate complaint, he decided. Even though she was wrong.

He snapped the pen out of its brass holder, stabbed it into the inkwell and proceeded to compose eleven letters to territorial newspapers and to enclose eleven photographs of Josie that had barely had time to dry. The twelfth picture he put in his desk drawer. As if he needed a reminder of the woman who was ruining his life.

When he got home, close to midnight, Josie was still sitting right where he'd left her, a bowl of cold, congealed stew close to her elbow. The minute he walked in, her glum face lit up. She left the chair and flew into his arms.

"I knew you'd come back, Will. I just knew it. You can take me now, if you want."

Will snagged her arms from around his waist and took a step back. "God Almighty—I *don't* want."

Josie flounced back to the table, moving as if she were still in short red satin rather than dignified dark blue. She plopped in the chair. "Well, maybe tomorrow," she said with a sigh. "I wish you wanted me, 'cause I've just gotta learn."

"I don't want you," he said through clenched teeth. "And, believe me, even if I did, there's nothing I can teach you. Nothing you don't already know." He flung his hat onto the sofa and ripped his fingers through his hair. "Hell, you probably know a lot more than I do."

"I doubt that," she muttered, planting her chin in her hands. "I just can't figure out why you don't want me. Free. Don't you think I'm pretty?"

Will let his breath out in a long, laborious sigh. "I think you're pretty, Josie. It isn't that. I just never did have much luck with women."

Her gaze lifted and her lashes fluttered. "With sex, you mean?"

"Yeah," he growled, feeling his face heating up all over again. "With sex. You sure call a spade a spade, lady."

"It's my job. Sex. Only..." She cocked her head to the side. "Is there something wrong with you? With your, well...equipment?"

"My equipment is just dandy, thank you kindly," Will shot back, intensely and painfully aware of that equipment at the moment. "And it's none of your business."

"So you're saying you're lucky at cards but unlucky in love? Is that right?"

"That's about the sum of it." Will slumped down on the sofa and started taking off his boots. He could feel Josie's eyes on him and looked up to find her grinning. "What?" he asked, tugging off a sock.

"Oh, nothing." Josie stood, stretched and yawned, then sauntered toward the bedroom. "I was just thinking," she said.

"Quit thinking," he muttered. "Go to sleep." With a weary, worn-out grunt, Will slung his long legs over the short arm of the sofa. He closed his eyes. Then opened one. Josie was still standing in the doorway, smiling at him. Lord have mercy. "Now what?"

"Nothing. I was just thinking what a shame it is for such a fine-handed man to have such bad luck. That maybe it's about to change." She gave a little shrug, smiled another odd smile, then disappeared behind the curtain before Will could tell her he sincerely doubted that.

Chapter Four

Will's luck did change later that week. For the worse. He'd spent every day since Monday feeling sorry for himself. He had a permanent crick in his neck from sleeping on the sofa, not to mention a perpetual ache below his beltline. Between suffering from the chilly glances and cold shoulders Helen gave him when she passed him on the street and fending off Josie's increasingly warm advances at home, Will felt like a man sweating in the grip of a weeklong fever.

Then, on Sunday morning, instead of being awakened by the bell in the tower of Padre Diego's church, Will was jolted out of sleep by the sound of gunfire, an unusual occurrence in Agate, where the drunks tended more to fists than firearms and the prospectors were generally worn out and therefore well behaved. At the sound of the shots, Will put on his pants and gunbelt. A minute later, he was standing in the middle of the excited crowd outside the Green Parrot.

"What's going on?" he asked Jake Vestal.

The weasel-faced barkeep sneered. "Joe Broder and Hiram Freeze," he said. "They broke my mirror the other night. Now they're back to break whatever's left."

When Will started toward the saloon's front door, Jake gripped his arm. "Not that way, Will," he cautioned. "They're popping anyone who goes near that door."

Will swore. "Is your back door unlocked?"

"The window is."

In the alley behind the Green Parrot, Will muttered a chorus of curses as he fit his sizeable frame through the narrow window. When his feet met the cool tile of the storeroom floor, he realized he'd been in such a rush he'd forgotten to put his boots on. Still, he thought, that made it easier to sneak behind the bar and get the drop on the two drunks.

Even though he'd been a lawman for a dozen years—and a soldier for several years before that—Will hated having to use his gun. Especially on belligerent drunks like Freeze and Broder, neither of whom had the intelligence of a horse apple.

Thank God he only had to draw on them to bring them to their senses.

"We was only fooling around, Will," Hiram Freeze mumbled when Will muscled both him and Joe through the front door.

"Well, you can fool around in jail for a few days, boys, and then you can get out of Agate for good." Will shoved the two drunks toward Burley Watson, who had joined the crowd outside. "Lock 'em up, Burley," he growled.

"Sure thing, Will." The deputy's gaze lowered to the dirt street. "You best see the doc about that foot. It looks bad."

Bad? Will glanced down, thinking his bare foot seemed fine, even though it was at the end of a distinct trail of blood that led from the saloon into the street. While he stood there staring, a pool of glossy blood spread around his toes and mixed with the dirt in the street. Then, suddenly, as if seeing were believing, as if believing were feeling, his foot started to hurt like all hell and Will felt as if he were standing on a red-hot coal.

"Hold still," Josie said, echoing the elderly doctor's command, but with a good deal more softness and sympathy when Will kept trying to jerk his foot out of the man's gnarled grip. She brushed a hank of damp hair from Will's forehead and then rested her hand on his shoulder while Doc Reese continued his assault on the sole of Will's foot.

"Those are awful big tweezers, Doc," she murmured.

"These are awful big cuts, Miss Josie." The doctor squinted up at his patient. "What'd you do, Will? Run barefoot through a shooting gallery or a fun house? Half of what I'm getting out of your foot is mirror."

In reply, Will snorted and took another swig from the whiskey bottle the doctor had produced from his cracked leather bag as soon as he determined the extent of his patient's injuries.

It had just about broken Josie's heart to see Will limping home that morning. In the week she'd known

him, she'd come to regard him as strong and inde-
structible, not to mention sober and stoic—none of
which he was at the moment. The whiskey that was
supposed to lessen his pain was also loosening his
tongue, and he cursed a dark blue streak when Doc
Reese dabbed tincture of iodine on him after he finished sewing up the deepest of the cuts.

"I want you to soak that foot in hot, soapy water
later on," the doctor said as he took his leave. "And
see that you stay off it for at least a couple of days. I'll
try to locate you a pair of crutches, but in the meantime, Miss Josie can do for you. You're lucky to have
her here, Will."

Will snorted again and muttered, "Lucky."

He had the same reaction, Josie noticed, when his
deputy stopped by.

"You just rest easy now," Burley said. "You're one
lucky son of a gun, Will, to have such a pretty lady
seeing to your needs."

"You're lucky you weren't shot," Josie said after
she waved goodbye to Burley and closed the door.

"Lucky," Will said again after another long pull
from the bottle. He put his bandaged foot up on the
arm of the sofa and, sighing, stretched out his long
frame, then turned his head toward Josie. The look he
gave her was one she had never seen before. His eyes
were dark under their half-mast lids. When he spoke,
there was a sultry timbre in his voice. "Come over
here."

Josie was tempted to glance over her shoulder to see
if he was talking to somebody else. She approached
the sofa slowly, not knowing what to expect, as if she

were afraid the worn piece of furniture might explode into flames at any moment. Or as if Will might.

He reached out, found the hem of her skirt, fumbled through her underskirt, then slid his hand up her leg.

Josie gasped. "What the devil are you doing?"

His lips slid into a grin and his fingers splayed out on her bare thigh. "What you've been wanting me to do ever since Las Vegas."

"Oh, no, you're not, Will Curry." She stepped back from his errant hand. "Of all the fool ideas. You're going to soak that foot, just like the doctor told you to."

Turning her back on him, Josie marched to the dry sink, grabbed a pail and almost ran outside to the pump, where she set the handle going vigorously—the same way her heart was pumping. What in the world was wrong with her, saying no when she'd been dying to say yes all week? She could still feel that fine hand moving up her leg and feel the warmth on her thigh where Will's fingers had clutched her. At his touch, a wave of wanting had surged through her, more powerful than any she'd ever imagined. And she had turned him down.

While the water pounded into the pail, Mrs. Schumacher's voice sounded in Josie's head. *This man you will choose, Josie. You will probably fall a little bit in love with him, and that will be good. It will help you feel. But don't take it so seriously,* liebchen. *You cannot be a success in this business if you fall so very much in love. You must learn all you can from him and then leave him.*

Water sloshed over the side of the bucket onto Josie's feet, bringing her back to the here and now. Maybe she was a little bit in love with the handsome sheriff, she admitted to herself. Her heart had certainly melted when she saw him limping home. Maybe she was afraid of falling in love too much. Or maybe, she told herself, she'd only spurned his advances because she was a little bit afraid of what would follow the feel of that fine hand on her leg or where that hand might go next.

Whatever it was, it made for a pretty dismal picture. A whore whose heart had melted and whose insides were quivering with fear now that Will was so, well . . . willing. Best just get on with your lessons, she told herself. Then she picked up the full pail and walked back inside the house.

"I'm sorry." Will meant it, but he wasn't accustomed to apologizing so it had taken him awhile. As long as it had taken Josie to heat up a kettle of water and to shave some soap flakes into a shallow pan. All the while, he'd lain there watching her, blaming his bad behavior on too much liquor and too bad luck and too long without a woman and too long with one whose every movement seemed designed to get him stirred up.

Even her clothes. Josie had put her prim, high-collared white shirt aside a few days ago and had taken to wearing the low and loose-necked *camisas* favored by the local Mexican girls. She'd traded her long blue skirt for a calico that showed off her shapely ankles.

Clothes that went on easy and—in Will's imagination anyway—came off easier.

He *was* sorry, too. Not so much that he had touched her the way he had as that he'd broken the vow he'd made to himself not to do it. His resolution was only partly based on the fact that Josie was a prostitute. In spite of all his hard luck, Will still placed enough honor on the exchange between men and women that he didn't want any part of sex for money. Mostly, though, it was Josie herself and the way he thought about her all day, every day. The way he couldn't wait to get home to see her. The way he'd begun to wish he hadn't been quite so hasty in mailing her pictures off to those eleven papers.

It was the way she'd looked at him with such sweet concern when he hobbled home this morning, and the way she'd fluttered around trying to help the doc, and the way she was moving toward him now, chewing her lip and glaring at the brimming pan of warm soap water, as if that alone would keep it from spilling.

It was because he was a cautious man and couldn't see the profit in caring for a woman who was a mystery. Who would be gone once that mystery was solved.

"I'm sorry, Josie," he said again as he sat up and unwound the bandage from his foot and then proceeded to scrunch up his pant leg. "That was the whiskey talking before. And touching." He felt the blood rise in his face. "I won't be doing that again."

Kneeling on the floor, she helped guide his foot into the pan, then lifted her dark lashes. "Didn't you like it?"

Will gritted his teeth, as much to keep from yelping at the hot water as to keep from admitting he could still feel the heat of her flank burning his fingertips. He was staring down the loose neckline of her *camisa* now, imagining that same heat. No. Different. Hotter. More lush. "Of course, I liked it," he finally snarled. "What man wouldn't?"

Josie didn't answer that. Nor did she remove her hands once his injured foot was settled in the water. Her warm, soapy fingers slid up his calf and began to knead the tight muscles there.

"Feel good?" she asked idly.

"Oh, yeah..." Will leaned back and closed his eyes. He'd ask her to stop, he told himself, in a minute or two. It just felt so damn good being touched. So good. He told himself he could ignore the way the rest of his body was responding to the slow, strong glide of her fingers.

"Poor thing." Josie clucked her tongue softly. "It must hurt something awful, Will."

He blinked stupidly, wrenching his thoughts from his groin to his head. "What must hurt?"

"Your foot, silly." Her hand executed another of those long, smooth strokes from his ankle to his knee. When Will groaned, she said, "Maybe you should have a little more of that whiskey."

No. He thought he'd probably had too much already, but before he could say so, Josie was reaching across his lap for the bottle at the far end of the sofa, and he was reaching for her.

"Stop it. I don't want the whiskey."

Josie stopped, but not because of Will's command or even the surprising huskiness in his tone. It was the spread of his hand on her rib cage, which didn't restrain her so much as take possession of her. The match went streaking across her heart again, and this time it flared into a flame. Will's fingers twitched as if he felt it, too.

"I want you, Josie. Damn it."

She suspected there were dozens, maybe hundreds, of more courtly ways to get a woman into bed. Will's gruff statement sounded more like a criminal's confession than a lover's urgent plea, and his expression was more grim than amorous, but right then Josie didn't care. He wanted her! She scuttled off his lap and headed directly for the curtained bedroom, wrenching her shirt off as she went, twirling it over her head like a victorious banner.

She was under the covers when Will limped into the room. Looking even grimmer than he had before, he shoved aside her discarded skirt and petticoat, then lowered himself heavily onto the edge of the bed.

"Maybe this wasn't such a good idea," he said, all traces of huskiness gone from his vice, replaced by a kind of strained quaver.

Josie sighed. She was about to tell him she thought it was probably the best idea he'd ever had when the silence was broken by a distinct thunk against the side of the house, followed by laughter and a rush of footsteps.

Just outside the bedroom window, a boyish voice called, "How can I catch it, Aaron, if you're always throwing the durn thing over my head?"

"Butterfingers!" came a taunt from the street.

"Here!" yelled the boy in the yard. "Now toss it right this time, will you?"

Will growled and started to rise, but Josie clutched at his sleeve.

"It's just those Carson kids," he said. "I'll run 'em off."

"No. Don't go, Will. Don't leave me," she begged just a second before the sound of breaking glass in the living room and a cry of "Cripes! Now you've done it, Aaron. You broke the sheriff's window."

Will muttered an oath. All he needed now was more broken glass, he thought, not to mention Josie's sharp fingers digging into his arm like eagle talons. He was likely to bleed to death before the day was done.

Her face was whiter than the sheet she was clutching to her chest. Her green eyes were huge and blank of all but fear.

"Josie. Honey." Will disengaged his arm from her grip and held her hand in his. "It's okay. Just some boys playing catch." He shook his head and added under his breath, "Not too well, either."

She stared over his shoulder, seeing, not seeing. Surely not comprehending. Will recognized the hundred-yard stare of a soldier in the thick of battle.

What battle? He grasped her fragile shoulders and shook her gently. "What is it? What are you remembering, Josie?"

She blinked and brought her eyes into soft focus on his face. "What?"

"What was it? Those boys playing ball? Did they make you remember something?"

"No. I..." Her gaze got faraway again as her green eyes glazed with tears. "Nothing."

"Tell me," Will urged quietly. "I want to help you." He brushed a stray hank of hair from her cheek. "Your memories are important."

A frail smile touched her lips. "Are they? Why?"

"They'll help me figure out who you are, where you came from. That's why." He gave her another little shake for emphasis.

"What difference does it make where I came from?" She shrugged his hands from her shoulders, then lay back and pulled the covers up, tucking them tightly under her chin. "What's important is where I'm going, isn't it?" Her voice sounded dreamy and distant. "And right now, Will, if you don't mind, I'm going to sleep."

He didn't mind all that much being forced back into playing a lawman instead of a lover. At least it was a role he was good at. But Will did mind that Josie kept running away from her memories. Whatever the hell they were.

While he hobbled around sweeping up the broken window glass, he kept wondering what it was about those boys playing ball that bothered her so much. And, if it bothered her so much, why wasn't she the least bit interested in following the threads back to the whole cloth of the person she really was?

He sat on the sofa and put his foot into the pan of tepid soap water, wondering what it would be like if his mind was suddenly erased. If there was no Ma or Pa to keep in his heart. No sister's sweet face to recollect, even though she'd been dead for twenty years. No farm back in Tazewell County, Illinois. No rich black dirt. Nothing.

He'd miss that, he thought as he reached for the bottle and took a medicinal swig. On the other hand, he wouldn't miss having a few memories chopped out of his brain. A couple of bloody moments from the war. Evie and their sorry wedding night and her final deathbed accusation. He was thinking that maybe there was some solace in not remembering, after all, when he heard the woeful little sob that signaled the beginning of Josie's tortured dreams.

Will took one more swig of whiskey—for courage—before he rose and walked into the dark bedroom where Josie tossed and turned.

"It's all right, sugar," he whispered, easing beside her on the narrow bed, pulling her against him to offer what comfort he could.

Chapter Five

There was moonlight streaming, cool as a high-mountain creek, through the shuttered window. There was moonlight striping the walls and falling across the bed in silvery bars. Will wasn't exactly certain if he was awake or dreaming. All he knew for sure was that he was kissing Josie and touching her sleek bare skin. If it was a dream, then he didn't want to wake up. Awake, in daylight, he was too much the coward to get things under way. But now, in this moonlit dream, he and Josie were already beyond the awkward preliminaries. Well beyond.

Not that he knew what he was doing, quite frankly. But his hands seemed to be operating independent of his head and taking their cues from Josie's every warm shiver and each of her encouraging little moans. Up until this very moment, tears and silence and disappointment had been all that Will had ever known in bed. Never the sighs or the glad little noises this woman was making. Josie was nearly singing when his fingers skimmed her hip to the inside of her thigh. And she didn't quit or slap his hand away when it discovered the slick, satin warmth of her most intimate part.

Her song deepened to a low thrumming against his lips, and she moved against his hand—sinuously, urgently—as if she knew exactly what she was doing and precisely where she was going. For the moment, Will was more than happy to abandon himself to her journey.

At the touch of that fine hand, Josie let out another soft cry in a voice she barely recognized as her own. If she was supposed to be learning things, she thought, she'd best make an effort to clear the various pieces of her brain that kept fogging up every time Will touched her in a different place or shifted the angle of his kiss. She ought to be taking careful mental notes, she told herself, and making an effort to remember everything those fine hands were doing, but instead she kept giving in to the urge not to think at all, allowing herself to simply feel.

To feel everything. The scrape of Will's whiskery jaw on her skin and the wild sparks it shot all through her. The slow warmth of his wonderful hands. The coolness of his damp skin and the sheer heat of the muscles beneath it. His solid weight above her. His heart beating hard against hers, and his breath catching, and the urgent gruffness in his throat when he told her, "Now."

Yes, now. If she knew nothing else, Josie knew she needed him closer. Impossibly close. She needed him to touch that place deep inside her that she'd never been aware of until now, when it had suddenly become the burning core of the world. She needed him to put out those glorious flames. Or to fan them higher. Right then she didn't know which.

She felt a tug inside, a tearing that didn't hurt so much as surprise her, and then Will quit.

"Don't quit," she gasped. "Oh, don't stop."

Only a part of his warm weight was on her now. He had levered up on his elbows and was staring down at her. Half his face was in moonlight. Half was in darkness. All of it was confused.

"Josie." He exhaled her name, then promptly inhaled an oath. "Why didn't you tell me."

She blinked. "Tell you what?"

"That you're a virgin, for God's sake!"

She blinked again. "I am?"

Will shook his head, then let it sag into the warm crook of her neck. He might not know *who* she was, he thought bleakly, but he sure as hell knew *what* she was. Or rather what she'd been till just a minute ago.

"Jesus," he breathed. "How could you not know?"

"That's a stupid question," she snapped.

Yeah, Will guessed it was. About as stupid as what he'd just done. Making love to a sporting girl was one thing, but a man with a sliver of conscience didn't take a woman's maidenhood without serious, even matrimonial intentions. And all Will had intended was sex. Pure and simple. Which it wasn't anymore. Which *she* wasn't anymore.

He lifted his head and gazed down at her face. It was all pretty and silvery with moonlight, all composed in a thoughtful expression. Gently he brushed back the wild tangle of her hair.

"I'm sorry, Josie," he whispered.

"For what?"

"For hurting you." He kissed a corner of her mouth. "It never occurred to me that a prostitute would be a virgin, too. I mean, I just assumed . . ."

"You didn't hurt me, Will. And I was only learning my profession, you know. Doing what you might call an apprenticeship." She sighed. "I guess that's over now, though. Will?"

"Hmm?"

"That was nice." She reached up and curled a lock of his hair around her finger at the same time she moved her hips beneath his. "Could we do it again? Only slower this time, so I can take some notes?"

Will swallowed hard, thinking *again* wasn't quite the right word. *Finish* was more like it. "Now?" he asked, amazed and a little abashed by the crack in his voice.

But Josie didn't even seem to notice. She nodded happily. Her whole body, in fact, nodded gleefully beneath his. "Yes. Now, please."

By the time Will's foot had improved enough for him to go back to work two days—and two *nights*—later, the rest of his body was exhausted. Pleasantly worn out. Gloriously used up.

"You're looking a mite peaked, Will," Burley had said when Will walked into the office. "Foot feeling all right? Did you stay off it like you were s'posed to?"

"Yep."

He'd stayed off it nearly the whole time. In fact, he and Josie had barely left that narrow bed where they'd made love again and again. This way. That way. Every possible way two human bodies could align and attach themselves. They had been the best two days of Will's life. For a man who'd spent the major part of his life believing that physical pleasure had passed him by, it was as if he'd finally tumbled, quite by accident, into paradise.

Josie was still under the impression that he was the experienced one, and after a while he hadn't bothered to correct her anymore. He felt, well...pretty damn pleased with his newly discovered abilities.

The wonder of it was, though, that it went far beyond mere physical pleasure. While their bodies had touched, so had their minds. In the quiet spells between making love, they had talked and talked. Not that they'd said anything much, but Will couldn't remember ever having taken such delight in simple conversation. He couldn't recall any time in his life when he'd felt so damn happy.

Now, at the end of those two days—and *nights*—in bed, Will was beginning to think he'd fallen half in love with Josie Dove. Half, he cautioned himself, because he still didn't know who she really was. Half, he warned himself, because—for all his newfound talents as a lover—he was still a lawman and Josie was still a mystery.

Will leafed through the stack of legal notices and Wanted posters on his desk. He slit open an envelope addressed to him personally, only to discover it was an advertisement from a saddle maker in Albuquerque. "I don't suppose anything came in the mail while I was recuperating, did it, Burley? Something from one of the newspapers?"

"Nope. Just what's there."

Will didn't know whether to be happy about that or not. With a little sigh, he opened his desk drawer and stared at Josie's picture, mentally divesting her of the high-necked blouse and skirt, conjuring up a more intimate portrait. The Josie his hands and lips knew so well. The pretty, dark-haired woman he didn't really know at all.

"I expect you'll be hearing something one of these days," Burley offered, peering over Will's shoulder.

"I expect." Will closed the drawer. Right now he was just about as nervous as Josie at the prospect of what that something might be.

Josie stood in the doorway, watching Will walk home, thinking how she'd missed him ever since he'd left at eight o'clock in the morning. It had seemed like the longest day of her life, and even though she'd busied herself with cooking and sewing and laundering the well-used sheets, time had gone all too slowly. By four o'clock, she'd been glancing out the window every few minutes, hoping for a glimpse of Will.

He was favoring his good foot, she noticed, and not disguising it all that well by trying to make his limp look like a saunter. Nor could he hide the badge that was pinned to his shirt and glinted in the late-afternoon sunlight. For the past two days, it had been all too easy for Josie to forget that Will Curry was a lawman. That tin star was a pointed reminder now, and she felt her forehead wrinkle with worry as that dark spot inside her made its presence known. She closed her eyes for a moment in an effort to ignore it.

When she opened them again, she was standing in the sweet coolness of Will's shadow—where she'd longed to be all day.

"You're limping again," she said softly, raising her eyes to his face.

"Doesn't matter." He grinned almost sheepishly. "I missed you today. The damn clock in the jailhouse took twenty hours just to get to noon, then another twenty till it was quitting time." His hand curved around her waist, bringing her against him. He sighed as he rested his chin on her head. "I've been thinking, Josie."

"What about?"

"You. Me. Us. This is happening pretty fast."

"I guess." When Josie lifted her shoulders in a little shrug, one point of Will's badge pricked through the thick cotton of her blouse. She stifled a little gasp and stepped back from the sharp and painful reminder that she had secrets, perhaps evil ones, in her lost past. She was gripped for a second by an urge to flee, but then Will's arms surrounded her and pulled her against him again.

"You make me happy, Josie. And I'm not just talking about in bed. I couldn't wait to get home to you today. Just to see you. To hold you this way. Hell, I'm half in love with you, honey, only..." His chest expanded, then settled with a rough sigh. "Only I don't feel right asking you to marry me until I get some answers."

The answers, Josie thought bleakly, that would lead him to put a noose around her neck instead of a ring on her finger. "I'm not looking to get married, Will," she lied, trying to convince herself, as well, trying to infuse her voice with lightness. "You're sweet to ask, though."

It was Will who took a step back now, and who scowled down at her. He hadn't intended to propose. It was as if the notion of marriage had occurred to him at the very moment he was speaking the words themselves. And as much as it shocked him that he had actually proposed, it shocked him worse that Josie had turned him down. Hurt him, too, but he'd be damned if he'd let her know that.

"It was just a notion," he said, then wrenched his lips into a grin. "Forget I even mentioned it."

Her lashes fluttered up coquettishly. "I missed you today, too. In the worst way." She linked her arms around his waist and pressed her cheek to his chest. "Can't we just keep on the way we have been? There's still so much I want to learn."

What could possibly be left? Will wondered. But it wasn't a minute after that that Josie had him by the hand and was tugging him toward the bedroom where those surprising lessons resumed.

Later, in the dark, when he was holding her and keeping her bad dreams at bay, he told himself that their present arrangement was best. He wasn't the sort of man to go off half-cocked and marry a woman whose true name he didn't even know. A woman whose haunted dreams might come to haunt him, too. Josie was right, he assured himself. It was best not to make things permanent. At least not till he knew who the hell she really was.

Of course, if she had it in mind that sooner or later she'd be moving on, taking all the things she'd learned here in his bed and sharing them with others, Miss Josie Dove—or whatever the hell her name was—had another think coming.

But only the summer moved on. June gave way to July and August. September arrived, turning the cottonwoods and aspens to yellow candles against the deep blue New Mexico skies. And Josie was still there.

Will had discreetly acquired a bigger bed, asking Burley to haul it up from Albuquerque and to deliver it in the dead of night. There was no point, he figured, in pointing out the obvious to the citizens of Agate, who for the most part had taken the sheriff's living arrangements in stride, once they got to know Josie Dove.

Amazingly enough, Will felt he'd gotten to know her, too. Not that he'd gotten any answers to his inquiries about her. Her past was still as much of a mystery as ever, in spite of his inquiries around the territory. His letters to the authorities in every New Mexico county had not included photographs this time but rather a description of her that had taken him half a day to compose because he kept getting distracted.

He'd write "dark hair" and then spend the next ten minutes thinking about how the sun tended to pick out blue threads in Josie's ebony tresses or how pretty they looked every morning spread out on a white pillowcase. Or he'd write "green eyes" and then put the pen down absently while he contemplated the inability of a simple word to capture the complex color of those eyes or the sadness that often flickered in their depths.

Often he'd find himself daydreaming, trying out names that might have suited her far better than the one the madam had given her. It irked him to no end that her sporting girl's name fit her so well with its perfect balance of gaiety and mournfulness. The Josie who was bright and happy during the day was the dove who still cried out in her sleep.

She was a puzzle who continued to resist his efforts at putting her together.

"Don't you miss not having memories to look back on?" he'd asked her one afternoon when they were picnicking on San Angelo Hill.

Josie had chewed thoughtfully on a pickled egg before she replied, and Will had imagined he saw a flicker of sadness in her eyes before she smiled and said, "What's important is now. Being here with you. These will be my memories, Will. I don't need any others."

"You need a birthday," he'd argued. "Damn it, Josie, you don't even know how old you are."

"Well, how old do I look?"

"I don't know. Twenty, maybe. Twenty-one."

"Sounds fine to me. What's today's date, Will?"

"August seventeenth."

She'd reached into the picnic basket for a chicken leg, then twirled it gaily and winked. "That sounds as good as any other day for my birthday, don't you think? Wish me happy birthday, Will."

He'd growled in reply. "It's not your confounded birthday."

"It could be."

Will had ripped his fingers through his hair. It was a gesture he'd perfected over the summer during similar confrontations. "Damn it, aren't you the least bit curious?"

But Josie, as always, had shaken her head adamantly, saying, "Nope."

"Josie . . ."

"It's *my* past, Will. I'll thank you to leave it alone. I figure if there was anything good in it, I wouldn't have forgotten it."

"Oh, for Christ's sake. That makes about as much sense as saying today's your birthday," he'd shot back right then, but ultimately that attitude had started to make complete sense to Will. And, though Josie never said it in so many words, it made sense, too—considering her bad dreams—that there probably was something bad, or at least unpleasant, in Josie's past that she was happy to run away from. Still, he wasn't the sort of man who ran from things. Or the sort of man who bought a pig in a poke—or married a mystery.

But as the summer wore on, Will's efforts to discover Josie's past seemed to become more and more halfhearted. He didn't mention marriage again, but it was always on his mind. It felt almost like a splinter in his brain, festering, worrying him. He decided, finally, that he liked Josie just the way she was—sweet and fresh, unburdened by a past or a glut of relatives or even a recorded birthday. Instead of puzzling him, Josie's lack of memory had begun to have a certain strange appeal for him. It made her belong to him exclusively.

By September, he found that he was going through the mail with more trepidation than curiosity. Maybe, he thought, he didn't want to know, either. Maybe he should just go ahead and marry her, live happily in wedded, if ignorant, bliss.

Will was about as torn as any man could be. He was still straddling what felt like a barbed-wire fence when, without warning, Helen Hogan and Josie Dove pushed him off. Helen with an ultimatum. Josie by throwing up her breakfast for the second day in a row.

Chapter Six

It was raining the morning Helen came into the jail-house, looking like a storm cloud in the shape of a woman. She shook her black umbrella and snapped it closed just inside the door.

Will glanced up from his paperwork, realizing all of a sudden that this was as close as he'd been to Helen in months. Her yellow hair seemed particularly pale and limp now that he was accustomed to Josie's dark, rich tresses. Helen seemed too tall, too thin despite her bustle. A reed trying to pass for a rosebush. Just all wrong. It nearly shocked him to remember he had shared this woman's bed on all those dismal Mondays. His breath hitched in his chest as if he were looking at a ghost. He almost wished she were.

"Morning, Miz Hogan," Burley said from the corner stove where he was pouring himself a cup of coffee. "This enough rain for you?"

"I'd like to speak with the sheriff," she announced, and when Burley just grinned and cocked his head toward the desk, she added a chilly "Alone."

Will rose from his chair with a soft sigh. Whatever Helen had to say to him—assuming she could get out any words at all from between her tightly clamped lips—he figured he had it coming. He handed Burley a stack of Wanted posters and a hammer. Then, after his deputy lumbered out into the rain like a sorrowful hound, Will gestured toward the chair on the other side of his desk. Helen sat on its edge, her back as stiff as its oak spindles, her fingers knotted in the strings of her handbag.

Angling a hip onto the desk top, Will crossed his arms. "It's good to see you, Helen," he said, when what he was actually thinking was that in her prissy little straw hat, her fussy bustle and her starched cotton gloves, Helen Hogan made Josie Dove look like a wild creature in comparison. Like a woman raised by coyotes. Hell, for all he knew, she had been. His heart gave a little kick against his rib cage and he bit down on a grin.

"I've been patient, Will," Helen said. She kept her gaze fixed somewhere between his kneecaps and the tips of his boots, and spoke slowly, distinctly, as if she were addressing a guilty child, which Will supposed was the case. She made him feel guilty, anyway. She always had.

"I've been extremely patient, as a matter of fact."

"I guess you have, Helen," he murmured.

"And I do believe I've been understanding, as well. Perhaps too much so. But my patience has worn thin and my tolerance has dried up." She gave her gloves a tug. "That . . . that woman's been in your house for three months now, Will. I simply won't stand for it anymore. You're going to have to choose."

Choose? Will could only stare at her. He'd made his choice months ago, only it just seemed to be truly dawning on him right this minute.

"That's fair," he said, not knowing how to continue. He didn't want to hurt Helen or her stiff-boned, thin-lipped dignity.

"It's more than fair. It's the decent thing to do. And then, after you've turned that harlot out of your house, I expect you to ask me to marry you, Will." Her hazel eyes ratcheted up to his face. "I expect you to make an honest woman of me. Otherwise, I feel I have no choice but to leave Agate and move someplace where my reputation hasn't been sullied."

Sullied. Will had a vision of those wretched Monday nights—of Helen, sighing with soft disgust and sneaking out of bed to wash. Helen, cool and prim on Tuesday mornings, as if he'd never touched her. Helen, making him feel ashamed of his physical needs, but willing to barter herself anyway—as Evie had done—in exchange for a wedding band.

He was sorely tempted to tell her he couldn't make an honest woman of her if he married her twenty times in twenty different churches.

"I'm going to marry Josie Dove," he said quietly, without cruelty. Just said it. And meant it, by God. He'd never meant anything more.

Helen's eyes flicked open wide. For an instant she looked shocked, even wounded, as if she were going to cry. But then those autumn-colored eyes narrowed to dry slits and she just looked mean.

"Marry her? Marry that . . . that . . ."

"That's enough, Helen," he cautioned.

"Damn you, Will Curry," she said, twisting her purse strings and winding herself tight before fairly springing from the chair. "All those years. Every filthy week, you were just using me. Using me despicably. I put up with it because I thought you were going to marry me. And now...*now* you're going to marry a whore, some piece of trash you've only known a few months." She shook her fist in his face. "Have you no morals at all? Have you no decency? You should be ashamed for what you did to me."

Will drew in a long breath. Yes, he was ashamed, he thought. And, yes, he was just about as decent as any man who had at least his fair share of morals. And, damn it, he would've stopped anytime Helen told him to, only she had been gritting her damn teeth so hard all the time, she never said no.

No use telling her, though. The more he said, the longer she'd wave her indignation—and her fist—in his face. Will stared at a gouge in the floor just beyond his boot tips, trying to look contrite. "I'm sorry, Helen."

After a little more poisonous invective, Helen stormed out of the office and slammed the door behind her.

When Burley came back in, he slapped his wet hat against his leg and grumbled, "Helen about put my eye out with that umbrella of hers. I always said that woman had the disposition of a rattlesnake. What'd she want, Will?"

"She's leaving town. Just wanted to say goodbye."

"Good riddance." The deputy tossed his hat toward the rack on the wall and missed.

Will hardly noticed on his way to the door.

"Look after things here for a while, will you, Burley? There's something I've gotta take care of at home."

Josie was bent over the woodpile by the side of the house, alternately muttering and throwing up, when she felt a warm hand settle on her back. She glanced through the wet cascade of her hair and had just enough time to identify Will and give him a weak smile before another wave of nausea racked her.

She wasn't sick. At least she didn't think so. But she had listened to the girls at Mrs. Schumacher's and at Sharkey's long enough and hard enough to know she was in trouble. Big trouble.

The rain eased off, but Will kept rubbing her shoulders and smoothing back her hair, standing behind her silently, his breathing even and his big hands as gentle as Josie supposed a mother's would be. For a bleak second, she wanted to cry out for her own mother, the one she didn't remember.

Without a word, Will offered her his handkerchief when she finally straightened up. His eyes were shimmering with a soft light, and his face was so full of sweetness and sober concern that Josie wanted to cry again. How she loved him, she thought, from the furrows on his forehead to the scarred soles of his feet and everything in between. She loved him to pieces, only she wasn't supposed to. Mrs. Schumacher had said she should only fall a little bit in love in order to learn her profession. And the madam had never said anything about...

"A baby, Josie?" Will asked in a voice as gentle as his hands. "Is that what this is all about?"

Josie nodded and shrugged. She felt wrung out, but still she tried to laugh. "Not such a good sign for a girl in my line of work, is it?"

"Pretty good sign for a wife, though."

Her gaze lofted to the yellow spires of the aspens by the river. "I'm not your wife."

"You should be." He coaxed her face back with a finger to her chin. "You will be as soon as you tell me yes."

"What are you saying, Will?"

"I'm asking you to marry me." He grinned sheepishly as he scraped his hat from his head. "Hell, Josie, maybe I didn't use all the flowery words a woman naturally expects, but..."

"That isn't what I meant," she said with some urgency as she stepped back, out of his reach. Suddenly she felt sick again, but for a far different reason. Sick and clammy with cold fear. "You told me you wouldn't ask me until you found out about my past. You said that you couldn't marry me until you knew who I was. Isn't that what you said, Will?"

"Yeah, that's what I said, but—"

Her hand flew to her mouth and she sucked in a sharp breath. "Oh, God. You found out something."

"Josie..." Will reached out for her, but she took another step back and batted his hands away.

"No! Stop it! I don't want to hear it!" she wailed. "I don't want to know!"

Josie spun away from him and clamped her arms around herself in a protective embrace. "Whatever you know about me, Will, I don't want to hear it."

She would have run then if Will hadn't looped his arms around her and pulled her back against him. His belt buckle pressed into her spine like a branding iron, and his words were warm at her ear.

"I'll tell you what I know about you, Josie Dove. You're beautiful and good and generous. You're soft and sweet and you make me feel like a hell of a man when you're lying in my arms. A hell of a *lucky* man. That's all I know. That's all I'll ever need to know."

Drawing in a breath, he let it out on a long, rough sigh. "As far as I'm concerned, darlin', neither one of us started living until we found each other. Nothing else counts. Nobody else counts. Just you and me."

His hand moved to her stomach and his fingers splayed out warmly. "You and me and this baby we've made. We have the future, Josie. Neither one of us needs a past."

She stood there for a long time, silent and still. Between the heat of Will's body behind her and the possessive spread of his hand, Josie felt like a sponge soaking up all the warmth her size would allow, like a cold-blooded creature taking on the sweet heat of a rock. She closed her eyes. The dark burden within her seemed to lighten. The fear began to fade. She was safe here in the present, in Will's fine hands. And she was glad for the future.

"Marry me, Josie." Will's voice slipped a rough notch. "I love you. I need you, darlin'. Always. Just the way you are."

Later, in bed, Josie drew up the jumbled linens, then plastered herself to Will's side. He could feel the warm swell of her belly against his hipbone, the soft weight of the leg she draped over his.

"I didn't hurt you, did I?" he whispered. "I've been thinking, honey, maybe we shouldn't..."

"Shh..." Josie reached up and pressed a finger to his lips. "You didn't hurt me. You couldn't. You're the dearest, gentlest man I've ever known."

A chuckle rumbled low in his throat. "I'm the only man you've ever known. Or," he growled in a mock warning, "ever will."

Will lay quietly a minute, just enjoying the feel of silky hair drifting through his fingers and the warm, feminine give of Josie's flesh everywhere he touched her. "Any regrets, Josie? This didn't turn out exactly the way you planned when you first latched on to me."

"Part of it did."

"Which part?"

"The loving." She sighed. "Somehow I lost track of the leaving. I'm sure I'd be a terrible disappointment to Mrs. Schumacher."

Will frowned in the dark. "But you're staying because you want to, right? Not because of the baby, or because you just forgot to go?"

"I'm staying because I love you, Will. Because this is where I belong."

"It's just that I can't help worrying—"

"Will," she said, cutting him off, "you promised to leave the past alone."

"I'll keep that promise, too, Josie. You can count on that." He slid his hand along her flank, loving the shape of her and the feel of her. Loving *her*. Nearly crazy with it. "Josie," he whispered.

"Hmm?" she answered sleepily.

"You can have any birthday you want, darlin'. You can have a different one each year, if it tickles your fancy. As long as you spend them all with me."

He could feel her mouth curl up in a smile as she nestled more closely against him.

"A wedding day is all I want, Will."

"You'll have that, too, as soon as the circuit preacher comes through next week. I don't suppose we could work out anything with Padre Diego, not knowing whether you're—" Will gritted his teeth. Of course she didn't know her religion. What difference did it make anyway? Except for upsetting her, it made no difference at all.

Josie made a tiny mewing noise then. In light of her condition, Will wasn't sure what that meant. He'd fathered a child over a dozen years ago, but he'd had precious little experience with pregnant women since Evie had taken that opportunity to sleep in the spare room.

"You feeling all right, Josie?" he whispered, tucking in his chin for a glimpse of her face.

"Fine," she murmured. "Safe. So safe . . ."

Her words trailed off, and in a minute or two her body went slack with sleep. And for the first time since he'd met her, Josie slept peacefully, without tears. Will held her anyway, just in case.

He didn't fall asleep until long after the moonlight gave way to the deep and quiet dark before dawn. Listening to the soft sound of Josie's breathing and savoring the warmth of her beside him, Will was glad—perhaps even a little proud—that he had finally made her feel safe.

That was what a husband was for, wasn't it? To be a watchman in the night as well as a good provider by day. So he couldn't tell her that he was worried sick.

It was all well and good to promise that he wouldn't turn so much as a hair trying to find out about her past. But what he couldn't promise was to keep her past from coming after her. In a dozen years of marshalling, he'd seen few men or women outrun the shadows that dogged them. Puzzles had a way of working themselves out, and people rarely escaped the natural consequences.

He reminded himself that he'd already made a significant effort in trying to discover her identity by sending out all those letters. Of course, it had been three months, and none of those lines he'd cast had gotten so much as a nibble. But you never knew. A wind could blow a scrap of newsprint any which way. A man might be unwrapping a sandwich one day and stare down at his beloved, amazed. Or a woman could be unpacking her best dishes and discover her long-lost daughter gazing up at her from a crumpled heap.

The same way a man could be dealt four kings and find his life changed forever.

He gathered her more closely against him and whispered her name. "Josie Dove." She was no longer a mystery he needed or wanted to solve. Just the love he wanted with all his heart to keep.

Chapter Seven

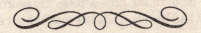

"Will Curry," Josie snapped as she yanked the last curling rag from her hair, "I want you out of here. Now." She glared into the mirror at the reflection of the man stretched out on the bed behind her. That lazy pose and those warm, appreciative eyes almost made her regret her words. Almost.

"Go on," she said, picking up her hairbrush. "Get. Go do whatever it is grooms do on their wedding day. You're not supposed to be here. It's bad luck."

His mouth curved up in a smile. The rest of him didn't move. "I didn't know you were superstitious, Josie."

"I didn't, either, until Señora Perez was pinning my dress yesterday and telling me about weddings." The boar bristles snapped through her hair. "We're already tempting fate, you know, by merely laying eyes on each other before the ceremony."

He laughed, a low sound deep in his throat. "Kinda hard not to, darlin', when we wake up in the same bed."

Wake up and make slow, sweet love, Josie thought.

It was a habit she hoped they would never break. Still, this was their wedding day.

"Go." She aimed a finger at the blanket-draped doorway. "I'll see you in the hotel lobby at noon and not a minute before."

Will sighed and rose from the bed. He left then, but only after he'd kissed her—a long, languorous kiss that nearly had her changing her mind about sending him away.

Josie stood in the window, watching him walk down the street. His new black frock coat was snug across his broad shoulders, and although she couldn't see it, she knew his black silk cravat was knotted perfectly, because she'd done it herself when Will wasn't able to manage it.

"Here. Let me do that," she'd said, and her fingers had whisked that flimsy silk into shape in a mere second, as if she'd been tying men's ties all her life. Which she hadn't. To her knowledge, she'd never done it before.

A little shiver had rippled along Josie's spine then, and she'd felt her forehead crumpling in a frown as the darkness surged inside her. She had swallowed hard, forcing it down. She had tied a cravat, that was all. The fact that she'd tied it perfectly was just beginner's luck. But before she was able to set her worried features straight, Will had seen her expression.

He had taken her face in both hands, quizzed her with his eyes and a softly spoken "What?"

"Nothing." She'd patted his tie and smiled up at him as brightly as she could. "There. Your noose is knotted properly, Sheriff. Now all you have to do is wait for the trapdoor to drop you into eternal matrimony.''

''Eternal bliss,'' he'd murmured, and that was what Josie was thinking now as she watched Will turn the corner at the livery and disappear from sight. In a little over an hour, she would be Will's wife. Next spring, she would be a mother. Surely there was enough bright future and bliss on her plate to crowd out any dark portions of her past.

Burley stood in the door of the jailhouse. Daylight, Will noted, could barely seep around his deputy's bulk.

''Just thought you'd like to know the stage pulled in 'bout ten minutes ago, Will. The preacher was on it, along with a couple other gents. I'll check them out this afternoon if you want. I don't s'pose you'll be coming back to the office after the ceremony.''

Will glanced at the clock. Twelve minutes till—as Josie had put it—the trapdoor dropped him into matrimony. Twelve long minutes.

''I'm considering not coming back at all, Burley,'' he said. He'd been more than considering it. He'd just about made up his mind. Will wasn't a man to run from a problem, but it didn't make much sense to him to just sit in Agate, twiddling his thumbs and worrying while he waited for Josie's past to catch up with her.

When he saw concern darken his deputy's face, Will added, ''I'm sure you could keep the town from falling apart until they located a new sheriff.''

"You aren't leaving on account of your bride, are you?"

"Partly," Will admitted.

"Aw, shoot, Will. Folks will accept her just fine. Now that Helen's not spreading any of her vicious gossip around town, I've hardly heard a peep out of anybody. There's a dozen folks already gathered at the hotel, oohing and aahing and fussing over Josie. She looks right pretty, too."

"It isn't that." Will's eyes sought the clock again. Two minutes had ticked off. Ten to go. Hell, if he sprinted across the street now and the preacher talked fast, they could be married in five minutes. But Josie had been adamant about all that superstitious clap-trap, and he'd promised her he wouldn't show up until noon.

"I'm just thinking it'd be nice for Josie and me to have a fresh start someplace."

Burley cleared his throat and leaned a beefy shoulder against the door frame. "Fresh start, huh? Is this your roundabout way of saying there's a kid coming along?"

"Could be," Will muttered, feeling an uncomfortable heat creeping above his tight collar. "Yeah."

"Aw, hell. That don't make no difference, Will. You've been here long enough to know most of the firstborns in Agate are big for six or seven months."

The deputy droned on, ticking off name after name—the Beasly girl, the Carmichael twins, his own Clarence—but Will's attention was claimed by the sound of boots drawing up on the boardwalk just outside.

"Excuse me, mister. I'm looking for the sheriff."

Burley stood aside, letting in daylight and a young stranger. From habit, Will's eyes sought the clock—five damn, blasted minutes—before they took in the young man standing just inside the door. He was twenty, give or take a year. A well-built kid with brown hair that straggled across his forehead and tickled the collar of his plaid shirt. That shirt, Will noticed, still sported its factory folds under clean suspenders, and the boy's jeans were stiff and indigo-new.

Courting clothes. The thought drifted through Will's head while he scrutinized the newcomer, who wore a determined expression and no discernible weapon, but instead carried a folded, faded bit of newspaper that, for all its lethal potential, might just as well have been a gun. Will felt his heart shift heavily within his chest.

"I'm looking for the sheriff," the young man said again. His glance fell to the paper in his hand. "Sheriff Curry."

Will remembered he wasn't wearing his badge because he hadn't wanted to punch a hole through his brand-new coat. The coat that had begun to feel as hot as sheepskin all of a sudden. "I'm Will Curry," he said, and leaned back a bit in his chair. "What can I do for you?"

"You best talk fast, kid," Burley called from the door. "In just a couple of minutes, the sheriff here—"

"It's all right, Burley," Will said. "You go on across the street. I'll be there directly."

When his deputy was gone, Will drew in a long breath before returning his gaze to the young man with the tattered paper in his grip. It could have been anything, he told himself. Maybe he'd read about one of the silver mines up in the hills and just stopped in for directions. It wouldn't be the first time that had happened. Hell, maybe—please, Lord—the kid was a peddler who was looking to sell him the latest thing in padlocks or hair slicks. Maybe he was looking for a stolen horse, or a damn lost dog, or a job.

Or maybe he was looking for Josie.

For a lunatic second, Will pictured himself putting a bullet in the kid's young heart and hauling his body out the back door, then up San Angelo Hill. For a mad instant...

The minute hand jerked straight up and the clock shivered a little on the wall before beginning its longest toll. When it quit, Will asked in a similar, measured tone, "What's your name, fella? What's your business here in Agate?" As if he didn't know.

"Lon, sir. Lon Spreckles. I've come from Union County on account of this." He dropped the paper on the desk top. Will read half a headline: Mystery Woman...

"Is she here, Sheriff?" His Adam's apple sprang up over his collar button. "Francie Cotton? Is she still in town?"

For one blank moment, Will thought the boy meant somebody else. A mistake! That was all it was. Just a damned mistake. Then Lon Spreckles leaned forward and ran a finger across the page.

"Or," he added, "I guess maybe you'd be better acquainted with her as this Josie Dove."

"Maybe. What do you want with her?"

When Will shot him a hard gaze, the boy straightened up. Less coltish boy now than mulish man, he replied, "I don't know that that's any of your business, Sheriff."

"Everything in Agate's my business. And everyone," Will growled.

He opened his desk drawer, grabbed his badge, then stabbed it through the stiff fabric of his lapel. Just for good measure, he opened a second drawer and withdrew his gun and holster. He hadn't planned to wear it on his wedding day, but he felt more comfortable with it now, better able to defend himself or Josie from this sudden stranger and whatever unexpected danger he presented.

"I'll ask you one more time," Will said as he strapped the holster down. "What do you want with her? What's this Francie woman to you?"

The kid's mouth crimped, and tears glossed his eyes. "She's... Well, sir, she's my betrothed."

Josie paced the fifteen steps across the lobby, then retraced them, counting them off once more. Fifteen. It felt like more—a mile—between the grandfather clock, with its brass pendulum sawing the stale air inside its walnut case, and the guests who were growing restless in their mismatched chairs.

Señora Perez, the dressmaker, stopped Josie to clip a thread from her hem. Then, with a look that was half sympathy and half apology, the woman slipped a darning egg and a sock from her handbag and bent her head to her mending. On the *señora*'s right, Curtis Malone, the photographer, crossed his legs this way, that way, then crossed his arms and clenched his teeth against a yawn.

When the long brass hand slid forward a notch and the clock banged out a quarter chime, Josie came to a standstill in the middle of the room. The preacher—she thought his name was Tate, but she'd been so excited when they were introduced that she barely listened—lifted his gaze to the clock, then draped a frayed blue ribbon down the seam of his Bible and closed it with a soft thump.

He made a similar sound in his throat. "I, uh... I have a baptism at one o'clock. Two miles south. On the... the Chivo Arroyo," he stammered, while his round face grew as pink and moist as a fresh cut of ham. "Is it possible that the groom... uh, that Will misunderstood?"

Josie only shook her head. When no one else answered, Lucinda Watson shot an elbow into her husband's well-padded ribs.

Burley blinked and snorted. "What?"

"Do something," his wife hissed.

"Like what?"

"Get him."

"Oh, hell, honey." He fumbled for his pocket watch, checked it against the grandfather clock, frowned. "Clock in the office must be off some. He'll be along."

When Burley reached over to pat her hand, Lucinda's lips thinned. They barely moved when she repeated, "Get him."

The deputy looked at Josie. He looked at the clock and then back at his wife. After a helpless shrug of his shoulders, he got to his feet. "I believe I'll just wander over to the jailhouse and see what's—"

"No need, Burley. I'm here."

Will's silhouette filled the hotel door, his dark wedding clothes even darker against the bright noon light behind him.

A sigh of relief riffled through the lobby like a welcome breeze. There was a rustling as Señora Perez put away her darning, as Curtis Malone uncrossed his various limbs, as Burley sat down again and his wife smoothed her skirts and murmured, "Well, it's about time."

Josie smiled at the sight of him so solid in the door frame, at the thought of his child so secure within her. She felt safe and warm inside and out, almost giddy with it. What a fool she'd been to worry, she thought. What a superstitious ninny to think for a moment that this day could be ruined by something as silly as the lack of a blue garter or an early glimpse of her wedding dress.

"Shall we commence?" The preacher clutched his Bible in both hands and popped out of his chair. Everyone sat up a little straighter, leaned forward a bit.

But just then, a shadow broke from behind Will's dark form. Shorter. Smaller. A shadow whose angular shape was as familiar to Josie as the darkness that lodged inside her. Familiar and frightening.

Still backlit from the bright street, the shadow edged forward. Spoke. "Francie?"

The name skimmed by her like the rush of startled wings. Josie shivered.

"Francie? Is it really you?"

The darkness inside her rose up, roiling like a thunderhead, clouding her vision. But not completely. Not enough. She could see the shadow's face now. She could see everything.

"Lon." It wasn't a question. Oh, God. She knew him. She knew everything. Remembered it all. The darkness, always black before, turned to a bloodred haze.

From the doorway, Will watched Josie's face change from delight to despair, then rinse of expression altogether. When Lon Spreckles stepped forward, so did Will—to lock a hand on Josie's elbow before she crumpled.

"Francie," the boy said, his round eyes pooling with tears, "you gotta listen. I've felt so damn bad ever since... But I was drunk. We all were. All fired up. We never meant... We were just horsing around before it all got out of hand. Before it all went mean and crazy."

Josie was staring at Spreckles with stark recognition, with a keener sense of awareness than Will had ever seen on her face. She was trembling, her bones gritting against her skin, and her breath, instead of slow, smooth glides, was coming in rough little chunks. He knew he ought to shove the kid away, ought to tell Lon Spreckles to shut up, but something in his gut prevented it.

Will's heart heaved. God help him, he craved the truth. He needed to solve the mystery. God help Josie, too. But there was no other way he knew. The truth, however painful, had to be better than ignorance. Didn't the good book say, "The truth shall make you free?" Josie could be free, and Will could do something with hard facts. Build a solid life for his baby and his wife. For she was going to be his wife, no matter what.

The preacher was fingering the worn leather of his Bible while shifting from one foot to the other. The other guests sat with their hands neatly folded in their laps, with careful smiles on their mouths. One moment they were all looking down at the floor or up at the ceiling or out the door, but then all their gazes converged on Will, as if they were asking who was in charge.

He was, damn it, despite his bewildered heart.

"Sit down," he ordered Lon Spreckles, who was openly crying now and gouging his wet eyes with his knuckles.

After the kid complied, with a meek "Yessir," Will guided Josie to a chair and sat her down before her legs went out from under her. She hadn't spoken a word yet, other than Lon's name, and she was still staring at him with no expression on her face. Will bent to kiss the top of her head and whispered that everything would be fine. It would. He'd make it fine. But he knew damn well that before things got fine, they were going to get a lot worse. A whole lot worse.

A glance at the clock told Will that Josie should have been his wife half an hour ago and warned him that she might never be if he didn't take the situation in hand.

Will turned to the preacher. "Reverend, I expect there are several souls out there—" he angled his head toward Agate's main street "—in need of a few hours' worth of saving. You might want to tend to them while we get things settled here."

The preacher nodded with silent understanding and, with a firm grip on his Bible, headed for the door.

Will turned to his deputy then. "Burley, I'd be obliged if you'd lead the rest of this little flock out of here, so Josie and Mr. Spreckles and I can put this puzzle together."

The big deputy nodded, as well—not so much with understanding as with staunch obedience—before announcing to the others, "Y'all heard the sheriff. Come on now. Let's give these folks some open range."

Then, after Will had glared the curious desk clerk into a quick retreat upstairs, it was just the three of them in the little hotel lobby. Lon Spreckles, wet-faced and shaky in his chair. Josie, limp and wan as a muslin doll in hers. And Will, standing between them in his wedding suit, with the gold band in a pocket, with his mouth dry as cotton and his heart feeling spiked on one of his ribs.

"Something happened two years ago," he said as calmly as he could, directing his remarks to the young man, who obviously remembered. Will shrugged his shoulders then and worked the muscles in his neck to ease the tension there before continuing. "I've got nothing else to do. No place else to go. I'm listening, Spreckles. I'm all ears."

The kid's mouth merely quivered.

"Start talking. Now," Will growled. "Josie doesn't remember anything. What happened two years ago?"

"It wasn't my fault." Lon's eyes darted in Josie's direction, then returned to Will. "It was the rest of them. The Daggetts. Tom Slade. Harlan and Shorty McKay. Hell, they hated half-breeds. Hated Joe Cotton worst of all."

"Joe Cotton?" Will said quietly.

"Francie's pa." Lon looked at Josie again. "I never hated him, Francie, honey. I swear I never did. You remember how I—"

Will cut in. "She doesn't remember. Tell me about Joe Cotton."

"Well, he—"

"No. Don't," Josie said in a voice that was empty of emotion. Her eyes, when both men looked at her, were hollow and dry. Lightless. Lifeless.

Will moved to stand behind her chair. He placed his hands gently but firmly on her shoulders. "Go ahead, Spreckles," he said.

The young man sucked in a breath, then exhaled roughly. His gaze sought the window and fixed there, as if he couldn't bear to look at Josie, as if he were afraid to meet the eyes of the man who stood so solidly behind her. Finally, Lon spoke.

"Two years back," he said, "in the summer of '76, after we got word of what happened to General Custer, some of the folks in Union County—the men, mostly—got pretty riled. They wanted to get in a few licks of their own at the redskins. Full-bloods. Mixed. It didn't matter." Still staring out the window, Lon shrugged. "It was just talk. Whiskey talk. Until that day we headed out to Joe Cotton's place."

Will felt a tremor work through Josie's shoulders. "Go on," he told Lon.

"We just pushed him around at first. The others did, mostly. I'd had so much liquor by then, it was all I could do to plant one foot in front of the other. Hardly even remembered why we were there." He stared at the floor and shook his head. "Guess I never really knew how far the others meant to go until Shorty McKay put the rope around Joe's neck. And then—oh, God, after they'd hanged poor Joe..."

Will bit off a harsh curse when the kid paused to swipe at his tears.

"I'm sorry, Francie, honey. I'm so damn sorry. I ain't a bit surprised you lost your mind after seeing what you did."

"She witnessed it?" Will's grip tightened on Josie. "She watched you hang her father?"

Lon Spreckles raised his stricken gaze. His voice was a wet whisper. "Yessir. And then, after Shorty got an ax, she saw a whole lot worse."

Chapter Eight

Josie wanted to run. She wanted to tear herself away from Will's firm grasp on her shoulders, from Lon's sickening gaze on her face. She wanted to ruck up her skirts and run. Run till she couldn't run anymore. But she couldn't move.

"I did what Papa told me to do."

She heard her own voice, but it sounded like a stranger's, distant and hollow—the voice of a woman calling out from the depths of a cave, from a time in the past when she'd been Francie. Francie.

"I always did just what Papa told me to."

She heard her father's voice now, more clearly than her own.

Close that book, Francie, and douse that light. You'll wear your eyes out, girl.

Yes, Papa.

Tie this tie for me, will you, Francie? I'm all thumbs today.

Yes, Papa.

You get to the barn and lie low, child. And don't you come out, no matter what happens.

Yes, Papa.

No matter what, Francie. You promise me.

Yes, Papa. I promise.

She had kept that promise, too. From her hiding place in the barn, she had watched the men push her father around. Punch him, then kick him, then put the rope around his neck. She could see it happening now, as if no time had passed, as if the scene swimming before her eyes were real.

No matter what, Francie. You promise me.

Yes, Papa. I promise.

He'd been a long time dying, twisting, heaving, clawing at the rope's end. The whole tree had trembled, while the men stood by and laughed and drank to Custer and the Seventh Cavalry. While Josie watched. While she kept her promise. No matter what.

The darkness inside her surged now. It rose like bile in the back of her throat, and Josie swallowed hard to suppress it, to make her mind a blank again. A blessed, peaceful blank.

She stood up. "Take me home, Will," she said with calm decisiveness, adding, "Now," almost sternly in the face of his surprise.

"Francie, don't...don't go." Lon Spreckles grabbed a handful of her skirt. "At least not without telling me you forgive me. You gotta. That's why I came.'

Josie pulled away. "I'm not her," she snapped, then bent to fuss at the wrinkles his damp hand had made in her wedding dress, cursing softly as she tried to smooth them away, to make them disappear.

"I'm not Francie. I'm Josie. Josie Dove." Her hands kept worrying the wrinkled satin. "Just go away. I don't know you, and there's nothing to forgive."

"But, Francie..."

Lon reached out for her again, but when Josie drew back, Will stepped in.

He'd heard about all he needed to hear, and so had Josie, in his estimation. But hearing the brutal truth and coming to grips with it weren't the same thing. Josie was already several miles down the road to denial, and he sensed he might lose her forever if he didn't bring her back.

"Come on." He took Josie's arm in one hand, Lon's in the other, and led them out the door and across the street to where Burley was waiting on a bench outside the jailhouse.

"Is the wedding on?" his deputy asked hopefully.

Will answered his question with a dark glare and a quick shake of the head. "Put young Spreckles in a cell, Burley, and see that he's comfortable, will you?"

When the youth protested, Will turned on him and snarled, "Telling Josie and asking for her forgiveness might set things right by your conscience, boy, but it doesn't satisfy the law. Not by a long shot. I expect you know that. Once things are straightened out here—" Will angled his head toward Josie before continuing "—I'll be taking you back to Union County and whatever's waiting for you there."

"Yessir." Lon gave Josie a last wet glance before staring down at his boot tips. "I won't give you no trouble, Sheriff," he said when Burley reached for his arm to lead him away.

"Let's go home, darlin'." Will curved his arm protectively around Josie's waist.

Then she grabbed his gun. She lurched away from him, her face paler than Will had ever seen, her eyes clearer, more full of recognition and rage—a rage that burned like fire, all of it directed at Lon Spreckles. She pointed the big .45 at the boy's heart. Burley took a step away from him, out of the line of fire.

When Josie spoke, her voice was eerily calm and quiet, as if it came from a great distance, from far in the past. "It wasn't enough just to hang him, was it, Lon? Was it?" Her gaze flicked to Will. "Are you listening, Sheriff? You need to listen to this. You need to know why I'm about to shoot this man dead. Why I'm going to find his friends and do the same to them. Why I'm going to do what I should have done two years ago.'

"I'm listening, Josie." Will's voice was even calmer than Josie's, despite the fact that he was barely breathing and every muscle in his body was primed for action. Lon Spreckles had begun to sweat profusely. The boy didn't know what Will knew, which was that he never carried his gun with a chambered cartridge. If Josie pulled the trigger, the big Peacemaker would only make a harmless click. Will was prepared to give her that first empty shot by way of revenge. But not the second shot that would rip into Lon Spreckles's young heart.

"They couldn't just hang him, Will," Josie continued. "That wasn't enough to satisfy their blood lust. Shorty came in the barn—so close to where I was hiding I could have reached out and untied his shoelaces.

He got the ax. Then, after they cut my papa down from the tree, they kept swinging that ax. Again and again. On him. And even that wasn't enough for the bastards. Because... because—'' Hot tears began to streak down her cheeks and pool in the corners of her mouth. ''—because after they were all done chopping, they played catch. Laughing. Yelling and screaming like wild animals. Drunken beasts. And you know what they used for a ball, Will? Do you have any idea what they used while I sat there, watching? They used my papa's severed head. While I sat in the barn like he'd told me to do. Sat and watched. Then, after they had their fun and went away, I buried him. All the pieces. I put... I put my papa together again in his grave.''

Her voice lowered to a wet whisper. The heavy gun trembled in her hand, but she managed to keep it trained on Spreckles nevertheless. ''But I'm not just going to sit and watch now, Lon. I'm going to kill you. And then I'm going back to Union County to find the rest of them, to hunt them down and kill them the way I should have done that day.''

Her finger twitched once, then squeezed the trigger. Will let her have that shot—the one with no legal consequences—and then he took the gun away and holstered it, just in time to catch Josie as her legs went out from under her.

A week later, Will rode hard and without a stop for food or sleep on his way back from Union County. Before he left with young Spreckles in handcuffs, he'd locked Josie up, as well, so that she wouldn't do anything foolish or lethal. He knew he could count on Burley to keep an eye on her and make sure she was all right physically. What he didn't know was what her mental state would be when he returned. Would she be Josie or Francie? Would she love him, or would all that—their love and their hopes and dreams—be another puzzle piece from the past now, put away in a tight compartment of her mind? Would she remember, or had she erased him from her brain and her heart the way she had all those other events?

He knew, too, that he wasn't the same man he'd been a week ago on his wedding day. The man he'd been then had a code of honor as a lawman. He brought men to justice; never exacted it himself. But the man he was today had turned a blind eye on that code during the past few days. He'd been judge and jury both. Most of all, he'd been executioner. Would Josie see that when she looked at him? Could she still love him knowing what he'd done for her sake?

It was dark when he tethered his horse outside the jailhouse in Agate. Inside, a lamp flickered dimly in the cell. Josie was sitting on the rickety cot, drinking a glass of milk. Over the rim, her eyes met his as he came through the door.

"I'm back," he said. Stating the obvious seemed a better choice than spilling out all his hopes and fears the minute he walked in. Was she still his Josie? Or a stranger named Francie Cotton who just happened to be carrying his child? He couldn't fathom her mood in the murky light of the jail, although he could see she was still wearing her wedding dress, as she had been when he saw her last.

Will slapped at the trail dust on his legs. "I'm pretty dirty," he said, when what he wanted to do was ask, "Do you love me, Josie?" He could feel the tension in his face. The hot sheen of his eyes. The fierce ache blooming in his throat.

"Burley been treating you all right?" *Josie? Francie?*

Will fell silent. What could he say when he didn't know who he was talking to? Or whether that person wanted to marry him or wished he was dead?

She put her empty glass down on the floor, then rose from the cot—a little stiff, giving her spine a twist and realigning her shoulders before walking to the cell door and grasping the iron bars with both hands. Her face appeared stern for a moment, then confused. And Will couldn't tell if she was glad to see him or not.

"Will Curry, I'd be willing to bet my life that you're the only lawman ever to put his bride in jail on her wedding day. You owe me an apology, mister."

She smiled then, and Will felt his own mouth crook up at one corner, but he tamed the grin. "I'm sorry. But it was for your own good, darlin'." He lowered his gaze to the floor. "There's something I need to tell you."

He was planning to tell her the truth about how he'd hunted her father's killers down, one by one, in Union County, how he'd brought them to the local authorities there and gotten Lon Spreckles to implicate them in her father's murder. How he had done everything by the book and according to territorial law. With one exception. Shorty. The one who had wielded the ax.

Will had saved him for last, and when the man sneered at him and laughed about what he'd done and said he'd gladly do it again, Will had shot him dead. Without warning. Without pity. Without regret. He had broken every oath he'd ever taken as a lawman, exacting Josie's revenge—or Francie's—so she would never be tempted to do it herself.

Maybe she'd love him for that. Or maybe, Will thought, she'd hate him. He had risked hellfire for her by killing Shorty the way he had, but now Will felt as if he were about to risk heaven itself by confessing.

He swallowed hard, trying to find his courage as well as his voice, but before he did, Josie laughed softly.

"There's something I need to tell *you*, Will Curry," she said. "I was mad as all hell, Will. The first day or so, all I knew what that I had murder in my heart and iron bars in front of me. But then something happened. Something, well . . . wonderful."

Will raised his head, looking at her silently, trying to figure out the wistful smile on her face, waiting.

"Our baby." Josie's smile widened. "I felt our baby flutter inside me. I felt our baby, Will, and suddenly I knew I'd do just what my papa did to protect me. And I knew I was alive because he made me hide that day. I could almost feel his spirit inside me, glad and proud and relieved that I'd obeyed him, no matter what. I knew my papa's soul was at peace because I had survived. And I was at peace then, too. I knew I couldn't have saved his life, and that his death would've been so much worse, so unbearably painful, if he'd seen me die, too, that day."

She sighed softly. "I don't have murder in my heart anymore. Or a fog up here." She lifted a hand to touch her temple. "All the darkness inside me is gone. There's only light now. Only love. A lifetime of love for you and for this baby of ours."

The ache in Will's throat loosened as he crossed the room. Josie's hands were still curled around the bars and he covered them with his own. She was gazing up at him now through the iron bars, innocent as God's favorite angel, her conscience at peace at last. Will meant to keep her that way. His Josie. His dove. No matter what name she chose for herself.

Her green eyes clouded then, and worry darkened her face. "What was it you were meaning to tell me, Will," she asked, "before I interrupted you?"

He laughed as he walked to his desk for the key to the cell. "Well, now, doesn't that beat all?"

"What?"

"Whatever it was I meant to say to you, darlin', I just plain forgot."

The whole town turned out for the wedding the next day. When the hotel lobby couldn't accommodate one more guest, they moved chairs out onto the street. It gratified Will to no end to see how the citizens of Agate had taken to his bride-to-be. At least a dozen people had drawn him aside that morning to express their hope that he'd stay on as sheriff.

It seemed like a good idea to Will. There was no reason to leave now that Josie's past wasn't shadowing her anymore. Or Francie's past. Hell, he still wasn't sure just who he was marrying since they'd barely had time to speak last night before she'd tossed him out of the house.

"No waking up together tomorrow, Will. We're going to do it right and proper this time," she'd told him in no uncertain terms. "Old. New. Borrowed. Blue. All of it. Not that I'm a superstitious person, mind you, but..."

Will glanced up over the heads of the assembled townsfolk now and frowned when he saw a line of thunderheads piling up in the sky to the west. "Just what we need," he muttered to the preacher, who stood patiently at his side.

"You never know," the man said. "I've heard rain's a good sign on a wedding day, Sheriff. Don't quote me on that, though." He nudged Will's elbow then. "Here comes your bride."

She was the prettiest thing Will had ever seen coming down the street in her white dress and carrying a bouquet of goldenrod and wild hydrangea leaves. His heart felt as if it might pop right out of his starched shirtfront when she stood beside him and the preacher began his speech. He thought he was probably the luckiest man alive ever since he'd turned over those four kings and won Josie Dove. Or Francie. Or—well, hell—both of 'em.

"Repeat after me," the preacher said. "I, Will..."

"I, Will..."

"Take thee...um..." The preacher looked up from his prayerbook. He crooked a finger, motioning the bride closer, then whispered in her ear. After she whispered back, he smiled and began again. "Repeat after me. I, Will..."

Will Curry swallowed hard. "I, Will..." he said. "Take thee, Josie..."

Will smiled. "Take thee, Josie, Josie Dove, my true love, to be my wedded wife."

*   *   *   *   *

If you enjoyed

THE BALLAD OF JOSIE DOVE

*by Mary McBride, turn the page
for an exciting preview of her next
full-length historical*

DARLING JACK

*Coming in July 1996 from
Harlequin Historicals.*

Prologue

Anna Matlin was invisible.

As a child in the grim coal-mining hills of southern Illinois, she had learned her lessons well. In a family of thirteen, the squeaking wheel got backhanded and burdened with extra chores. In any forest, it was the tallest tree that suffered the lightning.

So Anna, early on, had decided to be a shrub.

She had blossomed once—and briefly—at the age of sixteen when she eloped to Chicago with Billy Matlin. But Billy had soon looked beyond her, to Colorado and the promise of gold.

"I'll send for you," he'd said. But Billy never had. He'd died instead, leaving his young widow pale and even more invisible.

Under bleak winter skies, in her somber wools and black galoshes, Anna Matlin was barely distinguishable from the soot-laden banks of snow along Washington Street as she made her way to Number 89, the offices of the Pinkerton National Detective Agency, where she had been employed for six years, filing papers and transcribing notes and more or less blending into the wainscoting.

In summer, in her drab poplins and sensible shoes, she seemed to disappear against brick walls and dull paving stones.

Whatever the season or setting, Anna Matlin was—by her own volition—invisible.

But every once in a while, particularly in summer, when the sun managed to slice through the smoke-dense Chicago sky, it would cast a rare and peculiar glint from Anna's spectacles, a flash, that for an instant made her seem exceptional and altogether visible.

As it did on the morning of May 3, 1869...

Chapter One

Chicago
May 3, 1869

"I need a wife."

"That's impossible, Jack. Entirely out of the question." Allan Pinkerton leaned back in his chair. He raised both hands to knead his throbbing temples, then closed his eyes a moment, wishing—praying, actually—that when he opened them again, both the headache and Mad Jack Hazard would be gone.

But—damn it—they weren't. The nagging pain was still there, and so was his best and bravest operative. The man was a headache in human form, slanted back now, with his arms crossed and his brazen boots up on the boss's desk.

"I need a wife, Allan," Hazard said again in that voice that still had a touch of English mist, even after all these years.

The founder of the world's largest, most successful detective agency sighed as he continued to massage his forehead. "You work alone. Damn it. You've worked alone since the war. It's the way you've wanted it."

"Not this time."

Something in the man's tone made Pinkerton lean forward. Jack Hazard made demands. He didn't plead. But now there seemed to be a tentative note playing just beneath the usual bravado.

"If it were possible," Pinkerton told him. "But it's not. Right now all of my female operatives are assigned. There's no one—"

Hazard cut him off, jerking his thumb toward the closed office door. "There's a roomful of females out there, and you bloody well know it."

"Secretaries." Pinkerton dismissed them with a wave of his hand. "They always gather when you come. You know that. They flock like silly pigeons at a popcorn festival."

"Surely one of them—"

"No." Pinkerton banged a fist on his desk. "Absolutely not. They're clerks, not operatives. None of them has been trained or is qualified."

"They're women, for God's sake. That qualifies any one of them to play the part of my wife. It's not as if you're asking them to use a gun or to wrench a confession out of a counterfeiter."

"I understand that, but—"

"What you need to understand is this, old friend." As Hazard's voice lowered, his eyes lifted slowly to meet Pinkerton's straight on. Gray to gray. Steel to stone. There was a spark. And then it died. "I can't do it alone. Not this time."

Suddenly Pinkerton did understand. He understood all too well, and his voice softened considerably. "Perhaps I ought to assign someone else . . ."

"No." In one swift and fluid movement, Jack Hazard's boots hit the floor and he was out of his chair, towering over Pinkerton's desk. "She's mine. If anybody's going to bring Chloe Von Drosten down, Allan, it's going to be me. Nobody else. Me. You owe me that, damn it."

Pinkerton didn't answer for a moment. He studied his folded hands, then let his eyes drift closed. When he spoke, it was quietly, with calm deliberation. "The woman did you considerable damage, Jack. More than I had imagined."

"I'm over it" came the terse reply.

"And the drinking?"

"That, too. It's been five months." Hazard yanked his watch from his vest pocket and snapped it open. "Five months. Hell, it's been a hundred twenty-two days, ten hours and thirty-seven minutes."

Pinkerton sank back in his chair, out of Hazard's towering shadow. He massaged his temples a moment before asking, "You don't believe you need more time?"

"I've had time. Now I need something else."

"Revenge?" Pinkerton lifted a wary brow. "I won't have one of my agents rolling around like a loose cannon, bent on nothing more than wreaking havoc."

Hazard shook his head. "No, not revenge. That isn't it. What I need, Allan, is redemption." He smiled grimly as he closed the watch and jammed it back into his pocket. "And a wife."

And then his voice didn't break so much as unravel, coming apart in a thready whisper.

"Allan. Please."

The commotion down the hall had drawn Anna Matlin to the door of the file room. She stood there now, shaking her head and watching two more secretaries as they attempted to enter Allan Pinkerton's anteroom simultaneously. After a collision of shoulders, a collapse of crinolines and a good deal of elbowing and hissing, the women somehow managed to squeeze through and join the throng already inside.

It didn't take a Philadelphia lawyer or a Pinkerton spy to figure out what was happening. *He* was back. It happened once or twice a year. The arrival and departure of Johnathan Hazard sent the entire office into a tizzy, a frenzy of swishing skirts and sighs and giggles. Last spring, Martha Epsom had broken her ankle racing down the hall. Today Judith and Mayetta had nearly come to blows while wedged between the door jambs. All for a glimpse of Mad Jack Hazard. All for the sake of a fluttering heart. A fleeting sigh.

Such silliness.

Anna was about to turn and go back to her filing when someone grasped her elbow.

"Come along, Mrs. Matlin." Miss Nora Quillan's voice was brisk and efficient. Her grip on Anna's arm was secure. "There's a batch of expense sheets somewhere in there." The woman cast a dour glance at the door of the anteroom. "Perhaps you'd better get them before they're trampled."

There was no refusing Allan Pinkerton's steel-willed longtime secretary. Not if one had a thimbleful of sense, anyway, or if one prized one's employment at the agency, which Anna most certainly did.

"Yes, ma'am," she said, even as the tall, broad-shouldered woman was ushering her down the hall.

"I'm glad to see at least one of our young ladies has a sense of decency," Miss Quillan muttered. "Some modicum of pride."

They had reached the door to the anteroom now. Beyond the threshold was pandemonium—the sighing, simpering and swooning of a dozen or more of Johnathan Hazard's devotees.

Miss Quillan clucked her tongue in disgust. "I'm helpless. Mr. Pinkerton insists this...this frenzy is good for morale, although for whose I really couldn't say. Certainly not mine!" She narrowed her eyes on Anna now, and her mouth crimped in a small smile. "I'm glad to see you're immune, Mrs. Matlin."

"Well, I'm not exactly..."

"Yes. Well. You're a sensible girl. You'll find the expense sheets over there by the window. I hope. Good luck." Nora Quillan sniffed and waded into the feminine melee, clapping her hands and shouting, "Ladies! Ladies! Could we have a little order in here, please?"

It wasn't that she was immune, Anna thought as she made her way to the window. That wasn't the case at all. It was rather that she didn't believe in expending useless emotion. She wasn't the sort of person who wasted dreams. Not that she had any. But if she had...

She gave a little shrug and was reaching for the sheaf of papers on the library table when the door of Allan Pinkerton's office opened. There was a last-minute jostling in the anteroom, a flurry of movement, followed by a communal sigh that dwindled to a breathless hush as Pinkerton's most illustrious spy appeared.

Anna's hand halted in midair. Her heart, like countless others in the room, gathered speed, bounded into her throat and then plummeted to the pit of her stomach.

Johnathan Hazard—Mad Jack—was the most beautiful man in the world. From his jet-dark hair to the tips of his high-glossed boots. He was broad of shoulder, narrow of waist and perfectly tall. His bearing was straight and military, although Anna knew he had never been a soldier. His air of command was that of a duke or baron, even though he was the fourth son of an earl. Still, he was beautiful. Hazard was fashioned, Anna thought suddenly, not as a man at all, but as a model for what a man might be if all the gods could agree on a single definition of masculine beauty. Or if they consulted her.

Which they hadn't, Anna reminded herself quickly and firmly, redirecting her gaze to the stack of papers and the task at hand.

"Well?" Allan Pinkerton stood at Jack Hazard's shoulder. He spoke with the hushed tone of a conspirator. "That's the lot of them. A bevy, if you will. Take your pick, Jack. And be quick about it. I'd like to get back to business."

"It doesn't matter." Hazard shifted his stance and crossed his arms, surveying the roomful of women. "I'll need her for a month or so. Which one can you spare?"

"None of them, damn it," Pinkerton shot back. Then he demurred. "Well, anyone but Miss Quillan, I suppose. The whole place would come undone without her."

"I don't want your ramrod, Allan. God forbid." Hazard laughed as his gaze cut to the dark-haired secretary who was poised like a pillar of salt behind her desk. And then, just at the edge of his vision, there came a sudden flash of light, a glint of gold that made him turn toward the window.

"What about her?"

"Her?"

"Over there. The little mouse. The one in the brown dress and the spectacles who's doing her best to blend into the woodwork."

Pinkerton squinted. "Oh. Mrs. Matlin."

"Mrs. Matlin?" A frown creased Hazard's forehead. "Is she married?"

"No. At least I don't believe so. She's a widow, as I recall. Been here for years."

"I never noticed her."

"I don't suppose many do."

Jack Hazard grinned. "A widow ought to do nicely. See that she's on the train tomorrow morning, will you?"

Pinkerton cleared his throat. "I'll ask her, Jack, but I can't promise—"

"Don't promise, Allan. Just do it."

Then, with what seemed like a gust of audible sighs at his back, the Pinkerton National Detective Agency's most illustrious spy walked out of the room.

Nora Quillan already had her hat and gloves on. As on most days, she had worked late. Today in particular, with all the commotion, she had been hard-pressed to get the agency back to some semblance of order. Having done that, Nora was ready to go home to a cold supper, a single glass of ale and a good night's sleep. Still, she knocked on her employer's door and walked into his office before he was able to call, "Come in."

"You're making a dreadful mistake, Mr. P.," she said.

"Another one, Nora?" Allan Pinkerton turned from the window, hands clasped behind his back, an indulgent grin upon his lips. "And just what is this dreadful mistake?"

"I know you think the world of Johnathan Hazard, but—"

Pinkerton interrupted her. "He's the best man I have."

"He *was*." Nora sighed now as she crossed the room and settled on the arm of a chair. "His imprisonment during the war changed him. And now, after that Von Drosten woman sank her claws into him—and probably her fangs, as well—he's worse. Much worse." She narrowed her gaze on the man at the window. "Frankly, I'm surprised you haven't noticed it. And I must say I'm shocked that you'd risk letting him fall into her clutches again."

Allan Pinkerton was accustomed to his secretary's candor. He valued her opinions. Nora Quillan was rarely wrong. In this instance, however, he prayed she was. Dead wrong.

"Did Jack say anything to you?" he asked her.

Nora sniffed. "He didn't have to. I've known him for over ten years. Nearly as long as you have. The changes are obvious, although I must say he's done his best to mask them."

Pinkerton nodded—in agreement, in dismay. He was remembering his detective's uncharacteristic plea earlier that day, the way the man's voice had shattered and the tremor in his hands that he'd been hard-pressed to disguise. But he had, damn it. He had.

"He isn't drinking anymore, Nora."

"That doesn't mean he won't. Especially if he's under *her* influence again. That woman is evil, Mr. P. Surely you recognize that now, if you didn't before.

The Baroness Von Drosten is the devil in silk and ermine."

"She's a fake," Pinkerton said through clenched teeth.

A harsh laugh broke from Nora's throat. "It doesn't seem to matter, does it? Fake or not, she still manages to cast her evil spell on—"

"That's enough, Nora." Allan Pinkerton sagged into the chair behind his desk and began massaging his throbbing temples. His own worries about Jack Hazard were legion; he didn't need Nora's to aggravate them.

"Hazard has a plan," he said, attempting to put an end to the discussion.

"He had a plan *before,*" Nora shot back, as soon as the words were out of her employer's mouth. "He was going to seduce her last year, wasn't he? But instead the baroness seduced him. And worse."

"This time he won't be alone."

Nora rolled her eyes. "That's the other mistake I was intending to bring to your attention. To send little Mrs. Matlin along on this...this devil's business...is like sending a lamb to the slaughter."

"She agreed, Nora. We spoke at length this afternoon," he muttered. "The woman even seemed rather pleased."

"She wants to keep her job! How the devil else would you expect her to behave?" Nora shot up from the arm of the chair now, planting her fists on her hips. "You're determined to carry through with this, aren't you?"

Allan Pinkerton closed his eyes and slowly nodded his head.

Nora threw up her hands. "I knew it. Sometimes I don't know why I bother wasting my breath," she muttered on her way to the door. "Nothing good will come of this. You mark my words. Jack Hazard will be lost forever, if he isn't already. And God only knows what will happen to poor, unsuspecting Anna Matlin."

"Is that all, Nora?" Pinkerton asked wearily.

"I should think that would be quite enough," she said with a sniff. "Good night, Mr. P. I'll see you tomorrow."

After his secretary had slammed the door, Allan Pinkerton leaned forward, cradling his aching head in his hands, praying that for once in her life the infallible Nora Quillan was fallible and dead, dead wrong.

* * * * *

New York Times Bestselling Author

JAYNE ANN KRENTZ

Appearances can be deceiving. Find out how in

LEGACY

Honor Mayfield was about to walk into a trap. She thought that her chance meeting with Conn Landry was a fortunate stroke of luck. In fact, he had cleverly set her up a long time ago. With their pasts mysteriously linked, can Conn and Honor escape from a tangled web of deception and desire?

Available in June, at your favorite retail outlet.

BRIDE'S BAY RESORT

UNLOCK THE DOOR TO GREAT ROMANCE AT BRIDE'S BAY RESORT

Join Harlequin's new across-the-lines series, set in an exclusive hotel on an island off the coast of South Carolina.

Seven of your favorite authors will bring you exciting stories about fascinating heroes and heroines discovering love at Bride's Bay Resort.

Look for these fabulous stories coming to a store near you beginning in January 1996.

Harlequin American Romance #613 in January
Matchmaking Baby by Cathy Gillen Thacker

Harlequin Presents #1794 in February
Indiscretions by Robyn Donald

Harlequin Intrigue #362 in March
Love and Lies by Dawn Stewardson

Harlequin Romance #3404 in April
Make Believe Engagement by Day Leclaire

Harlequin Temptation #588 in May
Stranger in the Night by Roseanne Williams

Harlequin Superromance #695 in June
Married to a Stranger by Connie Bennett

Harlequin Historicals #324 in July
Dulcie's Gift by Ruth Langan

Visit Bride's Bay Resort each month wherever Harlequin books are sold.

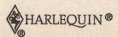

HARLEQUIN®

BBAYG

HARLEQUIN®

Don't miss these Harlequin favorites by some of our most distinguished authors!
And now, you can receive a discount by ordering two or more titles!

HT #25645	THREE GROOMS AND A WIFE by JoAnn Ross	$3.25 U.S./$3.75 CAN.	☐
HT #25648	JESSIE'S LAWMAN by Kristine Rolofson	$3.25 U.S.//$3.75 CAN.	☐
HP #11725	THE WRONG KIND OF WIFE by Roberta Leigh	$3.25 U.S./$3.75 CAN.	☐
HP #11755	TIGER EYES by Robyn Donald	$3.25 U.S./$3.75 CAN.	☐
HR #03362	THE BABY BUSINESS by Rebecca Winters	$2.99 U.S./$3.50 CAN.	☐
HR #03375	THE BABY CAPER by Emma Goldrick	$2.99 U.S./$3.50 CAN.	☐
HS #70638	THE SECRET YEARS by Margot Dalton	$3.75 U.S./$4.25 CAN.	☐
HS #70655	PEACEKEEPER by Marisa Carroll	$3.75 U.S./$4.25 CAN.	☐
HI #22280	MIDNIGHT RIDER by Laura Pender	$2.99 U.S./$3.50 CAN.	☐
HI #22235	BEAUTY VS THE BEAST by M.J. Rogers	$3.50 U.S./$3.99 CAN.	☐
HAR #16531	TEDDY BEAR HEIR by Elda Minger	$3.50 U.S./$3.99 CAN.	☐
HAR #16596	COUNTERFEIT HUSBAND by Linda Randall Wisdom	$3.50 U.S./$3.99 CAN.	☐
HH #28795	PIECES OF SKY by Marianne Willman	$3.99 U.S./$4.50 CAN.	☐
HH #28855	SWEET SURRENDER by Julie Tetel	$4.50 U.S./$4.99 CAN.	☐

(limited quantities available on certain titles)

	AMOUNT	$
DEDUCT:	**10% DISCOUNT FOR 2+ BOOKS**	$
ADD:	**POSTAGE & HANDLING**	$
	($1.00 for one book, 50¢ for each additional)	
	APPLICABLE TAXES**	$_____
	TOTAL PAYABLE	$_____
	(check or money order—please do not send cash)	

To order, complete this form and send it, along with a check or money order for the total above, payable to Harlequin Books, to: **In the U.S.:** 3010 Walden Avenue, P.O. Box 9047, Buffalo, NY 14269-9047; **In Canada:** P.O. Box 613, Fort Erie, Ontario, L2A 5X3.

Name: _____

Address: _____ City: _____

State/Prov.: _____ Zip/Postal Code: _____

**New York residents remit applicable sales taxes.
Canadian residents remit applicable GST and provincial taxes.

HBACK-AJ3

Harlequin® Historical

Don't miss your opportunity to read a very special historical romance from three-time RITA Award winner

Cheryl Reavis

The Bartered Bride

Keep an eye out for this unforgettable story. Coming this June from Harlequin Historicals!

Coming in July from

DARLING JACK

by

MARY McBRIDE

He was the country's number-one Pinkerton
operative…she was his pretend wife.

"I can hardly wait for her next one! She's great!"
—*Affaire de Couer*

Available wherever Harlequin books are sold.

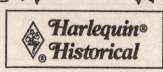

Harlequin® Historical

If you're a serious fan of historical romance,
then you're in luck!

Harlequin Historicals brings you
stories by bestselling authors, rising new stars
and talented first-timers.

Ruth Langan & Theresa Michaels
Mary McBride & Cheryl St. John
Margaret Moore & Merline Lovelace
Julie Tetel & Nina Beaumont
Susan Amarillas & Ana Seymour
Deborah Simmons & Linda Castle
Cassandra Austin & Emily French
Miranda Jarrett & Suzanne Barclay
DeLoras Scott & Laurie Grant...

You'll never run out of favorites.

Harlequin Historicals...they're too good to miss!

HH-GEN